The Diamond Syndicate

www.melodramapublishing.com

Library of Congress Control Number: 2009938153
ISBN-13: 978-1934157602
ISBN-10: 1934157600
First Edition: January 2010
10 9 8 7 6 5 4 3 2 1

Editors: Brian Sandy, Candace K. Cottrell
Interior and Cover Design: Candace K. Cottrell
Cover photo of woman: Frank Antonio

The DiamonD Syndicate

A Novel by

ERICA HILTON

Also by Erica Hilton

10 Crack Commandments
Dirty Little Angel

Part One

✦ ONE ✦

Diamonds in the Rough
1956

Diamond Reed was raised by her father Chester after her mother Betty walked out on them when Diamond was a child. After putting up with Chester's cheating, manipulation, and physical and mental abuse, not to mention Diamond's vindictive ways, Betty had finally had enough.

Betty was raised in a household with fourteen brothers and sisters, and had to fight and work hard for anything she wanted, so she believed that people should work hard for what they want. In her eyes, Chester was raising Diamond all wrong, spoiling her and never making her take responsibility for her actions. When she tried to teach Diamond how to cook and clean, Chester simply objected and reprimanded her for trying to make a slave out of his only daughter.

Diamond was a daddy's girl, and nothing her father did would change the love she had for him. Chester gave her everything she ever wanted and worshipped the ground she walked on, and she, in turn, worshipped him.

Diamond learned at an early age how to manipulate her parents, always going against her mother because she knew her father would give in to her. She became quite the little schemer at getting what she wanted. One time she asked her mother for a new doll she saw on television, but Betty said no.

"But why can't I have it, Mommy?"

"Because, Diamond, you have a closet full of dolls and toys that you don't even play with. Your father just bought you a brand-new dollhouse with two dolls two days ago. Go play with that," Betty told her without taking her eyes off the television.

Betty was a full figured woman, with unwanted extra weight that stayed with her after giving birth to Diamond. Her beautiful doll-like eyes sat perfectly behind her long eyelashes.

"But, Mommy that is the best doll ever." Diamond pleaded with the same baby-doll eyes as her mother. She wore two ponytail braids that reached her shoulders with ribbons tied to each end.

"Diamond, please go somewhere and sit down. Let you tell it, every toy on TV is the best ever." Betty wrinkled her wide nose, which sat over a pair of full lips. Her chin came to a point, making her cheekbones look high.

Diamond stood there fuming, her bushy brows furrowed, and the little wheels in her head began to spin as she plotted a way to get the doll. The dimples deepened in her pecan-colored cheeks, and the nostrils in her button nose began to flare. She stomped off to her room and slammed the door.

Betty simply ignored her temper tantrum.

Not even twenty minutes later, Diamond reappeared in the living room with her Barbie suitcase in her hand. She'd decided to run away.

Betty looked over at her, and a smile crept across her face. "What are you doing?"

"I'm running away. Now give me some money to catch the bus," Diamond demanded.

Betty fell out in laughter so hard her D-cup breasts jiggled. "You're kidding me, right? Where do you think your little butt is going? You aren't old enough to do anything."

"I'm leaving because you don't love me. You won't buy me the doll." Diamond stood there pouting and crying.

"Diamond, get your behind back upstairs before I give you something to really cry about." Betty folded her arms the best she could over her large breasts and refocused her attention on her stories.

Diamond wasn't satisfied with her mother's reaction. She'd expected her mother to run to her crying and then buy the doll for her. Mad that her plan hadn't worked, she stomped off to the kitchen.

She whipped her head around and her shoulder length hair swung. "And you better stop all that stomping before I get up for real and whup your behind!"

"No, you won't!" a fresh Diamond sassed her.

"What did you say?" Betty yelled narrowing her eyes.

"I'm leaving because you don't love me. Now give me some money!" Diamond continued to scream while standing in the middle of the kitchen floor.

Betty appeared in the doorway with a belt, having heard enough, and began to give Diamond a spanking she would never forget. She snatched her up and dragged her kicking and screaming to the front door. In the other hand she held Diamond's suitcase. "You want to run away, go right ahead, but I'm not giving you any money. You think you're grown, then fend for yourself." She put Diamond on the front porch. She was only going to leave her in the enclosed porch for a few minutes to teach her a lesson.

Betty closed the front door and peeked out the window. Diamond sat on the floor crying. She then got up, sat on the porch sofa, and pouted. Happy with the results of her punishment, Betty sat down to catch up on her stories, knowing Diamond would be knocking on the door in due time.

About an hour and a half later, Chester came walking through the door. "Hey, baby," he greeted her. He stood at six feet three inches of pure gorgeousness. The soft black curls in his short afro fit his narrow head perfectly. He had German in his bloodline, from which he acquired his soft hair.

Betty immediately became tense. She was so wrapped up in her stories, she'd forgotten to get Diamond off the porch before Chester came home. "Hi, honey, h-how was your day?" she asked.

"I had a good day! Where's my pumpkin? I want to take her to the store with me." He looked around. His caramel complexion was even-toned, and he bore the same deep dimples as Diamond.

Betty began to shake. Hadn't he seen Diamond sitting on the porch when he came in? Maybe she was hiding, but where? She walked over to the door and stepped out onto the porch. She looked around, puzzled.

Chester stood at the door watching her. "What are you looking for?" His bushy eyebrows now rose with suspicion.

"Diamond," she said, fearing the worst.

"What do you mean, Diamond? Where is she, Betty?" His voice deepened. The muscles in his slim but muscular arms began to flex.

"Well, she was sassing me earlier and told me she was running away. Chester, she was really being disrespectful, so I thought I would teach her a lesson and let her sit on the porch for a while." Betty was more petrified of Chester beating her than of her own child going missing.

"Wait a minute, you what? You put my daughter on the porch alone because of what?" he yelled, moving closer to her with his hands now balled into fists and his already deep dimples appearing like two drilled holes in his cheeks.

"She was right here, Chester." Betty pointed toward the porch sofa in a panic as she backed up a little.

His button nose had become red. "With all the child molesters and kidnappers in the world today, you hand a sick rapist my daughter on a platter!"

Before Betty could react, she felt a blow on the side of her head.

She immediately saw stars and couldn't keep her balance. Falling to the floor hard, she curled up in a fetal position, waiting for the kicks she knew would come. But there were no kicks. Instead Chester grabbed her by her legs and dragged her across the shag carpet, giving her rug burns on her back and buttocks. Then he dragged her up the stairs, letting her head hit each step, causing her to become dizzy.

He pulled her into the bathroom and made her stand. Betty didn't know what Chester was going to do to her, but she was gonna fight him with all her strength. She tried to defend herself, but each time she fought against him, the next punch was even more brutal. She heard her nose crack, and then he punched her in the eye, and she heard the bones crack. She was barely conscious when he stripped off her clothes and tied her wrists to the showerhead in the bathtub, where she hung like a side of beef in a freezer.

Chester turned on the shower, and Betty began to regain consciousness. Her head felt like it was going to explode from the broken nose and broken eye socket. With swollen eyes, she looked over at Chester and saw a look on his face that she'd never seen before. He turned off the water and left the bathroom. She wondered what he was going to do next, because she knew he wasn't finished with her. She also wondered why he wasn't out looking for Diamond, instead of torturing her to death.

He reappeared in the bathroom carrying a thick all-weather extension cord he used for the hedge trimmer. He wrapped the cord around his hand and began to beat her with it. If there was anything worse than feeling the pain from being hit with the thick cord, Betty didn't want to experience it.

Every time Chester came down on her with the cord, excruciating pain shot through her body. He would hit her several times in a row, and then he let hot water run down her body. Betty was in so much pain, she could no longer scream. Her dark complexion didn't show much sign of brutality, but the swelling was obvious.

Sitting just outside the bathroom door listening and snickering was Diamond. She'd gone around the corner and waited for her father to come home. After he'd walked in the house, she followed him inside. Once the beating started, she revealed herself to Chester, but stayed hidden from Betty.

That day Chester beat Betty far worse than he'd ever done in the past.

After he was finished, he called for his daughter. "Come here, baby," he said, reaching for her.

Diamond ran into her father's arms.

"I'm gonna teach you how to be a real woman. I'm gonna show you how to have every man eating outta the palm of your hand. You are a diamond in the rough. Do you hear me?" He looked at her.

"Yes, Daddy."

"Diamond, sweetheart, if anyone asks you what happened, you don't know."

"I know, Daddy, just like before."

"Now go to your room and don't come out. I'll be up later."

"OK, Daddy."

With Betty bedridden and unable to move for several days, Diamond had the run of the house.

Two weeks later Betty was released from the hospital after suffering a broken arm, a concussion, and several other broken bones on different body parts, all at the hands of Chester. She realized then that she was a prisoner in her own home. Chester and Diamond walked around the house in bliss, while she had a broken heart and no self-esteem, her spirit shattered. But what Chester and Diamond didn't know was that Betty Reed vowed to herself that she would never receive a beating like that again.

About two months after being released from the hospital, Betty got a call from the school to come get Diamond, who was being expelled for fighting. Betty assumed Diamond had a little scuffle with one of the little girls at school, but to her surprise, Diamond's actions were far worse than she'd imagined. Diamond had actually kicked a little boy in his penis and then taken a pencil and stabbed him in the leg.

On the ride home Betty looked over at Diamond and saw her serene face. "Diamond, why did you do that to the little boy?"

"Because he wouldn't give me his snack."

"Didn't you get a snack?"

"Yes."

"So why did you want his, if you had your own?"

"Because I wanted his too, and Daddy said if I want something, then I have to go after it." She looked over at Betty.

"Diamond, he didn't say fight for it. He didn't mean it that way." Betty was furious. She had always told Chester that Diamond was too young to understand his lectures. Now the little boy's parents were pressing charges.

"Mommy, I'm not gonna let nobody take anything from me, and Daddy showed me how to hurt a boy in his privates. He said that if I did that, the boy would give me anything I wanted."

"Well, that's wrong, Diamond, and I don't want you to ever do that again!"

"I do what Daddy tells me, not you!" Diamond looked at her mother with pure evil in her eyes.

When they got home, Betty beat the living hell out of Diamond, not caring about the repercussions when Chester got home.

When Chester arrived home from work later that night, Betty was in the kitchen preparing dinner. She was hoping he was in a good mood since he had been out with one of his flings. It was later than his usual time to get home.

As soon as Chester walked into the living room, Betty grabbed the dish towel from off of the counter to wipe her hands. She headed for the living room to greet Chester and tell him about the incident with Diamond in school and the young boy's parents pressing charges on them.

As Betty entered the living room, Diamond raced down the steps and jumped into her father's arms. Betty was outdone. She had told Diamond to stay in her room until she was called.

"Hey Pumpkin!" Chester planted kisses all over her cheeks.

"Mommy beat me," she pouted, looking deep into Chester's brown eyes with anguish.

Betty could see the thick vein begin to swell on the side of his neck and knew the rage was building.

Betty was terrified. "Diamond! Now you tell your father why I beat you!"

"Daddy, she beat me for no reason." Her innocence continued to play on Chester's heart.

"No! Chester, your daughter has gotten in the worst trouble at school today. She's caused charges to be pressed against us for striking another child." Betty did the best she could to get the story out before Chester could react.

She noticed that he was putting Diamond to the floor and she could see the scary, distant look in his eyes. It was as if he was staring right through her. She began to back away from him into the kitchen. Chester followed her slowly, not blinking once. He seemed like a trained robot out to kill.

"Chester, please just think about what I said. She's gotten us into a lot of trouble, and it's gonna cost us money. The boy's parents is gonna press charges! Are you listening to me?"

But Chester never said a word. He continued to walk toward Betty with Diamond on his heels, peering around him at Betty.

Betty backed herself up against the refrigerator and immediately covered her face, expecting the blows to begin. Chester stood in front of her and didn't throw one punch. By now Betty was crying. She knew he was standing in front of her, but she didn't know why he hadn't struck her.

When she lowered her arms some so that she could look at him, that's when the hot oil and fried chicken from the skillet she'd just turned off came flying her way. She screamed in agony as the hot oil and fried chicken pieces singed her skin. Even Diamond had to hide her face from the sight, and this was a first. Betty's skin seemed to burn right off of her. The white meat underneath her dark skin became visible.

Betty fell to the floor, kicking and screaming as her skin burned. Diamond covered her ears but continued to watch her mother squirm. Chester however, stood over her and watched her suffer in pain.

Betty lay in the hospital for three weeks, healing from the burns and stewing about her mistreatment. She decided she had had enough of Chester and Diamond and their wicked ways. The day after she was released, after Diamond went to school and Chester went to work, Betty packed her bags and never returned.

As Diamond grew, Chester continued to school her on how to get whatever she wanted.

"Baby girl, you're thirteen now, and I know these little niggas are gonna try to get in your drawers. I'm gonna give you something to help protect yourself with." Chester walked into the dining room, reached into his coat pocket, and presented his daughter with a pearl-handled .22. "Only use this when necessary," he told her.

Diamond's eyes bulged at the sight. "Thanks, Daddy!" She threw her arms around her father's neck and hugged him tight.

"I'm gonna show you how to use this."

"OK." She smiled, examining the gun.

"This is for them niggas that don't take no for an answer. You haven't let them get any of your coochie, have you?" he asked with a raised eyebrow.

"No, Daddy. I know better than that. Can't none of these boys do nothing for me that I can't do for myself, so if you give nothing, you get nothing," she said with attitude.

"That's my girl." Chester smiled a proud smile. "Are those young punks tryna date you?"

"Yeah, they tryna be with me, but I do my schoolwork and ignore them little boys." She waved her hand in dismissal, still gawking at the gun she held in her hand.

"Sit down, baby girl." He patted the sofa. "Just because your mother walked out, I don't want you to think she wasn't a good mother. She was a damn good mother and wife. It's just that, when it came to you, we didn't agree on things. I don't ever want you to think that it's OK for a man to lay his hands on you. I know you saw me do that to your mother, but that ain't cool, Diamond." Chester looked deep into his daughter's eyes. He was missing Betty so much, and looking into Diamond's face reminded him of her.

He added, "If a man ain't bringing nothing to the table, then he don't need to sit down to eat. These young punks ain't shit in this day and age. Use your brains and what I taught you, and you will go far in this world. Don't accept anything less than perfect. If you gonna lay down with dogs, then you bound to get up with fleas. A flea is one of the lowest insects that feed on meat, biting and sucking blood from the living, just like a tick."

Diamond nodded, giving her father her undivided attention. She knew she deserved to get whatever she wanted, whenever she wanted it, and no one could tell her anything different.

"Now, if you pull that thing out, then you better use it. That's why I don't want you to pull it out on no one unless it is an extreme emergency. You understand me?"

"Yes, Daddy, I promise." She hugged him.

"You're my diamond, and diamonds are forever. I would kill a nigga over you."

By the time Diamond graduated high school, she had the sex game on lock. She was a female pimp, tricking the high school boys to her advantage. All the boys in the school wanted to sex her, but they had to pay a hefty price.

✦✦ ✦✦ TWO ✦✦ ✦✦

Virgin No More

As the years passed, Diamond continued to get in trouble in school, often getting into fights, and she didn't have a problem displaying her lack of respect for her teachers either. Diamond knew all she had to do was play on her father's emotions and he would get her out of trouble.

Chester lacked book smarts, but he made up for it in street smarts. Everyone knew his reputation, teachers included, and no one wanted to get into a confrontation with him. The principal of the school, especially, didn't want any part of Chester after he'd witnessed firsthand how ruthless he could be. Chester at one time worked as an enforcer for one of the most ruthless drug cartels back in the day. His reputation preceded him, and most didn't cross him because of the rumors that still lurked. So instead of expelling Diamond from the school system, they simply allowed her to have her way, and she slid through high school.

In her senior year a bunch of the seniors planned to go to Atlantic City for an overnight stay. Diamond had never stayed away from home overnight, but she really wanted to go on this trip. She had a crush on the captain of the basketball team, Maurice, but he didn't feel the same way about her. She figured the trip would provide an opportunity for them to get closer.

Maurice knew who Diamond was, and all he wanted was to get in her drawers.

But Diamond really did like him. She wanted to experience sex with him, and not the way she'd sexed the others for gifts or money. She wanted to be his girlfriend.

She knew her father wouldn't let her leave home for an overnight stay, the one thing he didn't allow. She could have as many friends stay overnight with her as she wanted, but she could never spend the night at their houses or attend sleepover parties. There were times, though, when she snuck out of the house when her father was asleep, and she made sure to be back home in bed before dawn.

She knew Chester wouldn't budge on her staying out all night in Atlantic City, so she had to formulate a plan quickly.

"Dad, you home?" she yelled as she walked in the door after school.

"In the kitchen!"

"Hey, Daddy." Diamond walked over to him and kissed him on the cheek as she did every day.

"Hey, Pumpkin."

Chester was washing the dishes that had piled in the sink for three days. Diamond had still not acquired domestic skills, and wasn't accustomed to manual labor. Most of the time Chester hired someone to come clean the house for them, but he had been laid off from his job and needed to cut back on expenses, not knowing how long the layoff would be.

Diamond sat down at the kitchen table and opened her books to do her homework. "Dad, Tina wanted to know if I could spend the night with her tonight," she said, never lifting her head.

"You know the rules, Diamond." Chester kept scrubbing the pan.

"But, Daddy, I'm seventeen. I'm gonna be graduating high school this year, and you mean to tell me you still don't trust me?" She looked up at him with pitiful eyes, something he usually couldn't resist.

Chester looked over at her and quickly turned back to washing the dishes. He could never look into her beautiful eyes. They weakened him when he stared too long at them.

"When you graduate high school you can do whatever you want, but until then you are still a minor in my house. I don't trust these clowns out here today. Times have changed, and they around here raping young women, killing them, and stringing them out on drugs, only to put them on the stroll. That's not gonna happen to my baby."

"You're kidding me, right?" Diamond laughed. "Daddy, you taught me everything I know. Do you honestly think I am that naïve to let something happen to me? Besides, I'm gonna be in the house."

"What y'all gonna be doing over there, Diamond?"

"Well, we plan to go to the movies, but Tina's mother is taking us and picking us up," she lied. "We're gonna go to an early show so we can be back at the house early."

Diamond had mastered the lying game at an early age.

"I don't know." Chester shook his head.

"OK, listen, Daddy, I promise you I will call you at least a couple of times during the night so you know I'm all right, OK?"

Chester stared at her for a few moments. "OK, Diamond, but you have to call me every hour until you go to bed."

"Thanks, Daddy! I love you!" Diamond leaped from the table and wrapped her arms around his neck.

He kissed her on the cheek. "You still got that piece I gave you, right?"

"Yup, I sure do. I keep it right here." She patted her breast.

For the first time, Chester realized his seventeen-year-old daughter had breasts like a grown woman. He started to protest the outing, but then dismissed his reservations, realizing she was packing and knew how to use it.

Diamond was the happiest teenager alive. For two hours that Friday night in a cheap motel in Atlantic City, she had sex over and over again with Maurice and one of his teammates.

When the boys were done pulling a train on her, their plan was to tag-team the other two basketball players waiting their turn in another room. But these boys didn't know Diamond was gonna get hers before anything else jumped off.

"So y'all about to bounce?" she asked, lying there in the bed covered by a sheet.

"Yup," Maurice said as they got dressed to leave.

The two boys looked at each other and smirked.

"So, what's up? I know y'all gonna leave me some cash before y'all leave." She rose up on her elbows.

Maurice screwed up his face. "How you sound? I ain't giving you shit, trick." He laughed and slapped five with his teammate.

Diamond's eyes narrowed as she nodded. "OK," she said quietly.

The boys finished getting dressed, and Diamond got out of the bed. Her flawless hourglass figure still glistening with sweat, she reached down into her jeans pocket and pulled out the gun. She then slipped on her pumps and walked toward the boys.

The boys were lacing up their sneakers and didn't see Diamond approaching. When they stood, Diamond kicked Maurice's friend in the groin, causing him to double over and fall to the floor. Before Maurice could react, she had her gun resting against his dick.

"Come on, man! What are you doing?"

Diamond smiled at him. "Oh, we ain't talking that smack now, are we?"

"Hey, what you doing?"

Diamond reached down into his pocket and pulled out the money he had in there. She looked down and counted thirty dollars. "Is this all the money you got?" She peered up at him.

"Yeah, man. Come on, Diamond!"

"I should shoot off your dick for this chump change! Get the fuck outta my room!" She rammed the gun farther into his groin.

"Ow! Come on, Diamond!"

"You better not say shit to nobody about this. Trust me, I know how to use this gun, and I won't have a problem using it either."

"I won't!" he said, still standing there, his hands raised in the air.

"Give me what your boy got in his pockets too," she said to Maurice, the gun trained on him.

After Maurice reached down into his teammate's pockets, retrieved the money, and tossed it at Diamond's feet, she struck him across the forehead.

He fell to his knees and held his head. "Please, no!" he yelled, now more frightened than ever.

Diamond placed the gun to the back of his head. "This is not a game," she growled at him. "You better not say shit!"

"I told you I wouldn't say nothing!"

"Get your boy and get the fuck outta my room!"

Maurice scrambled to get his teammate to his feet, and they both walked out of the motel room, never to cross Diamond Reed again.

Diamond, a satisfied smile on her face, lay on the bed naked with her pumps still on and counted her money.

After her mother had left home, Diamond secretly missed her with a passion, but she would never tell her father that because she thought he hated Betty. She thought that was the way it was supposed to be. In school she would get mad when other students talked about their mother, or their mothers would come to the school to attend functions. She had longed for her mother all through high school as well, but never told anyone.

Instead, Diamond began to hold resentment toward her mother for walking out on them, and the animosity mounted by the day. She never knew any of her aunts, uncles, or cousins because her father had kept her away from her mother's side of the family, and he only had a few family members, none of whom seemed to like him too much either.

Diamond eventually went off to college. But she stopped speaking to her father her sophomore year. Her father had stopped sending her money and hadn't made a payment on her tuition in over three months, and the school was threatening to remove her from her dorm unless a payment was made.

Diamond came home that weekend, which was something she rarely did. She didn't have to because she was living the life of a queen on campus. She had all the boys doing what she wanted them to do and taking care of her the way she wanted, so the money her father sent her was extra money for her to trick off on buying designer clothes.

She knew her father had sold the house and relocated, but she hadn't been to the new place. In her mind she thought it was another house, but when she arrived by taxi at the rundown rooming house, she knew it had to be a mistake. But curiosity damn near killed her she entered the building and met an elderly lady.

The woman greeted her with a warm smile. "Hello, chile."

"Yes, um, is there a Chester Reed staying here?" Diamond could barely stand looking at the woman in her dirty housedress.

"Why, yes. His room is upstairs on the second floor, second door on the left."

Diamond could have thrown up in her mouth. She turned on her heels and proceeded to climb the stairs, making sure she stayed in the middle to avoid touching anything.

But what she saw next was enough to make a grown man cry. She walked into the open room, which smelled of stale liquor and dirty clothes, and saw her father sitting on the bed looking at a thirteen-inch black-and-white television. He had lost considerable weight and looked weary and used-up.

He looked up at her, and shame filled his eyes.

"D-Daddy, what the hell?" Diamond couldn't even get the words out of her mouth.

Chester explained to her that once he was laid off from his job he never could find another job making the amount of money he was accustomed to. He found himself doing petty jobs here and there and moonlighting at night. He had told her he sold the house when, in all actuality, he lost the house. Chester had lost his life trying to please his daughter. He worked to pay her tuition and keep her pockets filled, but neglected his responsibilities. After that he turned to the bottle, further burying himself in debt and drowning his sorrows.

"You sorry son of a bitch! You ain't no man! How the hell are you gonna teach me how to stay away from certain types of men, and you the same trash I'm supposed to avoid?"

With no remorse, Diamond walked out of her father's life, never to return.

✦✧✦✧ THREE ✦✧✦✧

Shot
1997

The bright rays from the sun nearly blinded the three fifteen-year-olds who sat on the front steps of the three-story garden apartment building marked A. Music came from the huge speakers that sat in the open trunk of a tan Nissan Maxima. The car was parked in front of Building C, two buildings away, but with the volume raised so high, the speakers acted as surround sound for the neighborhood. They all rocked their heads to the beat as Biggie spit game.

Notorious B.I.G. did his signature call over the beat, "Uh, uh," and the bass line dropped, sending "Hypnotize" blaring from the speakers.

The young dealers who stood in front of Building C jumped up and down and rapped along with Biggie while they smoked weed and drank beer.

The sad look on the faces of the three teens in front of Building A was because they couldn't hang with the Building C crew. They knew the crewmembers, but they didn't live the life that the young dealers did. In fact, they only spoke to them in passing.

"All I know is this shit is for the birds!" Trey said, looking down the street at the young dealers.

"So what you 'bout to do, kid?" his friend Al-Malik asked.

Trey, Al-Malik, and Dante were bored on this lazy summer day and wanted something to do. The neighborhood they lived in always had something going on, whether it was a street fight or a drive-by. Just about every week somebody got shot at, robbed, or killed in Newark, New Jersey. It was just the way things were.

"I'm saying, I ain't tryna sit here all night. Ain't nothing popping off tonight," Trey said.

"Not so far, but give it some time," Al-Malik said. "Somebody bound to get they shit pushed back. I mean, what you tryna get into?"

"I dunno. Anything but this shit!" Trey stood, walked down two steps, and began to look up and down the street as if searching for someone.

"Well, you ain't saying nothing, nigga," Dante finally said. "All you doing is bitching right now."

Unlike Dante, Trey and Al-Malik had siblings, so they were used to excitement, and spent most of their time sitting on Dante's porch or in his room playing video games, trying to escape the chaos of their own homes.

"I'm saying, man, anything is better than this. Let's just go take a walk or something," Trey said, bored out of his mind.

The three of them continued to watch the group of teens at the other complex who seemed to be having a ball. They watched cars pull up to the curb in front of Building C. Then they watched the young dealers sell drugs to the occupants of the cars. At times it looked like a drive-thru at a White Castle, with cars waiting in line to get served.

But the three young men sitting on the steps of Building A had never wanted a part in that lifestyle. At least they pretended not to. Although they lived in a drug-infested neighborhood, they'd managed to avoid getting caught up. But on this day, with nothing to do and no money to go anywhere, Trey was getting restless, and a part of him wished he was part of the Building C crew.

"Where you wanna go, Trey?" Al-Malik asked. "We ain't got no loot."

"That's the problem. I'm tired of not having no paper."

"Trey, shut the hell up, man! You killing me!"

Trey scowled at Dante, not feeling like getting into another debate with him. They argued about everything. To the average person, it would seem as if they didn't like each other very much, but that was just the way they were. They had nothing but love for each other and would have each other's back in a heartbeat.

Dante was somewhat the leader of the trio. He tried to keep the other two from venturing into the belly of the beast. Dante had to get good grades in school or suffer the consequences at the hands of his mother. He knew the potential the other two had and made sure that Trey and Al-Malik did their homework and helped them with it if needed. He was the levelheaded one of the bunch. Trey always got into fights because he got picked on for his weight, and Dante always had his back, although Trey didn't need any help, because he could handle his own.

The boys had made an agreement about their futures in junior high, and Dante made sure he reminded them of it, to keep them focused. Dante wanted to do something with his life, but it wasn't easy. Sometimes he thought about selling drugs to get his own money, just like he knew Trey thought about it.

Trey was a handsome young man standing at six feet two inches tall. Although he was overweight for his height, he was quick on his feet. He weighed close to 360 pounds, but could play basketball just like the average-sized athlete. He was the oldest child in a household of six boys and two girls, all living in a small three-bedroom apartment. He shared a room with two of his brothers. The living quarters were cramped, and they didn't have much.

The one important thing that Trey always lacked was adult guidance. His mother was too busy playing cards, drinking, and having babies to pay him any attention. In fact, she put the bulk of the responsibilities on

Trey. Trey was stressed and felt overwhelmed at times. He had a good head on his shoulders and was a good kid, but his outbursts and temper came from the amount of weight and pressure he felt on his shoulders to be the man of the house. He was a time bomb waiting to explode.

Dante knew Trey was a good person underneath all his gruffness, and this was why he would never give up on Trey. Each and every time Trey hinted that he wanted to start selling drugs, Dante would reason with him until he relented.

Trey tossed his shoulder-length dreads out of his face and shoved his hands in the pockets of his size 46x30 jeans. The bottom of his jeans dragged on the ground as he walked down the steps and began to pace on the sidewalk.

After about another ten minutes of silence, while Trey paced, the front door to the building opened. The three young men looked up to see Diamond standing in the doorway.

"Fellas, what's going on?" she asked in her smooth, hypnotizing voice.

Dante and Diamond lived alone in the two-bedroom Section 8 apartment. They were on welfare and didn't have much, but what they did have Diamond kept neat and clean. She didn't work and didn't have the desire to answer to anyone. She relied on her looks and skills to overpower a man's mind and get by. Diamond had never wanted for nothing, until the well finally ran dry and she had to turn to public assistance three years ago.

"How you doing, Ms. Reed?" Trey asked, smiling brightly with lust in his eyes.

"How you doing, Ms. Reed?" Al-Malik asked.

Diamond knew she had it going on, and she loved the attention her son's friends gave her. She loved to play with their young minds. "How's your mother, Malik?" she asked, running her hand through her shoulder-length hair.

"Uh . . . she's a'ight," Al-Malik stuttered, ready to nut in his pants.

He secretly lusted over Diamond. In fact, all the young boys in the neighborhood wanted her.

"Dante, I'll be back," she said to her son. "You gonna be here?"

"I don't know, Ma."

"Well, I'll see y'all later," she said.

Trey and Al-Malik watched Diamond as she descended the steps, her hips rotating in a smooth, swaying motion as she walked away. She winked at Trey. Both boys stared awestruck at her ass while she walked up the street.

Diamond purposely added extra swing to her walk. She got off on teasing men, both young and old. But Diamond preferred a young man as opposed to someone her own age. Young boys were easier to train and didn't lack stamina. At her age she needed a man who could go the distance. Diamond needed the young boys for her other agenda as well, and unbeknownst to them, her son and his friends were on her list.

"Damn, man, your moms got a fatty!" Trey exclaimed.

"Word up!" Al-Malik cosigned.

"Yo! What the fuck, man? That's my mother!"

"I'm just saying, man." Trey laughed and gave a pound to Al-Malik, who was laughing with him.

"That shit ain't funny! Y'all muthafuckas gonna catch a bullet talking 'bout my moms!"

"A bullet? From where, nigga? You ain't got no gat." Trey continued to laugh, clowning Dante.

"Yeah, but I heard Ms. Reed got one," Al-Malik said.

Dante hated the way Diamond flaunted around the neighborhood. The men in the neighborhood would whoop and spew sex slurs at her, trying to holler at her. It seemed that Diamond loved the attention, though, and she would flirt outrageously with them. Dante got embarrassed sometimes, because they would talk about her in front of him with no respect. When he was younger he would get into fights at school because Diamond would come to pick him up wearing revealing clothing. The male teachers would simply drool over her with no regard for Dante and how their disrespectful behavior made him feel.

"What up, Trey?" a young boy walking by asked as he slapped hands with Trey. He held a stack of cash in his free hand.

"Damn! It's like that?" Trey asked, nodding at the wad of bills.

"Hell, yeah, man. I'm telling you, y'all niggas better jump on some of this loot," the boy said as he continued to walk down the street.

Trey said to Dante and Al-Malik, "That's what I'm talking about." He pointed at the boy.

"What are you talking about?" Dante already knew what Trey was referring to. Lately he'd been giving subtle hints about selling drugs.

"I'm talking about getting some paper!" He pointed to the dealers up the street.

"What . . . you tryna get put on with them niggas?" Al-Malik asked. The thought had also crossed his mind on several occasions, and Trey had been putting the bug in his ear, unbeknownst to Dante.

Al-Malik was a bit naive and, at Trey's prompting, was leaning toward hustling. He, too, had several siblings living in cramped quarters. Al-Malik was the youngest of four, and his siblings were drug users who used their sickly mother for a place to stay because they were lazy and had no ambition. Al-Malik's two older brothers were on the streets hustling, and his older sister was raising two kids of her own in the hostile environment of Newark.

"Why not?" Trey asked. "Everybody else is eating but us. We fucking sitting around not doing shit. Our mothers are on welfare and shit. I'm tired of living like this while them niggas getting paid." He looked over at the dealers chopping it up with each other.

"Yeah, I feel you, but we suppose to be staying focused in school. Isn't that what we said?" Al-Malik, his golden, silky cornrows laying neatly on his back, picked at a scab on his knee. His skin was light from his white father, who he'd never met.

The boys had been friends since elementary school. They'd seen a lot of crime go down in their neighborhoods. They'd even lost classmates while growing up. But the three of them had agreed a long time ago to finish school and get out of the hood the right way. After an ex-con visited their junior high school and told them about his experience in the drug game and spending twenty years of his life in prison, Dante, Al-Malik, and Trey made a pact never to get involved in that lifestyle. They would finish high school and then go to college, making it possible for them to get far away from the streets.

"Yeah, I know what we said, but until then, we need to get a hustle, because I ain't built for this shit no more."

Dante and Al-Malik looked at each other and shook their heads. Dante knew selling drugs wasn't an option for him. He could hear his mother's words echoing in his head.

"You better take your ass to school so you can make something of yourself. You owe me a degree from college, and I better not ever catch you selling drugs. I ain't got no money to bail your ass outta jail! You owe me for taking care of your ass. You gonna get that college degree and get a good-paying job to pay me back for all the money I spent raising your dumb ass!"

He'd heard those same words for years. Every time his mother got mad about something or strapped for money, she started her ritual of blaming him for her shortcomings, beating him upside the head as she fussed at him. Then she would leave him lying there crying, only to return to the room to beat him some more for crying too loudly.

"Listen, yo, you can do whatchu want, but I ain't with that," Dante said.

"You's a pussy, man," Trey said. "Your moms got you wrapped around her finger."

"Yeah, a'ight." Dante waved his hand at Trey, dismissing him.

"Man, I'm outta here." Trey walked off, disgusted with his friend.

The two boys' watched Trey walk down the street over to where the other young boys were selling drugs.

"Come on, Malik, let's go in the crib," Dante said.

Al-Malik was confused. He didn't know whether to go in with Dante or to follow Trey. He too was tired of the struggle. He didn't want to sell drugs because he feared being shot, and most of all he feared going to jail. And even he knew from hearing his older siblings talk, that if you harbored fear in your heart, then you wouldn't be able to survive on the mean streets. He hesitated as he looked on and saw Trey laughing and joking with the young boys.

Another one of the young crewmembers pulled up in a brand-new cherry red BMW. Everyone ran over to the car, checking out the rims and the sound system the young dealer had installed.

"Malik," Dante called out, "whatchu gon' do?"

Al-Malik stood. He turned and looked at Dante.

"Come on, man, that ain't nothing but a dead end. He ain't even old enough to have a license. What you think gonna happen as soon as the cops pull him over?" Dante started to climb the steps, hoping Al-Malik would follow his lead. He breathed a sigh of relief when he looked back and saw Al-Malik behind him.

It was a constant struggle to avoid the life that surrounded them every day, but one way or another, Dante was determined to do it.

✦✦✦ ✦✦✦ ✦✦✦

Dante and Al-Malik had just finished playing their third game on the PlayStation Diamond had somehow managed to get for Dante. He never found out how she was able to afford the expensive game system, but he was too thrilled to pry too deeply.

They were getting ready to start up another game of *Resident Evil* when they heard shots outside. Though it was something they'd grown accustomed to throughout their lives, both boys dove to the linoleum floor. Shouts could be heard outside.

When the gunfire ceased, the Dante and Al-Malik raised their heads, assuming the coast was clear. It seemed like the shots had come from where Trey was talking with the young dealers a few buildings away. After standing and walking over to the apartment window, they saw two bodies lying on the ground.

As a small crowd formed in front of the house, an eerie feeling overtook Dante. "Come on," he said to Al-Malik as he bolted for the door.

Al-Malik wasn't far behind. They practically jumped down the two flights of steps, busted through the front door, and ran down the handicap ramp instead of using the stairs. They ran up the street and squeezed their way through the crowd to see who'd been shot.

The teen that had shaken Trey's hand earlier lay twisted on the concrete. Dante looked at the other body that lay by the curb and air escaped his body like a deflating balloon. The eerie feeling that washed over his body rang true. It was Trey. He made his way over to Trey and knelt down beside him.

Seconds later Al-Malik was kneeling as well. "Trey!" Al-Malik shook him.

Trey's eyes rolled around in his head. He'd been shot in the right shoulder, and shock was evident on his face. He took a deep breath, trying to suck in air.

"Yo, who did this?" Dante demanded as he looked up at the sea of faces that stared at Trey.

No one answered. In fact, no one cared about Trey.

"Fuck that! My boy is dead!" one of the young dealers yelled. He still held a smoking gun from the shots he'd fired at the fleeing vehicle. He waved it around frantically, clearly upset about a fallen soldier.

The other dealers continued to rant and rave as well.

"Them niggas is toast!" one stated.

"Who was it?" another inquired.

"I think it was them cats from the Neck!"

"Trey, can you get up?" Dante asked.

Trey simply moaned and groaned, unable to speak.

"Yo, we gotta get him outta here," Dante said.

Al-Malik, whose face was as white as a ghost, couldn't move or speak. This was what he'd always feared about the game, and if he was unsure about going into the game before, Trey getting shot turned him even further away from that lifestyle.

"Yo, man, somebody help me get him outta here," Dante said to no one in particular, realizing Al-Malik wasn't going to be of any help to him.

"Yo, man, fuck that nigga! Let's go buck off on these niggas!" the dealer who seemed to be the leader stated.

The crewmembers all concealed their weapons and began to pile into two of the cars, locked and loaded, and ready to do some retaliation damage.

Dante and Al-Malik remained there alone with a bleeding Trey as they listened to the sounds of an approaching ambulance.

✦ ✦ FOUR ✦ ✦

Scared Straight
1997

A week later Trey got out of the hospital and was at home recovering from the gunshot wound to his shoulder. As Dante walked to Trey's house to visit him, he thought about the past couple days' events. Al-Malik was now down at the Extra Supermarket working as a grocery bagger. Their math teacher had gotten Dante and Al-Malik jobs there. This was Dante's day off, so he decided to visit Trey.

One of Dante's old classmates ran to catch up to him from behind. He shouted, "Ay, yo! Tae, what up, man?"

Dante looked back and waited for Mike to catch up. He'd dropped out of school in the eighth grade.

"What up?"

"What up?" Mike gave Dante a pound. "Where you headed, kid?"

"I'm gonna go check out Trey. Why? What's up?"

The two of them began to walk together.

"Oh, naw, I'm saying, I thought maybe you wanted to get down with me on a package."

"You crazy as fuck, man! What made you think I wanted to get down with you?"

"I'm saying, you don't usually come through here, and I know you heard I'm getting paper. I thought maybe you came through looking for me to get put on."

"You know Trey got shot, right?"

"Yeah, I heard. He a soldier, man."

"How is that shit being a soldier? He coulda lost his life messing around with the same shit you doing! Naw, man, I ain't with that bullshit, so please don't step to me with that shit again!"

Mike stood there in shock for a moment, and then he shrugged his shoulders and went back to his corner to sell drugs.

Dante was furious. *The nerve of that nigga,* he thought.

Dante walked into Trey's house after his younger sister opened the door. The smell of month-old dirty clothes immediately assaulted his nose. "Where Trey?" he asked.

"He in his room." She pointed and walked away.

Dante walked through the dirty apartment. He stepped over several bags of laundry that littered the path down the hall. He knocked on the closed door of the bedroom.

"Yo!" Trey yelled from the other side of the door.

"It's Tae."

"Tae! What up, nigga? Come in."

Dante opened the door and stepped inside the room, closing the door behind him. He stepped over the clothes that littered the floor.

Trey shared the small room with two of his younger brothers, and there was barely enough space to walk around. His twin bed sat against one wall, and a bunk bed sat on the other wall. A six-drawer dresser with a 19-inch color TV on top stood on the wall by the door.

"Damn, man! You need to clean up this room." Dante sat down at the foot of the twin bed Trey lay in.

Trey was happy to see his friend. "What's up, Tae?"

"It's all good. How you feeling, man?"

"I'm a'ight. It's sore, but I'm a soldier." Trey rubbed his heavily wrapped shoulder.

"Yeah, a'ight, soldier, that's what got your ass in that position you in now, being a soldier. Soldiers can die too, nigga." Dante smiled.

Trey laughed. "But I'm one of the *real* soldiers."

"Yeah, OK, you keep thinking that."

They both sat there in awkward silence.

"But seriously," Dante said, "me and Malik got us a little job down at the Extra Supermarket."

"Doing what?"

"We bagging groceries and sweeping."

"Baggin' groceries?" Trey frowned. "Yo, that ain't no real job."

"Whatchu mean, that ain't no real job? We get paid with real cash, nigga."

"Yo, for real." Trey laughed. "I need to make some *real* paper."

Dante looked at Trey in disbelief. After all that had happened, Trey still wanted to hustle.

"Are you shitting me, man?" a shocked Dante asked. "Are you gonna lie there and tell me you still wanna bang, and niggas just got finished putting a bullet in your shoulder?"

Trey never said a word. He simply looked at Dante without blinking.

Dante took that as his answer, and the wheels in his brain began to turn. He was already trying to figure out a way to keep his friend off the corner.

"What about what we said, Trey?"

Trey switched his eyes to the television.

"You remember, right?" Dante persisted.

"Yeah, I remember, man. Stop sweatin' me."

Trey was quickly becoming irritated. Ever since he'd been home, he'd had to listen to his mother bitch about how getting shot was his fault, and now he couldn't help her with his younger siblings. Now he was lying there in his bed and his best friend was bending his ear back, bitching and complaining about him selling drugs.

Trey needed to do something—anything—to get out of the hellhole his mother called home. He wanted nothing more in the world than to make his own way and get his own place away from her. Also, unbeknownst to Dante, Trey wanted revenge. As soon as he got well, he was gonna try to find the cats who'd shot him.

The two boys sat in silence in front of the TV, not really watching it. They seemed to be off somewhere else in their own minds.

The bedroom door burst open and hit the wall behind it with force, jerking Trey and Dante from their trances. In came Trey's six-year-old brother, Evan, who shared the room with him. He slammed the door.

"What the fuck, man! Why you busting up in here like that?" Trey screamed.

"Shut up!" Evan said as he sat on the bottom bunk of his bed.

"Yo, man, get the fuck out!" Trey yelled.

"No! This is my room too!" Evan yelled back. "You get out!"

Trey grabbed one of the many pillows surrounding him and hurled it at Evan.

"Ha-yah!" Evan yelled as he jumped to his feet and blocked it with a karate kick and stood in a karate stance.

Trey yelled, "Get the fuck outta the room!" and reached for another pillow to throw at his little brother, but pain shot through his shoulder. He grimaced and held it, rocking back and forth.

Evan fell back onto his bed in laughter. "Good for you," he said and continued to laugh.

Dante sat there and watched the whole scene unfold. He'd always told Trey that his little brothers and sisters were bad as hell, just like in the cartoon *Bébé's Kids*.

"Evan, can you go up front, so me and your brother can kick it?" Dante asked him.

"Hell, no!" Evan yelled, rolling off his bed and onto the floor. "This is my room too!" he said, hiding on the other side of the bed.

"Ma!" Trey yelled. "Ma!"

The bedroom door opened, and Trey's mother stood there in the doorway. "What the hell you want, boy?"

Her pair of tight low-rise jeans were about three sizes too small. The fabric barely covered her behind. You could see the crack of her ass when her shirt rose. The crotch of the jeans choked her coochie, and her huge belly hung over the waistband. Her breasts were so large, they looked to be the same size as her stomach.

"Ma, tell Evan to get outta here while I got company," Trey said through clenched teeth, his shoulder now throbbing.

She put her hand on her hip, and the meat on her arms sagged like a balloon filled with water. "What the fuck y'all doing in here that he can't stay in here with y'all?"

"Ma, he in here clowning, and me and Dante tryna talk and shit."

"Watch your mouth, boy! If your ass was home helping me take care of these kids, then you wouldn't be in the predicament you're in now." She turned and left. "Evan, come on outta there, boy!" she yelled from the hallway.

"Maaa, I wanna stay! It's my room too," he whined, still hiding behind the bed.

"Bring your ass outta that room, boy!"

Evan climbed over the bed and stomped his way to the door. Grabbing the door handle, he pulled the door behind him as he walked out. Before he stepped completely out of the room, he stuck out his tongue at Trey. "You bitch!" he yelled and slammed the door.

"I hate that little muthafucka!"

"Come on, man, that's your little brother."

"Man, you have no idea what it's like living here. That's why I need to get me some paper up quick and move up outta here."

Dante couldn't argue, because he could only imagine what Trey had to go through living there. Dante thought, *At least Trey don't have to worry about his mother laying hands on him.* Dante sat there saddened as he thought about one of the times when Diamond had done just that.

Diamond had left a nine-year-old Dante home alone while she went out on a date, as she often did. She told him to stay in his room and not to make a sound so as not to alert any of the neighbors that he was home alone.

Late that night, while Dante slept, she busted into his room, turned on the light, and stood there snarling at him.

Dante lay in his bed awake as the light she'd just turned on shone on his innocent face. He sat up in bed, rubbing his eyes, trying to adjust them to the brightness of the light. "Hi, Mommy," he said.

Diamond didn't answer; she kept glaring at him.

"What's wrong, Mommy?"

"What's wrong? *You're* what's wrong! I was offered a trip to the islands tonight that I had to refuse because of you!"

Dante knew what was to come next, so he lay down and pulled the covers over his head.

Diamond proceeded to pull him out of the bed until he hit the floor. She beat him so badly that night, he couldn't attend school for a week because of the visible bruises on his body.

FIVE

Planting the Bait
One Week Later

Dante had just left to go to work, and Diamond sat on the front stoop of the apartment building and watched the young dealers make sales. They were running a serious operation, and her mouth watered at the thought of the paper they were stacking. She hadn't found a man in a long time to take care of her like she was used to. She was tired of struggling and wanted the finer things in life.

Diamond considered herself high-maintenance, but how could she be high-maintenance with no money and no means of being able to manipulate men the way she used to? It was as if she was losing her touch, or men were no longer going for the *you-gotta-pay-my-bills-before-you-can-hit-this* game. Either way, the money she was getting from welfare wasn't cutting it.

She didn't always think this way, despite the monster her father had created within her when she was young. She actually always wanted to be married to the fairytale prince, but she'd repeatedly ruin her chances by being so demanding. Diamond never had a problem as far as looks were concerned, and she had the body as well. Men always flocked to her, and she always managed to get the best of them to wine and dine her. The only problem with Diamond keeping a man was her controlling ways. Not long after she would lock a man down, she would start trying to control their lives. This ultimately turned men off or ran them away completely, and she'd be left alone again. But Diamond would just move on to the next victim.

As she sat there she thought about how sad her heart really was, which she covered up by behaving the way she did. Being aggressive and putting up a front was the only way she knew how to protect her heart. But, truth be told, she was missing her mother. She'd always missed her mother, and now as an adult she often wished her mother was still in her life. She thought about how her father couldn't teach her the womanly things her mother could have. Like how to mend a broken heart and how to deal with a man.

Diamond struggled and battled with her own mind, and she longed for someone to truly love her for herself and not what was between her legs. The one chance she did get at love was stripped away from her, which made her very bitter and abrasive toward people.

At one time in her life, she did manage to find who she thought was Mr. Right. His name was Byron. Byron was everything a woman wanted in a man. He had the looks, the money, and the charm. He was also a non-confrontational man. When Diamond would go off on one of her hissy fits because she couldn't get her way, he simply gave her time to calm down and used his mellow swagger to make her melt in the palm of his hands. It seemed as if Byron was that balance that Diamond needed in her life. He was the one who kept her grounded, and only gave in to her selfish and spoiled ways at just the right times.

Diamond eventually fell deeply in love with Byron. This was something she had never allowed herself to do—love. She'd always been the dominant one in her relationships, and now the tables were turned. Byron dominated the relationship without ever having to be forceful. But just when Diamond thought this was going to be her fairytale knight and shining armor to marry her and live happily ever after, Byron left her for another woman.

She was blindsided. She thought their relationship was fine. To say that Diamond was heartbroken was an understatement. She never got a chance to confront Byron or the mistress that he left her for. Diamond tried her best to find out any information on who the woman was that Byron left her for. But she always came up empty-handed. All she had was a letter that he left behind letting her know that she had a lot of growing up to do and that he needed a woman who wasn't so needy. He wanted a woman to equally give him back the love he gave.

Diamond must have cried for weeks on end, beating herself up and trying to figure out what she could've done differently. Never coming up with any answers, Diamond turned her sorrow into rage, therefore reawakening the monster within her.

And being picked on and ridiculed in high school didn't help much. It actually made her tough and numb to others' feelings.

She'd sometimes cry at night in her bed, thinking back on how she grew up being called a whore when she was really just looking for love. But Diamond didn't realize she was in need of counseling. Her father gave her any and everything she wanted and protected her to no end. He succumbed to her demanding ways, but he never gave her what she truly needed, and that was genuine love.

As she sat on the front step, Diamond watched one young dealer in particular. His name was Pop, and he seemed to be the one who ran the crew. He was tall and muscular, and his thuggish swagger turned her on. She watched him boast while the muscles in his arms flexed. Pop spoke with emphasis, although she couldn't hear what he was saying clearly.

And then he did it. He grabbed his crotch, and moisture seeped from Diamond's vagina. It was his swagger that turned her on. It made her think that he could get it popping in bed. Diamond began to picture him mounting her as she rubbed his muscular arms while he lay on top of her in a push-up position.

"Pop!" she called out to him.

Pop didn't hear her at first, so she called him again. He looked in her direction, and she waved for him to come over.

"How you doing, Ms. Reed?" he asked as he approached the steps.

"How you doing, Pop?"

"It's all good, Ms. Reed. What's up?" He stared at the mountain of cleavage that spilled over the top of the tank top she wore.

"Nothing much. I know you got all them little girls running after you," she said, crossing her legs in a pair of tight shorts.

Pop smiled and exposed a perfect set of white teeth, making him look like a movie star. He gawked at Diamond's thick, toned legs and licked his smooth, thick lips, envisioning what he would do to her if given the chance.

"Yeah, they tryna get with a cat, you know." He blushed as he ran his hand across the sea of waves that layered his small, round head.

"Well, if you ever get tired of playing with little girls, you come see a real woman," she said, uncrossing her legs and opening them so Pop could see the outline of her coochie.

"Word?" Pop asked almost in shock.

"Word, baby boy." She stood. She then winked at him before she turned to give him a full view of her fat ass as she walked up the stairs.

"Where Dante?" Pop asked.

"He won't be back for a while. He went to work." She winked at him.

Pop stood there licking his lips. He looked back down at the crew, and they were still talking amongst themselves. He looked up and Diamond had disappeared into the hallway. Pop quickly walked up the stairs and into the building behind her.

✦✧✦ ✦✧✦ ✦✧✦

About an hour later, Diamond and Pop lay on her bed catching their breaths after a rambunctious session.

"That was real good, baby boy," she said, panting.

Pop smiled. "Damn, Ms. Reed, you got the bomb pussy."

Diamond smiled. She already knew that much. "Damn!" she said, sitting up in bed.

"What's up?" a concerned Pop asked.

"I gotta figure something out. They about to cut off my lights, and I don't get my check for another two weeks." She placed her head in her hands, pouring it on thick.

"How much you need?"

Diamond smiled. It was just that easy.

A little while later, Pop walked out onto the porch of Diamond's building and put a blunt into his mouth. He walked down the steps and proceeded toward his crew, lighting the blunt on the way.

Back inside, Diamond lay in the bed naked, counting the money Pop had given her for her services. Her body glistened, and satisfaction was written all over her face. She thought about the fact that she didn't even have to ask him for the money outright.

Diamond walked back out onto the porch after taking a shower and changing her clothes. She'd just reclaimed her seat on the stoop when another one of the neighborhood dealers came walking up the street. When Diamond looked up, he was standing directly in front of her.

"What's up, Tyquan?" Diamond asked as she looked at a Mercedes driving by.

"What's up?" he asked. "Pop was up in the crib?"

Tyquan was another young boy she'd managed to slip into her bed without Dante knowing. At seventeen, he was a year older than Pop.

Diamond looked at him in a motherly way. "What did you just ask me?"

"I heard Pop was with you up in your crib."

"Do you hear the key words here? *My crib*," she said, rolling her eyes at him in disgust.

Diamond was over Tyquan because his street status wasn't as high as Pop's. Tyquan was a nickel-and-dime hustler, something she found out soon after she slept with him. Tyquan couldn't feed her the type of cash she was looking for. He talked big, making her think he could back it up, but when she told him she needed him to pay her two-hundred-dollar rent, he choked up and started stuttering, trying to make excuses. She'd been giving him the cold shoulder for the last several weeks, and now he was standing in her face, questioning her like she owed him something.

"I-I-I'm saying—"

"I, I, I nothing, nigga. You better raise up outta my face!"

Pop and the crew turned to see what was going on when they heard Diamond yelling.

Diamond may have been a sex symbol, but she was also one of the few women who could hold her own. She almost always carried a small caliber gun in her bra, and she wasn't afraid to use it. In fact, she had used it plenty of times during her life. Most people knew not to take Diamond there, but Tyquan wasn't from that side of town, and had never seen her get down like that.

"Oh, word? It's like that?" he asked, shocked by her sudden change in behavior.

"What the hell you think?"

"Listen, bitch. Don't forget I'm the one giving you money!" Tyquan was getting pissed. He really liked her and didn't appreciate the way she was flaking out on him.

Before Tyquan could blink twice, Diamond had leaped from the porch with her small-caliber weapon and forced the nose of the gun into Tyquan's nostril.

"Yo!" he protested.

"Yo, my ass! Don't you ever fuckin' disrespect me!" she growled.

Pop and two more of his crewmembers made their way up the street. "We got a problem here?" Pop asked, his arms spread open.

Tyquan looked at him with hatred in his eyes, and then he looked back at Diamond with pleading eyes.

Pop and Tyquan didn't particularly care for each other, but they tolerated each other only because they knew the same people. Although he wasn't from that side of town, Tyquan had originally set up shop there first because he knew people from that neighborhood.

Deep down Tyquan was jealous of Pop, who came on the scene and stole his clientele. But there was nothing Tyquan could do about it, because of the amount of people Pop had behind him. So Tyquan had slowly moved his dealings to another part of the neighborhood.

"We ain't got no problems, right?" Pop asked again as he walked up on Tyquan, looking in his face while Diamond held the gun steady, ice-grilling him. He looked back and forth between Diamond and Tyquan, waiting for an answer.

"Naw, B, we ain't got no problems," Tyquan said, as if trying to catch his breath.

"Come on, ma, put the gun down." Pop grabbed Diamond around the waist, trying to calm her.

Diamond pulled back a little, but she never took her eyes off Tyquan.

Pop slowly pulled her away, but Diamond still had her gun pointed at Tyquan. She then hit Tyquan hard in the face, sending his head snapping back.

A sarcastic smirk came across Tyquan's face. "So it's like that, right, ma?" He started to back away.

"Yeah, it most certainly is." Diamond rolled her eyes, acting like a high school girl.

"I got you, ma. No problem." Tyquan kept backing up until he got to his car. Then he got inside and quickly drove away.

Pop looked over at Diamond. "You a'ight?"

"No doubt." She smiled at him, remembering how he'd just slayed the hell out of her.

"A'ight, put that thing away," he told her and simply walked back up the street with his crew in tow.

Diamond had the young boy open already, and she planned to keep him in check. Everything was unfolding just as she'd planned it. She would have all the young boys balling out on her and providing protection for her, and she wouldn't even have to pull out her gun. She would line them up to be her muscle, providers, and lovers.

✦✦ ✦✦ SIX ✦✦ ✦✦

Struggling
September 1998

Alittle over a year had passed since Trey was shot. Dante and Al-Malik managed to get promoted from bagging groceries to stocking shelves. The pay was much better, and they were able to finally see some money in their pockets. The best part about the job was that they got paid under the table, which appeased Diamond. She didn't mind that Dante worked, but she didn't want him to mess up her welfare benefits by them finding out he was working. As long as Dante was in school, she was gonna milk the system for all she could.

Dante, Trey, and Al-Malik had all gone back to school. Dante was focused and still had his goal in mind, but the same couldn't be said for the other two. Trey was getting deeper and deeper into the game and had even developed a reputation for bullying other dealers out of their turf. He always carried a 9 mm gun, and people feared him.

Dante didn't agree with the way Trey was acting, but he left him alone, as long as he showed up for classes every day.

Al-Malik, on the other hand, was having a hard time keeping up with his schedule. Between work, school, and trying to maintain life at home, he was a bundle of nerves because of the constant drama his older siblings caused. Several days a week he would crash at Dante's house after work because he wouldn't be able to get any sleep if he went home. His mother found a new man to take care of her, and she spent most of her time at her boyfriend's house. So that left Al-Malik there with his two addicted older brothers, his unemployed sister, and her kids.

There were always get-high parties, loud music, fights, or some stranger in the house when he came home. His siblings had no regard for him when he was trying to study or sleep so he could get up for school the next morning.

Al-Malik wanted to quit work, but he needed the money to eat. His mother no longer bought food for the house, and his sister used her food stamps to supply food for her own kids. He had to take care of himself.

Trey offered on many occasions for Al-Malik to come on board with him and make more money, and Al-Malik was leaning heavy toward selling drugs. But whenever he was completely fed up and ready to take to the streets, Dante helped to steer him back to being focused.

Trey had finally gotten his wish and made enough paper to get his own studio apartment in the same complex where Dante lived. He was happy now that he was finally living the life he'd always dreamed of. He'd also lost a considerable amount of the baby fat he used to carry around. Already a handsome man, he was now turning heads more than ever.

One night around ten pm as Dante was walking home after work, he walked past the crew that hung out two buildings down from where he lived. They were blasting the new "Ruff Ryders' Anthem" by rapper DMX. Niggas were going crazy as they sang the lyrics.

As Dante walked by, he gave everybody pounds and handshakes. Trey called out to him. Dante turned around and saw him jogging toward him and waited for him to catch up.

"What up?" Trey asked, giving Dante a handshake and looking over his shoulder at the teens jumping up and down.

"What's good?"

"Where you headed? Home?"

"Yeah, man." Dante leaned against the metal fence that partially surrounded the building. "Why? What's up?"

"Yo, kid, I heard some shit, and I wanted to put this bug in your ear."

"What's up, man?"

"Yo, I heard niggas be running up in your moms, man."

"What?" Dante yelled, glaring at Trey.

"Yo, for real, man, chill." Trey knew how Dante was when it came to his mother. "I'm saying that's what the word is."

"Where you hear that dumb shit?"

"Niggas talk, man, and I'm out this bitch, so I hear shit."

"Man, fuck what niggas talking 'bout. I ain't pressed for that shit!" Dante turned and walked away.

Trey followed him. "Yo, man, I know how you feel about that shit, but I'm your boy, and I'm saying, I thought you should know what niggas talking 'bout."

"Whatever, Trey. You probably out here talking with them niggas too."

"Naw, man, it ain't like that. I know I be fucking around with you, talking 'bout your moms and all, but you know it ain't really like that. I just be fucking with you."

Dante walked up the stairs to his building, leaving Trey standing on the sidewalk. He walked into the house to confront his mother about what Trey had just told him, but she wasn't there.

In all honesty, Trey had been thinking about taking a crack at Dante's mother. He knew it wasn't right, but if she was letting other niggas run up in her, then why not him? He had always dreamed about being between her thighs and believed that, if he got with her, it would be better than the average fuck. At least he would be keeping it all in the family.

Trey made his way back up the street to get with the crew when he saw Al-Malik coming up the street carrying a duffel bag. "What up, Malik?" Trey gave him some dap.

"What's up?" Al-Malik asked. He looked exhausted.

"How was work, man?"

"I'm tired as hell."

"Where you headed, kid? You live that way." Trey pointed in the direction Al-Malik had just come from.

"Man, I went home, and all kinds of niggas is up in the crib. I can't stay there tonight." Al-Malik shook his head.

"So you just gonna go crash at Tae's?"

"That's the plan."

"Come on, man, you can crash at my spot for the night," Trey told him.

"You sure?"

"Word, man. Come on." Trey led the way through the complex to his building.

Once inside, Al-Malik plopped down on the sofa. "Yo, man, when you get that?" He pointed to the big-screen television.

"Oh, I copped that joint last week."

"Damn, man! You living large up in here."

"Yeah, man, life is good right now." Trey smiled.

"I see."

"Life can be good for you too, Malik," Trey said, seeing the sad look on his friend's face.

"Man, I can't live like this on the loot I'm making at the store."

"I ain't talking about that kinda loot, Malik. I'm talking 'bout making some real paper. I can put you on."

Al-Malik looked around the apartment and saw all the updated stuff Trey had, not to mention his wardrobe.

"It's real simple, Malik, and you can have your own crib in like two months."

"Word?"

"Word up, man. I'm telling you."

"They don't ask you for ID or nothing?"

"Naw, 'cuz all you gotta do is put it in somebody else's name. They don't ask no questions 'cuz as long as you got the loot, you got a crib."

"Word?"

"Money talks."

They both sat there in silence.

"Well, just think about it," Trey finally said. "You can crash on the couch right there. It's a pullout bed. I'm 'bout to get back out on the block." Trey turned and prepared to leave.

"Yo, Trey, how am I gonna do everything, man?"

"Yo, quit that lame-ass job you got and you do you. It's that's simple. How you think I'm doing it?"

"Yeah, but you said you ain't got time for school no more, and I ain't with quitting school."

"Well, that's on you, homeboy, but once I get my paper up, I ain't gonna need school no more. I'm out, man. I'll kick it with you later," Trey said, leaving Al-Malik sitting on the sofa, thinking.

✦✦ **SEVEN** ✦✦

The Plan

It was eleven at night, and Diamond had been talking with her friend Tammy for a few hours. She was venting to her girlfriend, "Girl, I gotta get me a man with some real money. I can't keep messing around with these bums that keep giving me chump change."

"Diamond, puh-lezze . . . I know what you doing." Tammy looked at Diamond like she was a fool. She handed Diamond a glass of cheap wine. "Don't you got them two little boys running after you, giving you money or something?"

Diamond scrunched up her face. "Why you gotta say it like that? 'Them little boys.'"

"Because they is. They still wet behind the ears, and you on your way to senior citizen age." Tammy burst into laughter. "You ain't nothing but a ho to them kids."

"Yeah, OK, you got jokes today. It is what it is, and yes, I got them young hotties giving me money, but it ain't popping off like I thought it would. It ain't coming fast enough."

"Yeah, but you popping something—popping that coochie for those children." Tammy laughed again. "You gonna mess around and get pregnant by one of them little sperm donors, girl. You know they got some strong sperm that will bust one of them old-ass eggs wide open." Tammy laughed so hard, she began to cough and choke.

"To hell with you, Tammy." Diamond smiled, but didn't think Tammy's jokes were as funny as Tammy did.

Tammy lived on the first floor of the building, and she and Diamond often had drinks together and talked. Tammy was handicapped and had to use a wheelchair because her legs were underdeveloped since birth. Her upper body looked huge because of her undeveloped lower half. She had short, lifeless legs, but she got around in her wheelchair better than most people who could stand on their own two feet. Although she grew up confined to a wheelchair, it never stopped her from claiming her own identity. Her beautiful personality made her special, and she could melt any heart with her charisma.

"So what's on your agenda next? Kindergartners?" Tammy chuckled.

"Enough with the smart-ass remarks, Tammy!" Diamond had had enough of Tammy roasting her on having sex with the young dealers. Sometimes Diamond wished she never confided in Tammy. But, really, she didn't have a choice. Tammy did live on the first floor and often parked her wheelchair in front of the window, watching all that went on out front, so she knew just about everyone and their business. In fact, nothing got past her.

Diamond took a sip out of her glass and smacked her lips on the cheap wine.

Tammy noticed the expression on Diamond's face. She could see Diamond was deep in thought and wasn't in the joking mood, so she decided to stop teasing her.

"Well, Diamond, you know there are some people out there who don't have nothing, so I think we should be grateful for at least being able to receive any type of assistance."

Diamond snapped out of her thoughts. "To hell with that! Do you know I had it going on not too long ago? I didn't ever have to want for nothing, and technically I still don't. But I'm high maintenance and these niggas ain't got enough to keep me laced. Shit, I had niggas that would peel off paper to me like they manufactured money in their bathrooms. Now I can't get none of these old, cheap, limp-dick niggas to hit me off 'cause they broke. That's why I mess with them young boys, because they would give up knots in a heartbeat. They appreciate me, Tammy. They appreciate the way I 'pop this coochie,' as you say it."

Tammy shook her head at Diamond. She was fed up with hearing how Diamond *used* to have it going on. Diamond lived a good life and she didn't appreciate it. In fact, Diamond didn't need to be on welfare, but she used the system because she could. Tammy had learned to appreciate life and the blessings that came her way. She couldn't understand most women and their complaints. Diamond's complaints seemed so silly to her. There were more important things than living a lavish life.

"So what are you gonna do?" Tammy asked her friend, deciding to humor her. "You don't want to work, and you can't find a man to take care of you like you want. It sounds like you're looking for a handout."

Diamond shot Tammy a look of contempt. "Wait a minute, Tammy. I don't look for no handout from no one. I can't help it if niggas fall all over me."

Tammy decided to let the issue rest as she so often did. Diamond would never face the truth about herself. "I didn't mean it that way, Diamond."

"Oh, 'cause I was getting ready to say"—Diamond finished her glass of wine and reached for the bottle to pour herself more—"I do got an idea that could make us both some money, though. I mean, hell, you struggling too, and you by yo'self."

When Diamond got pregnant with Dante, she was livid. Having a baby would not only mess up the perfect figure she had, but would throw a monkey wrench in the whole program. Diamond felt a baby would cock-block any and all victims in her sick circle.

But the man who she was pregnant by wouldn't allow her to get an abortion because he promised to take care of her and Dante. And she believed him. After all, she didn't have any reason not to. He was the one who she spent most of her time with because he dropped the most cash on her. But he met his untimely demise by committing a murder and being sent to jail for life, leaving Dante fatherless and her penniless. Diamond even tried to date while being pregnant with Dante. But no one would touch her with a ten foot pole. One, because of her being pregnant and two, because of who the father was. Diamond despised him for going to prison. She felt he betrayed her.

After Dante was born and his father in prison, Diamond had to get back out in the streets and nab other potential victims so they could take care of her and now her son.

Tammy reached for the bottle to refill her glass as well. "What are you talking about, Diamond?"

"OK, listen."

Diamond moved her chair closer to Tammy and leaned in like she had some juicy gossip to tell, and Tammy leaned forward, eager to hear what she had to say.

"I was thinking about opening up another claim," Diamond said.

"Huh?"

"Another welfare claim. I was thinking about opening up another claim so I can get two checks and more food stamps." Diamond smiled like she had just made a great announcement.

Tammy was taken aback by Diamond's proposal, but she made sure to keep a poker face, not wanting Diamond to know she disapproved. Tammy was older than Diamond and had done her best to live an honest life. She'd had her ups and downs and didn't claim to be an angel, but she didn't want any part of what Diamond had just proposed.

"Diamond, how do you suppose you gonna pull that off?"

"Oh, I got a way I can get it off," Diamond said matter-of-factly.

"Ooookaaay. You gonna tell me, or do you think I'm that damn stupid to go in on a scheme and not know what the hell the plan is?" Tammy took a sip from her glass.

"I'm gonna get my caseworker to help me out with it."

Tammy began to cough as she choked and gagged on her wine. Her fat belly shook like Jell-O with each cough.

Diamond patted her on the back. "You all right, girl?"

"Yeah, I'm OK. *Eh-hem!*" She cleared her throat.

"So what do you think?"

"Um, I don't know what to think, except how you gonna get your caseworker to agree?"

"Chile, please." Diamond waved a hand and sat back in her chair. "That chick is young and dumb. She is so green, I can get her to do anything. Hell, she struggling herself to take care of her kids, and she work for the system. Plus, we go out to the bars together from time to time."

"OK. So did you talk to her about it yet?"

"Nope, but I'm gonna call her and take her out. Then I'm gonna talk to her about it. I know she gonna go for it. So, do you want in or not?" Diamond looked at Tammy.

"I don't know. Let me think about it for a few."

"Well, don't take too long, because I'm rolling with it, with or without you."

Tammy already knew she wasn't going to do what Diamond was asking her to do, but Diamond was such a demanding person, she didn't want to say anything right away. She had to think of an excuse why she wasn't going to participate in the illegal action.

"Let me ask you something, Diamond."

"What?"

"You don't think that y'all could go to jail for welfare fraud?"

"How? I got the best inside connect to getting paid."

"Getting paid? How much do you think you gonna get from welfare?"

"Enough to start me off. Shit!"

"Start you off to do what?"

"What do you mean, do what? Girl, I ain't tryna live in this hellhole no more. I want my own castle. I can't find me no princes to get it for me, so I got to get it for myself."

"And you think by pimping these young boys and the welfare system you gonna get it?" Tammy looked at her sideways.

"And you know this," Diamond said with confidence.

Tammy shook her head at her crazy friend and her crazy schemes.

After sitting with Tammy and finishing off the bottle of wine, Diamond walked into her apartment and set her keys on top of the stereo by the door. She kicked off her shoes and walked into the kitchen.

"Ma," Dante called out to her.

Diamond jumped. "Boy, you scared the hell outta me! What you want?" She turned on the light and saw Dante sitting at the table. "Why you sitting here in the dark?"

"I got something I need to ask you, and I want you to be honest with me."

"What are you talking about, Dante?" Diamond opened the refrigerator door and peered inside.

"Word out on the street is that you letting niggas run up in you."

Diamond stopped what she was doing. She stood upright and turned slowly to face Dante. She slammed the refrigerator door and put her hands on her hips. "Excuse me?" she asked, a frown on her face.

"Word out—"

"I heard what you said! What I'm tryna figure out is, who the hell do you think you're talking to? I'm a grown-ass woman, and what I do is my business."

"Ma, do you know how that makes me feel to hear niggas talking about they running up in my moms?"

"I don't give a shit how it makes you feel. How the hell do you think I was able to raise you by myself? How you think you was able to get whatever you wanted growing up? By any means necessary, Dante. I had to do what I had to do as a mother, and yes, that meant I let niggas run up in me, as you put it. I raised you by myself. I'm the one who pushed you outta my pussy! No one else!"

Diamond walked closer to Dante, who had grown to be taller than her, so she had to look up at him. When Dante started to develop into a young man, she knew she was gonna have to make sure she still had a hold on him by getting up in his grill at times, even if that meant slapping him upside the head.

The two of them stood there staring each other down. Diamond's eyes glared with authority, and Dante lowered his and took a step back. Diamond was satisfied as she continued to tongue-lash her son.

"So what if I slept with one or two of these dudes out here? But I bet you a dime to a dollar them muthafuckas are sprung. They throw money at me, Dante. I can get them niggas to do whatever I tell them."

"Ma, in the streets they call that a *ho*. I can't take that."

"A ho? No, Dante, a ho is somebody who goes out there and looks for dick so she can get paid. I ain't a ho! The dick comes to me, and just so happens because I got the bomb pussy, they make it rain dollars on me."

"You know what, Ma? I can't take this shit no more. I had to deal with you acting like this all my life. I was always the one who got cracked on and picked on because of the way you are. I got into fights every day in school because somebody said something about you or called you a ho. Why can't you be like the other mothers and just act normal?"

"Because I ain't like these trifling bitches out here!" Diamond was now inches away from his face. "You have no idea what I had to go through to raise you. You took away my freedom. I gave up my life to raise you, and this is the thanks I get?" She pointed her finger in his face, tapping him on the forehead with each word.

"Maybe you shoulda kept your legs closed that one time and I wouldn't have been born for you to lose your freedom!"

Diamond brought her hand back and let it go across Dante's face.

He grabbed the side of his face, looking at his mother. It had been a couple of years since she'd laid a hand on him.

Diamond came at him again, but this time he grabbed her arm, stopping the smack from connecting.

Diamond's eyes grew wide when she realized how strong her son's grip was. She snatched her arm free, eyeballing him, still shocked that he had touched her. Reaching down into her bra, she pulled out her gun and placed it square against Dante's temple. "Anytime you feel froggish, little nigga, I want you to leap!" she said through gritted teeth. "I don't have a problem taking you outta the world that I brought your black ass in to. Now if you ever think you can take me, I beg you to try me. Because, muthafucka, I will become your worst fucking nightmare! Do you hear me?"

Dante stood there shaking in his Jordans, sweat glistening across his face as he twitched.

"Do you hear me?" she yelled.

"Yeah, Ma," he said in a low voice.

"Now get the fuck outta my face before the side of your head starts leaking from this bullet I'm tempted to put in it!" She pushed Dante on the side of the head with the gun.

Walking into his room, tears formed in Dante's eyes. He slammed his door and locked it. Dante wanted to die. He couldn't believe the woman who raised him actually held a gun on him because he was concerned about what people were saying about her. He loved his mother, and never in a million years would he cross her, but it didn't seem like she had the same unconditional love for him. No matter what, he still felt he owed her for raising him and in his eyes being the rock of their small family. He felt that she raised him alone doing whatever she had to do to keep a roof over his head, clothes on his back and food in his belly. If Diamond didn't have it, by any means necessary she went out and got it. Dante knew this and admired her for it. Yes, there was the abuse, but he had grown up with it thinking this was the way she had to be to teach him how to be a man. This was why he continued to take her abuse and still love and respect her.

✦✦ ✦✦ EIGHT ✦✦ ✦✦

Days Later

Diamond got out of Pop's car and sat down on the front steps of her building as he drove off.

"Hey, babysitter," Tammy teased. "I see the kindergartner took you out today," she said from her position in front of the window.

"Go to hell, Tammy!"

Tammy laughed. "Don't get mad at me."

Diamond smiled. "I ain't mad at you. You just nosy as hell."

"I was sitting here in my window minding my own business. You the one flaunting around town with the boy you babysit."

"That's the problem, Tammy, you always got your nosy ass sitting in the window." Diamond laughed. "Did you think about what I asked you?"

The smile disappeared from Tammy's face. She'd been ducking Diamond because she didn't know how to tell her she didn't want any part of her welfare scheme.

"Uh, no, not yet," she said. "Uh-oh, here comes another one of your playmates." Tammy was happy for the interruption.

Diamond looked up the street to see Trey walking toward the house. She sucked her teeth. "Shut up, girl! That's Dante's friend."

Tammy snickered. "What that mean? I thought they all were his little classmates."

"Hey, Trey-Trey," Diamond said, smiling at him playfully.

Tammy wheeled her chair away from the window, so Trey couldn't see her. In fact, she often kept the lights turned off at night so no one would notice her sitting there.

"How you doing, Ms. Reed?" Trey asked, blushing.

"Dante not here. He's at work."

"Yeah, I know."

"Oh? So who you come to see?"

"You, Ms. Reed."

"OK, first let's cut the 'Ms. Reed' shit. I told you and Malik before that you can call me Ma." She eyed him.

"Yeah, *Grandma* sounds more like it," Tammy whispered.

"Cool."

"So what's up? What you need?"

"I saw you sitting down here, so I thought I would come say what's up to you and see how you doing. I haven't been over much lately." He gazed at her.

Diamond didn't say anything at first. She sat looking over Trey's physique. She knew he was now selling drugs, and she liked the way the new Trey looked. Even his demeanor was different. He carried himself with a new confidence. He looked like new money, which turned her on. Dollars signs danced in her eyes.

"That's nice of you, Trey. I was just saying to Dante the other day that I haven't seen you over here much anymore. I know you been hanging out down the street, though." She raised an eyebrow, letting him know she knew what time it was.

He just rubbed his hand across the peach fuzz he was now growing, not saying a word. He wasn't sure if she was going to reprimand him for selling drugs.

"So you making a little money. It's all good. Just stay outta trouble."

"Oh, no doubt." Trey perked up, realizing she was OK with his new occupation. "You know I got my own crib now."

"Really?" Diamond was impressed. Dante never told her that Trey had his own place.

"Yeah. I stay in the J building," he said, pointing at it.

"Here?"

"Yeah."

"That's a good look for you, Trey. What a way to be a man. I know that's right. You're sixteen years old and you got out on your own." She commented.

There was an awkward silence between them. Diamond looked up at the window to see if Tammy was still there, so Tammy backed up her chair some more, just to make sure Diamond couldn't see her. Trey looked into the window also, trying to see what Diamond was looking for.

When she didn't see Tammy sitting there, she asked, "So when you gonna show me your apartment?"

"Oh, we can run by there now if you want," Trey said, eager to get Diamond in his apartment. His manhood started to rise just thinking about having his way with her.

Diamond stood and looked into Tammy's window one more time before she walked off with Trey to see his apartment.

Diamond wasted no time when they got to his apartment. Once inside she immediately began to undress him, and Trey didn't protest. In fact, he began to help her out of her clothing.

They panted and groped each other, and he smacked her ass a few times, turning her on even more, as moisture continued to seep from her treasure.

A few minutes later, Trey was knee-deep in Diamond's twat, pumping hard and long as he gripped a handful of Diamond's fat ass, hitting it from the back.

Diamond loved the way Trey was handling his business. Even

though he was still young, he had a lot of width and length.

Diamond hadn't had a dick that big in a long time. As soon as she saw what Trey had to offer, she knew he was gonna be her number-one dick.

Three positions and forty-five minutes of straight humping later, Diamond was worn out. She lay across Trey's bed panting like a lioness that had just tracked down a deer, and Trey, who was hardly out of breath, lay next to her.

As Diamond lay on her stomach, Trey watched her ass move up and down as she tried to catch her breath.

"You want something to drink?"

"Yeah, please," she said between breaths.

Trey squeezed her ass before he got up to get her something to drink. Fucking Ms. Reed was everything he'd imagined and more, but of course, he wasn't going to let her know he was in love.

As he poured her some Kool-Aid, he thought about how warm his dick felt inside her juicy pussy, and his manhood began to rise. He could definitely go for another round, and he was damn sure gonna try.

Diamond looked up at him when he stood over her with the glass of Kool-Aid. Face to face with his hard-on, she thought, *Shit!* She was too tired to go another round. She sat up and took a sip of the Kool-Aid.

"Trey, I gotta get up outta here. I want to be home when Dante gets there, so I'm gonna have to take a rain check on that," she said, pointing to his hard-on.

"Oh, no doubt," a cocky Trey said. "It's all good. You know where I'm at now."

Diamond looked at him and saw the arrogant smirk on his face. She simply laughed.

✦✧✦ ✦✧✦ ✦✧✦

Diamond could barely walk up the front steps to the apartment building because her legs felt like Jell-O. She was so fatigued by the pounding Trey put on her body, she needed to get in the shower and lay down in her bed as soon as possible.

"Well, well, well, I see you found one that got you walking gap-legged," Tammy said from her window.

"I knew your nosy ass was listening. You know what, Tammy? I think you're jealous of me."

"Jealous of you?" Tammy laughed. "Girl, you ain't got nothing I want, so how can I be jealous?"

"Oh, but I do, my dear, and you are jealous. You wish you could get you one of these big-dick young boys to come in there and rock your dried-up pussy, but you can't! 'Cause ain't nobody fucking with a cripple!" Diamond was tired of Tammy insulting her and judging her. She really didn't mean to call her a cripple, because she knew how her friend felt about that, but she was pissed that Tammy was trying to judge her.

"It's all good, Diamond. I don't have to belittle myself just so I can get fucked. I can still hold up my head with dignity, cripple and all. Can you?" Tammy then shut her window.

Diamond stood there for a few moments before she headed into the building. She hoped Tammy would forgive her in the morning. She walked into her apartment and went straight to her bedroom and sat down on the bed, thinking about she had hurt her only friend.

Sometimes Diamond would get really depressed. She knew some of the things she did and said weren't right. She wasn't totally evil, but to protect her feelings, she just seemed to feel better when other people suffered like her.

✦✦ ✦✦ NINE ✦✦ ✦✦

Puttin' in Work
November 1998

Shakeeda entered the lobby, a mixture of scents, from cheap perfume to old clothes, and where a sea of welfare and Medicaid recipients sat waiting their turn to see their caseworkers. Today was a busy day, and Shakeeda wasn't in the best of moods. It wasn't even ten am, and she was already in need of her lunch break. She walked over to the handheld device that they used to activate the intercom system. Looking down at the file in her basket, she pressed the button, and a beep came over the loudspeaker.

"Diamond Reed!" she called.

Diamond made her way through the crowd. Shakeeda looked Diamond up and down as she approached her. She couldn't understand for the life of her how Diamond was so well put together, while only receiving minimal benefits. Deep down she envied women who could do what Diamond did. Shakeeda worked every day and couldn't afford to look the same way.

"Hey, girl," Diamond said, displaying a warm smile. She had been trying to get in contact with Shakeeda several times, but couldn't reach her. So she decided to set up an appointment where she knew she could get to her.

"Hey, Diamond," Shakeeda said, suddenly feeling slightly better.

Every time she and Diamond were together, she felt at ease.

As they made their way through various crowded rooms where other recipients waited, they finally settled into the last cubicle in the office.

"What can I do for you today?" Shakeeda asked, taking her seat and placing Diamond's file on her desk.

Diamond settled into the hard plastic chair and placed her Coach purse on the desk. "I wanted to visit you and see how you were doing."

"I've seen better days, Diamond, really I have." Shakeeda exhaled.

"How are the kids?" Diamond asked, trying to show concern.

"Bad as hell. I swear, I want to send them back to the fathers they came from." Shakeeda rolled her eyes as she pecked away at the computer. She figured since her and Diamond were having small talk, she would finish her notes from the last file she was working on.

"Girl, you should send them back." Diamond chuckled. She was easing her way up to the real reason she came to see Shakeeda, but she wanted to feel her out first. "When was the last time you been out?" she asked.

"The last time you and me went out months ago. Please . . . I don't get many of them anymore. Why?"

"You need a break."

"Don't I know it." Shakeeda continued to type.

"You wanna go out with me sometime? My treat."

Shakeeda stopped typing and looked at Diamond.

Got her, Diamond thought.

"Sure, I'll go."

"Why don't we go tonight?" Diamond said. "I need some 'me time' anyway."

"Well, I don't know. I need to find a babysitter. Plus, I don't have any money to pay a babysitter tonight. Maybe next time, Diamond."

"Don't worry about that. I got you."

+✦+ +✦+ +✦+

Later that night, Diamond and Shakeeda sat at a table in a lounge, sipping on their second drinks. The waitress walked over to the table and placed two shots of tequila in front of them.

"Come on, girl," Diamond said and picked up her shot.

A partially drunk Shakeeda picked up her shot, and the two women clinked their glasses in a toast. Then they threw back their heads and downed the shots. They tapped their shot glasses on the table and drank from their bottles of Corona.

"Diamond, thank you so much for bringing me out. I am so stressed at work, it ain't even funny."

Diamond waved her hand. "You know how we do it, girl. It's all love."

"It's sad how two women gotta go out on a date 'cause none of these trifling-ass Negroes gonna spend their money," Shakeeda said, looking around at the small crowd in the establishment.

"You better preach, girl." Diamond gave Shakeeda some dap.

Shakeeda looked at her sideways. "What you talking about, Diamond? You can get any man you want. Shit, you know I know the deal. You got all them Negroes spending money on you."

"Yeah, that's what you think." Diamond downplayed Shakeeda's comments. It was all part of her plan.

"Yeah, whatever, Diamond. Girl, don't forget I know how you get down."

They both laughed.

"You know, Shakeeda, it's like you said. Men ain't tryna spend no money on a sister, so shit ain't like it used to be."

"Really?"

Shakeeda was surprised, because the last time she and Diamond had gone out was about three months ago, and things seemed to be all good with Diamond then.

"Yeah, really. You know I was thinking about a way we could both make some real cash."

Shakeeda turned the bottle of beer up to her lips and took a swig. "How?" she asked, looking at the bottle to see how much she had left in it.

"It's risky, but we can pull this off together, if you down." Diamond watched a tipsy Shakeeda drain what was left of her beer.

"Damn! What you talking about? Robbing a bank?" Shakeeda burst into drunken laughter.

Diamond laughed right along with her. "No, girl. You want another beer?"

"Sure. Why not?"

"All right, I'll order one when the waitress comes back around. So what do you think?"

"Think about what?"

Shakeeda clearly wasn't listening to Diamond. That shot must have gone straight to her head.

Diamond was getting agitated. Her plan was to get Shakeeda drunk, but not too drunk where she wouldn't remember their conversation. She decided not to order another beer. Instead she would continue to work on Shakeeda to get her to agree with her plan.

"Making some money," Diamond said.

"Oh, yeah, the bank robbery." Shakeeda giggled.

"No. Come on now, this is serious."

"A'ight, I'm listening. What's up?" Shakeeda tried to straighten up and focus.

"I figured, since you work for welfare, you got the inside connections to pull it off."

Shakeeda didn't say anything, so Diamond kept talking. She ran down the plan to Shakeeda, explaining how Shakeeda would be the key person to pull off the whole thing. She also told her that they would split everything down the middle.

"Wait a minute." Shakeeda held up her hand to stop Diamond from talking. She closed her eyes, trying to get her head straight. "You want me to help create a couple false full-benefit welfare claims, and you gonna split it down the middle with me?"

"Yeah, that's the plan. I mean, just look at it." Diamond moved in closer to make sure she had Shakeeda's undivided attention. Plus, she didn't want to talk over the music and risk someone overhearing her. "We could make a killing. You are the caseworker and have complete control over the amount of the benefits."

"No, Diamond, I don't have complete control, because my supervisor has to sign off on all my claims. He reviews them. The computer calculates benefit amounts. I don't do that."

"OK, I understand that, but the computer can only calculate what you put in."

"Yeah, but you gotta have valid social security numbers, addresses, and all that."

"You let me handle that. All you gotta do is put it in and let the checks start rolling in."

Shakeeda stared at Diamond, trying to figure out if this was a joke, or at least if Diamond was drunk. But when she didn't see a hint of laughter or drunkenness in Diamond's eyes, she knew Diamond was dead-ass serious.

"Shakeeda, look, you can make about another thousand dollars a month," Diamond said. "I know you could use the money. And let's not forget the food stamps. With them kids you got, I know you rather get food stamps for at least five hundred dollars a month to buy some food, right?"

Shakeeda just sat there looking at her nails while Diamond spoke. She couldn't afford the nail salon. *It would be nice to be able to get my nails done*, she thought.

She looked at Diamond. Diamond had it going on. If she got the extra money, then she would be able to ball out the same way. But she still wasn't sure. She could lose everything if she got caught—her job, her house, her kids, and her freedom.

The two of them went back and forth discussing the logistics for more than an hour. Diamond was very persistent and controlling. She didn't want to take no for an answer, but she finally gave up trying to convince Shakeeda in one night.

It would take a little more convincing and another night out on her dime to get Shakeeda on board. Diamond also needed to make sure that Shakeeda wouldn't rat her out, and another night out showing Shakeeda what she could have would only help. Once the ball got rolling, and Shakeeda got a taste of the extra money that was going to be coming in every month, she would soon feel better about the situation.

Shakeeda was definitely thinking about taking Diamond up on her offer, but a part of her was still afraid of getting caught. She needed more time and less alcohol in her system to make her final decision, but she knew Diamond had a way of always getting what she wanted. And she had a feeling this situation would be no different.

✦·✦✦ TEN ✦✦·✦

Getting the Ball Rolling
1999

It was a year later when Diamond finally convinced Shakeeda to go for the deal. Diamond had four fraudulent welfare claims set up under bogus names. Tyquan had started to come back around, and he proved to be a huge asset to Diamond's plan. His sister worked for the Department of Social Security, so Tyquan got fake social security numbers from her, which Diamond then used to set up the welfare claims. Diamond made sure she gathered two thousand dollars between Trey, Tyquan, and Pop, so she could pay Tyquan's sister for doing the favor. This way, she figured the sister would be less likely to snitch.

Shakeeda set up the claims so the checks came to her sister Tanya, Trey, Pop, and Tyquan's addresses. Diamond still received her regular benefits. With all the money that came in from welfare and the loot she was getting from her boys, Diamond was rolling in dough.

But Diamond's greed and selfishness took control, as it always did, and she started reneging on her deal with Shakeeda. What was once a fifty/fifty split was now a seventy-five/twenty-five split in Diamond's favor. Shakeeda was bothered by the excuses Diamond gave when she stopped sending Shakeeda's complete share of the profits. She was starting to think Diamond was trying to play her. Shakeeda already had to pay her sister a portion of her profits for letting them use her address, and now with her not getting her full share, she was hardly seeing any money for herself. Finally, she tracked down Diamond to talk with her about her concerns. She had spoken to Dante and he'd told her where to find her.

"Diamond, what happened last week?" Shakeeda asked as she walked over to a table in the restaurant where Diamond sat with Trey.

"What?" Diamond asked, clearly disgusted.

"You didn't send anybody by with the money. I was waiting on that money," she said as she helped herself to a seat.

Trey put down his fork, ice-grilling Shakeeda for interrupting their meal.

"How you know I was here?" Diamond asked her.

"Diamond, that don't matter right now. What happened to my money?" Shakeeda looked over at Trey, whose mean-mugging was starting to bother her. She knew his reputation and wasn't happy he was there.

"Wait a minute. You walk up in here and interrupt my dinner, making yourself comfortable, and you tell me my question don't matter?" Diamond rolled her eyes. "Are you kidding me?"

"Diamond, listen," Shakeeda said calmly, trying not to upset her. She knew Diamond could easily get someone to hurt her, and that wasn't what she wanted. Diamond had that kind of power over people and Shakeeda didn't want to one day be faced with death because Diamond ordered a hit on her. She'd heard the stories about her. All she wanted was her fair share of the deal they made. After all, she was the one who was taking the biggest risk. "All I want to know is what happened. That's all. I tried to call you several times, and you never returned my calls." Shakeeda smiled, trying to make light of the situation.

Diamond didn't smile at all. "Maybe I was busy and couldn't get back to you, Shakeeda. Did you ever think about that?"

Shakeeda shook her head.

"Of course not," Diamond said. "Listen, young girl, I don't know who the fuck you think I am, but I am not one of your little young girlfriends. I am a grown-ass woman, and don't you ever roll up on me again like you about to do something . . . because you really don't want what I got. Do I make myself clear?"

"Yes, Diamond." Shakeeda regretted coming to the restaurant.

"All right. I'm gonna entertain your little suspicions this one time, since you came all the way down here to find me. I didn't send anybody with your share of the money because I am investing it. I'm tryna flip it to make more money for you and me. I got this, and all you gotta do is just chill out and wait till I get this paper up," she said, using the street lingo she'd picked up from being with young boys.

Diamond wasn't stupid. Even though she had the upper hand, and she knew Shakeeda was afraid of her, she still had to play it safe. Shakeeda could drop a dime and blow the whole operation. So Diamond had to stroke her lightly to keep her quiet until she was able to start a new hustle.

"At least you got the one check coming in," Diamond continued. "Hell, you getting a six-hundred-dollar check plus four hundred in food stamps, and that's on top of your regular salary you make down at welfare. Don't get greedy, Shakeeda, because when you get greedy, you make mistakes that can fuck it up for all of us."

Diamond never took her eyes off Shakeeda while she spoke, but Shakeeda couldn't hold Diamond's stare. She was afraid.

"All right, Diamond, I'm gonna go. I'll see you later." Shakeeda jumped to her feet and made tracks out of the restaurant. When she got to her car, she broke down and cried. What had she done? What kind of a woman had she gotten herself mixed up with? Shakeeda knew she was in too deep, and she had to find a way to get out of it before it was too late.

"Do you want me to handle that?" Trey asked Diamond after Shakeeda left.

"No, she'll be all right for now." Diamond continued to eat her lukewarm food.

"I don't trust her. She gonna blow."

"Of course she will, but not right now. She's in too deep with us, so she ain't gonna say nothing yet. Besides, once I get this other thing up and running, we won't have to deal with this penny-ante welfare shit no more. It ain't enough money to feed my appetite anyway, and you know I got a big appetite." Diamond winked at Trey.

"Yeah, I know you do. You got another big appetite for something else too, but I can take care of that one." He smiled at her.

"You sure can, baby. You sure can."

Later That Night

"Dante!" Diamond called out to him when she heard the front door open and close.

"Yeah, Ma."

"Come here."

Dante walked into his mother's bedroom and found her sitting at the foot of the bed.

"What's up, Ma?"

"Have a seat." She pointed to a chair that sat in the corner of the room.

Dante did as he was told.

"All right, here's the deal. I need your help on something." She looked at him seriously.

"Ma, I told you before, I ain't with the welfare thing. I don't want to be a part of that."

"Boy, shut the hell up! You ain't a part of that, but I see you don't mind taking my money when I give it to you."

He didn't respond.

"I thought not. Anyway, I want you to help Trey move some weight."

"Uh? No, Ma, I can't. I got school, and my classes are getting harder. I got promoted at the store to team lead. I ain't tryna mess that up."

"You can make more money with Trey," she said, dismissing his reasoning with a wave of her hand.

"Ma, I don't want to quit my job. I like it there. Plus, I worked my way up. In another six months, I'll be manager."

"Manager? Boy, please. With the loot we gonna be making, you can buy the damn store."

"No, Ma, I ain't selling no drugs," he said, shaking his head.

"Dante, shut the fuck up for a minute and listen to what I'm saying!"

Dante patiently waited for his mother to finish.

"You ain't gotta sell shit, just move it from one location to another."

"I can't believe you. You of all people always drilled in my head that you didn't want me to sell drugs and how I better not be out there selling drugs, and now you asking me to get my hands dirty handling drugs."

Diamond thought about it for a moment. He was right, but she would never admit it to him. She just got caught up in the hype of it all. When Trey told her how much money they could make if he started dealing in weight, she got caught up. In her book she would rather Dante not be involved in the drug end of it anyway, since he wasn't street smart enough to handle the job.

"You always fuck up everything for me!" She pouted and walked out of the room mad.

Dante wished his mother would just act like a mother was supposed to act. Dante never liked his mother messing with boys who were his age or younger. He'd voiced his opinion, but she was gonna do what she wanted to do, no matter what he thought. He also saw how dumb most of these boys were—throwing paper at her like it was water. He reaped the benefits of their stupidity, so instead of continuing to fight against it, he embraced it and milked it for all it was worth. Besides, they'd made an agreement. She agreed not to bring them in the house anymore if he stopped bitching about her being with them. Diamond was known to tell a lie or two but Dante decided to trust his mother on this one issue because he felt she knew how this hurt him deeply.

Thankfully Dante still didn't know about his best friend Trey sleeping with his mother and being her number-one dick. He simply thought Trey was working for his mother, naïve as it may sound. Trey's reputation had climbed over the years, with him putting niggas on their asses. He thought Trey was watching his mother's back as a friend. Dante wouldn't allow himself to think anything other than Trey working for his mother in their little schemes. Trey had dropped out of school, and Dante gave up talking to him about it. And since they were no longer as close as they once were, Dante had no idea Trey was doing his mother.

Dante didn't respond. He just sat there with his head hanging low, preparing to hear the *I-raised-you-by-myself* speech that Diamond always made when ranting and raving.

"And another thing," she said, walking back into the room. "If I tell you to do something, then just do it. I raised you by myself. I'm tryna do something that's gonna get us back into a nice neighborhood like before, and you sitting here asking me questions, like you don't trust me or something. You don't trust me?"

"Yeah, Ma," he said in a low, exasperated tone.

Diamond stood and began to pace the floor. "I'm just saying, Dante, I want better for me. I had it going on when I was your age. I mean, I didn't want for nothing because my father gave me everything, and you asking me questions."

She went on and on and on about Dante being an ungrateful child. Dante heard his mother bitching and complaining, but he wasn't really listening.

"Do you hear me?" she finally asked, standing in front of him, her hands on her hips.

"Yes, Ma."

✦✦ ✦✦ **ELEVEN** ✦✦ ✦✦

Kids No More
Three Months Later

"A l-Malik!" Dante yelled as he stepped off the bus.

Al-Malik stood on the corner where the bus had dropped off Dante.

"What's up, man?" Dante asked as they slapped hands. "Where you been?"

"I been around," Al-Malik told him without making eye contact.

"Where, man? You ain't been in school or work for almost three months. Darren already fired you, man," Dante said, referring to their boss.

"Man, I don't care." Al-Malik shrugged.

"You don't care about school either? Darren said you called out sick and never called back. I called your crib, and your sister said she ain't seen you in a minute. What's up?"

Al-Malik didn't respond right away. He was searching for the right lie to tell Dante. Al-Malik had always looked up to Dante and loved him like a brother. Dante was always there for him more than his real brothers. Dante always took up for him in school and helped him with his homework when he had problems.

But Al-Malik had grown weary of the life he was living. Trey was in his ear more than Dante knew, and he saw firsthand how easy it was to make quick cash. He had moved in with Trey and was now slinging on the very block they stood on, right under Dante's nose.

Dante went to school and worked long hours, so he never saw this change coming. As long as Al-Malik showed up for school and work, he thought it was all good, but now he was about to find out that his friend had folded under the pressure.

Before Al-Malik could answer Dante, a female fiend walked up to him. She was skin and bones and desperately needed a bath, judging from the funk fog that surrounded her.

"Hey, Malik, can I get two bags?" she asked, referring to heroin.

Dante's mouth dropped open.

Al-Malik wouldn't look at Dante. He simply backpedaled over to a box of cereal that sat on the side of the building, reached inside, and pulled out the bags that held the dope. He walked back over to the woman and handed her the drugs once she gave him the crumpled bills she held in her fist.

Al-Malik carefully unfolded the money, observing his surroundings. He had become a pro at slinging. He pulled out a knot and put the money the fiend had given him with the other bills then placed it back in his pocket. Finally he looked up at Dante.

"Oh, word? It's like that, Malik?"

Al-Malik saw the hurt look on his friend's face. "Yo, Tae, man, my bad, but I couldn't take it anymore. It was too much for me, man. I couldn't even stay at home no more. I couldn't study, and the money we was making wasn't doing nothing for me. Besides, you got promoted, not me."

"All you had to do was come talk to me, Malik. I'm your boy. Haven't I always looked out for you?"

"Yeah, man, but—"

"We said we weren't gonna do this, man. We was gonna get up outta the hood the legal way. Al-Malik, you could have come to me, straight up. I would have let you crash at the crib, man. Shit! How many times before have you come and crashed at the crib?"

"Tae, man, for real, we getting older now. We said that shit when we was kids. It was a dream we had when we was kids. That's all it was—a dream. This is reality, man."

"That's not you talking, and you know it! That sounds like Trey to me."

"Naw, bruh, it's me. I'm my own man. I made this decision, not Trey." Al-Malik hit his chest for emphasis.

"Word? A'ight, cool. It's all good then. Do you. And you right, we growing up," Dante said as he waited for the cars to pass so he could cross the busy street. He hunched his shoulders as the winter air blew.

"Yo, Tae!"

Dante looked back at Al-Malik.

"We still boys, right?"

"Oh, no doubt, kid." Dante crossed the street, readjusting his backpack on his shoulders.

Dante was hurt. It seemed he was the only one still believing in their childhood dream. Was he wishing on a star? Was there something everybody else saw that he couldn't see? Did he need to let go and grow up? He felt positive about finishing school and getting out of the hood.

Through the years, Dante had to endure watching his mother bring one man after the next in and out of the house. He was always locked up in his room and most times left at home alone. When Diamond couldn't do something because of him, she made sure she told him every chance she got. Dante had to carry a lot of weight on his shoulders as a child, because his mother was so controlling, manipulating his small mind. But as time went on and Dante grew, Diamond seemed to lose the gift to pull men to keep her laced in the finest, causing her to go on welfare when Dante became a teen to bring in the extra money she needed to trick off.

Although his mother had come up with the crazy welfare fraud idea and talked about getting them a home out of the hood, he still wanted to finish school and make his own living legally. He had no intention of living with his mother for the rest of his life. But for now he would live with her—under her rules—so he could save his money.

TWELVE

Ready to Blow
Two Months Later

Shakeeda sat on her bed rocking back and forth. Diamond still hadn't come up with her missing percentage of the money. Although Shakeeda had gotten used to the extra money and benefits she did get, she was starting to feel guilty about spending it, but it wasn't until Diamond cut her off that she started feeling that way. While the getting was good, it was all good. She became dependent on the extra cash and benefits. She'd moved to a bigger and better apartment, furnishing it, and her children were much happier too, since they were able to go more places and get more toys and clothes.

Even after her encounter with Diamond at the restaurant five months prior, Shakeeda still managed to do all right with the one check that came in. At first she believed Diamond when she told her she was investing her money. She figured Diamond was putting the money in with drug money to flip it into an even bigger profit. Shakeeda was all for that, especially knowing the amount of money drug sales brought in. She had big dreams, and was even considering buying a home in Newark.

But all of that came crashing down when she wasn't able to get in contact with Diamond yet again. She had been trying to get in touch with her to go out and have a few drinks like they used to, to make sure things were all right between them. The encounter at the restaurant had her a little afraid. So when she couldn't reach Diamond, she decided to take her sister Tanya out. She needed to get out and clear her head. She was even becoming paranoid at work, thinking someone knew about the false claims. She checked on them periodically, making sure no one had been in the accounts investigating them, but she couldn't be one hundred percent sure.

When Shakeeda and Tanya walked into Marlo's Lounge, she thought she was gonna bust a blood vessel. Diamond, sparkling like a crystal ball from all the diamonds she wore, sat at a table surrounded by good-looking young men and two females, and they were laughing it up, clearly having a good time. Bottles of expensive champagne and liquor lined their table.

Shakeeda and Tanya walked over to Diamond's table and stood there waiting to be noticed.

Diamond finally looked up to see them standing there. "Shakeeda, what's up?" She half-smiled at her.

"Hey, Diamond. What's going on?"

"Getting my party on. What you doing here? This ain't your usual hangout." Diamond took a sip from her flute, filled with champagne.

Shakeeda placed her hand on her hip, looking around at everyone, who was now looking at her.

"It looks like you got played," her sister whispered. "You better check your girl. I'm going to get a drink."

Shakeeda's blood was beginning to heat up. "Diamond, can I talk to you for a minute?"

"Sure, you can. Pull up a chair."

"Alone, please."

"What?" Diamond placed her hand next to her ear, letting Shakeeda know she didn't hear her because of the music.

Shakeeda leaned forward and spoke louder. "I said, can I talk to you alone?"

Diamond got up from her seat and excused herself from the table. The two of them tried to find a place to talk privately, but it was impossible, since the establishment was small, and the place was packed.

"In the bathroom," Diamond said to her.

Once inside the bathroom, they made sure no one was in there before they spoke.

"What's up?" Diamond asked. It was evident that she was feeling good from the bottles she and her friends had been popping that night.

"I been tryna get in touch with you, and you ain't returned any of my calls."

"Oh, my bad. I've been busy."

"Diamond, I know you said you was investing the money and all, but I ain't heard from you, and I was just wondering what's going on."

"Oh, so we still on that?" Diamond asked.

Just then a woman walked into the bathroom and looked at the two of them standing there.

Diamond and Shakeeda stood there, not saying a word.

The woman looked in the mirror and began to fix her hair, after which she applied more lipstick. She hastened out of the bathroom, uncomfortable with the evil way Diamond was staring at her through the mirror.

"Listen, Shakeeda, what's the problem?"

"I don't have a problem, Diamond. I'm just saying, we had a deal, and it seems that you the one reaping all the benefits. I mean, I can't afford to do it big like you. How is it that you can live that large?" Shakeeda pointed to the jewelry Diamond was sporting.

Diamond laughed a little and shook her head at Shakeeda like she was a pitiful mess.

"Let me set you straight right now. This little jealousy thing you got for me needs to end. I been around a long time, sweetheart. I ain't new to this. You see them little niggas that's at my table?"

Shakeeda didn't answer. She continued to listen.

"I got all them little muthafuckas on a string. They will give me whatever the fuck I want, and if they ain't got it, oh, trust, they gonna go out and get it. You think that chump change we getting from them claims gonna do something for me? Naw, baby girl, I am high maintenance, and that ain't enough. So instead of riding my ass, you need to get your shit together and stay the fuck outta mine. Now this is the last time I want to have this conversation with you about this. Understand?"

"Yeah, I understand," Shakeeda said.

"Oh yeah, and if you think about cutting off the claims, just remember, I got some witnesses that will definitely say it was all your idea." Diamond looked at herself in the mirror, and then shot an icy glare at Shakeeda over her shoulder as she walked out of the bathroom.

Tanya came into the bathroom several seconds later. "You all right, girl?" she asked, looking her sister up and down, making sure Shakeeda was still intact.

"Yeah, I'm OK. I gotta get out of this shit with her. I'm scared." Shakeeda began to cry.

"What happened?"

"Tanya, that bitch is crazy. I know if I do something, she probably gonna have me killed or something. I gotta get out of it, but I don't know how." Shakeeda looked at her sister for help.

Tanya felt bad for her sister. She'd never thought about the consequences of what Shakeeda was doing, because Shakeeda had shared her ill-gotten gains with her. She knew Shakeeda was afraid for her life. "OK," she said, pulling Shakeeda into her arms for a hug. "We gonna think of something. We gonna get you out of it."

✦✦ ✦✦ ✦✦

After they left the club and went home, Shakeeda and Tanya talked for about an hour, trying to figure out what they could do to get Shakeeda out of her involvement with Diamond.

They came up with a plan that would have Shakeeda cancel the claims coming to her house and her sister's house. That way, they wouldn't be tied to the scheme. They agreed that once that was done, they would get together to go over the next step on how to take care of Diamond Reed.

First thing the next morning, Shakeeda went into work and canceled the two claims. The rest of the claims would have to wait until the time was right.

Shakeeda really wanted to report Diamond. She felt like if she reported her and had her arrested, she would go to jail for a long time and wouldn't have to deal with her at all. Tanya agreed with her, but that was something they really had to think long and hard about. The last thing Shakeeda wanted was for Diamond to find out she was the one who ratted her out. If the cat got out of the bag, Shakeeda would be in the next cell across from Diamond.

❖❖ ❖ THIRTEEN ❖ ❖❖

The Diamond Syndicate
2000

Diamond and her crew piled into two cars for a trip to Atlantic City to see a rap concert. She wasn't a fan of rap, but she decided to tag along and do some gambling. Dante didn't want to go with them.

In the first car Trey drove Diamond, with Tyquan and Al-Malik sitting in the backseat. The second car contained Pop and two newcomers to the crew, Seth and Devon, both seventeen. They made their way down the New Jersey Turnpike, music blasting, weed smoke filling the cars.

Once in AC, Diamond booked two suites at the fabulous Trump Plaza. After checking in and putting their bags in the room, the crew made their way through the hotel lobby to take the car service over to the Sands, where the concert was being held.

"So you sure you don't want to swing with us?" Trey asked Diamond as they stood in the lobby.

"No, you go ahead. I'll be all right."

Trey stood there gazing at Diamond. The others were talking loudly and clowning around. They both looked toward the door at the crew.

"You better go ahead and keep them in check," Diamond said. "Make sure they stay outta trouble."

"I don't know, man. I think I should stay here with you."

"For what? I ain't got nothing to worry about here."

Trey was Diamond's bodyguard. At least, that was the way he behaved. He was overprotective of her and never left her side, except when she was entertaining one of her other young boys. But, even then, he wasn't far away.

"A'ight then. I'll see you when I get back." He turned to leave and then stopped as if he forgot to tell her something. "It's me and you tonight, right?" he asked, trying to claim his spot for the night with her.

"No doubt, baby." She winked at him. "Oh, yeah, do me a favor, Trey."

"What?"

"No shit from Tyquan and Pop. Keep them two apart, you hear me?" She pointed to him in a motherly way. Trey was now eighteen as was with Dante. Pop and Tyquan were in their early twenties.

"*Psst.*" Trey waved at her. "Them niggas don't want it from me."

"All right, see you later." Diamond walked away after observing other guests staring at them.

Sometimes she felt out of place when she was with the crew. Mostly in nice places like where they were. Only because she looked as if she was the mother of the bunch, and yet she was behaving like their peer

A half-hour later Diamond found herself bored out of her mind. She had lost about one hundred dollars sitting there waiting for the slot machine to pay off. After about another ten minutes of feeding the machine, she decided to leave the quarter-gobbling monster alone. She found herself wandering into one of the lounges, where she took a seat at the bar and ordered a drink. The house band was playing, so she sat and people-watched. She thought about how she should have gone with the boys to the concert, and just as the thought entered her mind, it quickly left. She knew she would've had a headache by the second song.

"Excuse me, is this seat taken?" a male voice asked.

Diamond looked up to see one of the most handsome white men she had ever seen outside of a TV screen. "Um . . . oh . . . no . . . no," she said, stumbling over her words. Moving her Dolce and Gabbana purse out of the way, she made room for the handsome man to sit next to her.

"It's dead in here tonight, isn't it?" he asked, once seated.

"Yes, it is."

"I'll have a gin and tonic," he told the bartender, who was now standing in front of them.

The bartender walked off to make his drink.

"My name is Michael," he said, extending his hand for a shake.

"I'm Diamond." Diamond shook his hand lightly while staring into his gorgeous ocean-blue eyes.

When the bartender came back with the drink, Michael reached inside his suit jacket and pulled out his wallet. When he opened the wallet, Diamond glanced at the wad of cash that lay in a neat pile.

Michael pulled out a twenty-dollar bill to pay the bartender. "Are you here alone?" he asked Diamond.

"Yes."

"In that case, run a tab," Michael told the bartender as he replaced the twenty with a credit card, which he set on the counter.

The bartender nodded and made his way down the bar to serve another customer.

Diamond's pupils danced with dollar signs as she eyed the AMEX card. Michael L. Ricci, MD was clearly written on the bottom of the card.

"So what is a beautiful woman like you doing here alone?" Michael smiled a Colgate smile at her that caused her vagina to pulsate.

"Well, technically I'm not alone. I'm here with my son and his friends. They went to a concert over at the Sands." Diamond lied as she took a sip from her drink. Dante wasn't there in AC with them. But what else could she have told him on why she was there with a bunch of young male teens?

"You look like you could use another drink." He noticed her glass was almost empty. "Bartender!" he called.

The bartender looked in his direction.

"Give her another one." He held up Diamond's glass. "Now back to you. So you brought your son and his friends to a concert?"

"Yes." Diamond smiled nervously. She didn't know what was going on with her. For one, she had never before dated nor slept with a white man, not to mention she was always in control when it came to men. But there was something about this man that had her giddy as a teenager.

"Well, the way I see it, you are alone." He never took his eyes off hers.

"Well, yeah, if you look at it that way, then you're right."

"Are you staying overnight, or are you just down for the concert?"

"I'm staying overnight."

"Hmm."

Dr. Ricci nodded and took a swig from his glass, and so did Diamond. They were both silent as they sat there drinking. Every once in a while he glanced at Diamond's mountain of cleavage.

"Diamond, huh?" he said. "You must be a rare gem." He smiled at her.

Diamond smiled. "Something like that."

"Where are you from?"

"Newark."

"Really?" he asked, surprised.

"Yes. Why?"

"What a coincidence. My office is in East Orange."

She smiled. "Really?"

"Yeah, small world."

"It sure is." She chuckled.

"So, tell me something about yourself, Diamond."

The two of them drank, laughed, and talked for more than two hours. It was as if they had known each other for years. Diamond found out he divorced his wife because he caught her cheating with one of his colleagues.

"Are you kidding me?" Diamond asked, surprised.

"No, I wouldn't kid about something like that. I caught them in the act." Dr. Ricci drained his fifth gin and tonic.

"Oh my God! She was a fool!"

"Yeah, that she was," Dr. Ricci said, staring into his now empty glass as he remembered that day.

"Well, all I can say is, it's her loss to lose a wonderful man like you."

"You know, Diamond, it took me several years to realize that," he said, gazing into her eyes.

Dr. Ricci and Diamond sat there gazing at each other lustfully. It had been some time since Dr. Ricci had last had a sexual encounter. As for Diamond, she wasn't lacking in that department, but what she was missing was a real man's touch.

The two of them moved in slowly toward each other. Their lips touched, and Dr. Ricci gently and passionately kissed Diamond. Juices seeped from her treasures as his tongue gently danced with hers. They pulled back from each other, looking deep into each other's eyes.

"That was nice. You wanna go up to your room?"

"I'm sharing a room with my son. Do you have a room?"

"I sure do," he said and went in for another taste of her sweet lips.

✦✧✦ ✦✧✦ ✦✧✦

Diamond walked into Dr. Ricci's hotel room in her stiletto clad heels, 5-inch heels that made her feel sexy. She purposely took languorous steps, and as she walked Michael watched her ass jiggle in her formfitting dress.

One by one, she stepped out of her shoes and left them by the king-sized bed. Michael looked down at her perfect French pedicure and couldn't wait to suck each toe. The lust in his eyes said he wanted to do nasty things to Diamond, which aroused her endlessly. She inhaled his cologne and began to taste his skin. Gently, he clasped both hands behind her neck and kissed her softly. His tongue was exploring the inside of her mouth. His kisses slowly moved down to her earlobe and then he began to gently suck and lick her neck in circular motions. He'd suck and then gently blow, sending a tickly sensation through Diamond's entire body.

Slowly, she stepped back, pulled off her sweater dress, and let it cascade to the floor. After that, Michael pulled his shirt over his head and let it hit the ground. The two lovers stared at each other in silence as he pulled off his jeans. Diamond stood, posing provocatively as to let Michael see her flawless skin and voluptuous hourglass shape. As he stood there, gawking at her in her bra and panties, his skinny legs appeared awkward as his boxers swallowed his small lower body frame. His stark-white legs were in desperate need of some sun. Diamond's eyes were drawn to them immediately.

Diamond turned around so that she could refocus and unclasped her bra. Her large breasts fell into her hands as Michael nestled up behind her. She could feel his hard dick pressing against her lower back. Slowly, he turned her around to face him. Diamond was still discreetly holding her breasts until he removed her hands and slid her bra off. He licked and sucked her beige nipples and paused for a minute to admire her large areolas.

"You're so sexy," he whispered and continued to suck on her nipples until her pussy began to tingle.

Michael playfully pushed Diamond back onto the bed and then skillfully climbed on top. His heavy upper body weight covered

Diamond almost completely. He removed his boxers and then slowly slid her G-string off, then parted her legs and admired her nakedness. Slowly, he glided up in between her legs and gently teased her with his tongue. His wet tongue flickered rapidly, beating her clit, and then he'd slow down and suck it while murmuring, "I want to make you feel good ..."

He was definitely an experienced man when it came to kissing the pussy. He didn't bury his head and start licking like a dog slopping up water. He concentrated on the clit, softly and skillfully applying pressure at just the right moment and keeping each move steady. His tongue fluttered expertly, and the feeling was beyond pleasurable.

Diamond began to rock her hips back and forth, getting lost in the moment. As she felt waves of pleasure cascading through her body, her legs began to uncontrollably tremble.

Diamond came in silence. She wasn't a screamer; to her that meant she wasn't in control. The thick liquid gushing from her cave was the only evidence. As he lapped it up he whispered, "Ummm ... you taste like candy."

When he started sucking every single toe, one by one, Diamond tried to envision she was with Trey, and he was making love to her that good.

Moments later, Diamond reached down for Michael and pulled him up. Instead of letting him enter her, she turned him over to return the favor.

She started off slowly by lubricating the tip of his dick with her saliva. At first, she teased him by sucking only the tip. As his pickle-shaped dick went in and out of her mouth, Diamond watched him intently. She began slobbering all over his dick and making slurping noises. Diamond arched her neck and opened her jaws wide to deep throat him. Her jaws caved in and out and his moaning encouraged her.

"Ummmm, baby that feels soooo good," he murmured. "Damn, it feels good."

Next, she went to his balls. She took her left hand and continued to jerk his dick while her warm mouth took in both nuts. Her tongue expertly flickered rapidly while pulling them in and out of her mouth. When he started babbling, she knew he was ready to release his juices. Diamond took him fully into her mouth and sucked until he exploded. His cum erupted into her mouth and she eagerly swallowed his bitter tasting liquid.

Diamond slid back up and laid on her back in the missionary position.

"You sure you ready for this," he asked and began stroking his juicy dick while towering over her, preparing to put on a condom.

"I can't wait," she purred and parted her legs giving him easy access.

As he applied pressure her tight cave resisted only momentarily and he methodically slid in. Her wet pussy gripped his dick as their bodies moved in unison. The couple had sex in the frog's position, doggy style, and then Diamond flipped over and rode Michael's dick. As he pushed deeper and deeper into her walls, once again, they were both ready to come. Michael screamed out in ecstasy as they both climaxed. Diamond fell on top of Michael, breathing rapidly, as he wrapped his strong arms around her waist and held her firmly.

Dr. Ricci made passionate love to Diamond that night. He took his time and explored her body like no man had ever done before. Diamond was in heaven.

"I think I know why you were named Diamond," Dr. Ricci said while Diamond lay in his arms.

"Why?"

"Because diamonds are at the top of all the precious stones. Diamond, I have never made love to a woman who has made me feel this way, not even my wife."

Diamond lay there, her head resting on his chest, and a smirk on her face. She knew then that she could have her way with the doctor. "Well,

Michael," she said, "this doesn't have to end here. Your office is not far from where I live."

"You would really see me again?" a sprung Dr. Ricci asked.

Diamond didn't answer right away. She thought about settling down and having a good relationship with him. He seemed honest.

"Are you kidding me? You rocked my world, Michael, and I'm all yours for the taking."

Diamond's phone began to ring at one thirty in the morning. She got out of the bed to retrieve her phone from her purse. Looking at the caller ID, she saw that it was Trey. She sucked her teeth, not wanting to answer, but she knew he would only continue to call, if she didn't. Trey was persistent like that. She also knew he would tear up the hotel looking for her, and she didn't want that either, so she answered.

"Hey. Are you back?"

"Yeah, we back. Where are you?"

"I'm in the hotel. Are you in the room?"

"Yeah, I'm in the room. Where in the hotel are you?" a suspicious Trey asked.

"OK, I'll be there in a few. See you in a minute." Diamond disconnected the call. She placed her phone back in her purse and exhaled.

"Was that your son?"

"Yeah, that was him. They're back in the room. I better go up there. You know how teens are. I want to make sure they don't do anything to get us thrown outta here." A little paranoid, she smiled nervously.

He watched her pick up her clothes from the floor. "I understand. Do you want to have breakfast in the morning?"

"I won't be able to do that, Michael. We plan to leave first thing in the morning."

He sat up in the bed. "So when will I see you again?"

Diamond continued to get dressed. "Well, I'll give you my number, and you give me a call when you get back up that way, and we can set something up." She smiled at him.

"Sounds like a plan." He reached over onto the nightstand and grabbed his cell phone.

Diamond gave him her number and kissed him passionately before leaving.

When she walked into her room, the first thing that hit her in the face was the smell of weed. Pop and Al-Malik were sitting in the living room of the suite, smoking weed and playing PlayStation.

"What's up, Diamond?" Pop asked, the blunt hanging out of the corner of his mouth. He never looked up at her. His eyes were glued to the big-screen TV, while his thumbs worked on the video game control.

"Hey, Diamond." Al-Malik too was glued to the TV.

Diamond didn't say a word. She simply made her way to the master bedroom. As she passed the kitchenette, she saw the remainder of the crew stuffing their faces with some takeout food they'd obviously picked up after the concert.

Tyquan looked up and saw her walking past. "You want something to eat?"

"No," she said and kept stepping. She was wondering why they weren't in their room. She'd booked two suites for that reason.

When Diamond walked into the master suite, Trey was sitting at the end of the bed watching TV.

He stood when she walked into the room. "Where were you?" he asked like a jealous boyfriend.

Diamond wanted to curse out Trey. She was grown, and he was a child. Who the hell was he to question her? But she realized Trey was her right hand and would do anything for her. He was indeed young, and she had to remember that he wasn't a man like Dr. Ricci. Just thinking about Dr. Ricci made her want to turn around and go back to his room.

"So what's up, Diamond? Where were you?" Trey stood there fuming, waiting for an answer.

Diamond snapped out of her fantasy and began to stroke his ego. "Trey, baby, come on and take a shower with me." She grabbed his hand and led him into the bathroom.

"You still didn't answer my question," he said, although he didn't resist being led into the huge bathroom.

"I was down in the casino." She began to run the water for the shower.

He leaned against the vanity, his arms folded across his muscular chest. "I was down there looking for you. I didn't see you."

"I was sitting at the slot machines, Trey." She busied herself with preparing their shower.

"I checked the slots, Diamond. Don't bullshit me!"

She stood in front of him. "Oh yeah? You did, huh? Did you check the quarter slots?"

"Yeah. Where you think I checked? You weren't there."

"That's because I was sitting with two old ladies, having drinks and playing the penny machines. I had a good time with them."

She began to undress Trey, who kept his gaze on her, trying to read if she was telling the truth, but he let her take off his clothes.

Diamond began to plant soft kisses on his chest. Trey was a physically fit, handsome young man, and Diamond loved his eyes and couldn't get enough of looking into them. But Dr. Ricci had eyes like no other.

She stepped into the roaring shower, which had three showerheads, and pulled him by the arm. He finally stepped in behind her, still angry.

The hot water cascaded over their bodies, relaxing their muscles. Even Trey began to loosen up when the water soothed the tension in his shoulders. Diamond knew what to do to calm him down. After all, she had the experience, and technically, he was learning from her about how to treat a lady.

She eased down to her knees and swallowed his manhood whole. Trey grabbed on to the railing on the shower wall, bracing himself, because of the chills running through his body.

Diamond put her skills to work on Trey. She didn't usually give him this kind of treatment, but tonight it was time to show him who had the upper hand. When it was all said and done, Diamond had Trey in his place, laid out on his back, snoring like a grizzly bear.

✦ ✦ FOURTEEN ✦ ✦

Busted

2000

Diamond and Dr. Ricci had been going hot and heavy for the past four months. Diamond thought Dr. Ricci was gonna wine and dine her, but he was a chiropractic doctor who didn't have many patients nor much money. His wife was raping him of his money she was awarded in the divorce settlement, so he barely made ends meet. But the little he did give Diamond, she gladly accepted and even saved. She knew that with the hustle she wanted to plan with him, eventually the cash would flow in, so she needed to keep him around, regardless.

The crew was doing well with drug sales and extortion, and Trey had recruited more muscle to help with security.

Diamond kept Dr. Ricci a secret for as long as she could, until the shit hit the fan one day. Unbeknownst to her, Trey had been following her and Dr. Ricci all day. Dr. Ricci had just dropped off Diamond in front of the nail salon on Springfield Avenue, when Trey snatched her by the arm.

Diamond went to reach for her gun in her bra, not knowing who had grabbed her. She never saw Trey coming.

"By the time you pull your shit out, I'll already have you filled with the hot ones," he growled into her ear like a maniac. Trey's gun was in the front of his waistband and now pressed against Diamond's back.

For the first time, she realized how crazy he was. She may have had the upper hand on him mentally, but in brute force and strength, Trey was like a raging bull, and Diamond was no match for him.

He continued to press up against her back. It was broad daylight, and the avenue was busy with shoppers, but no one said a word.

"Trey, what are you doing?" she asked calmly, trying not to make matters worse.

"The question is: What are *you* doing?"

"I'm trying to go get my nails done and you out here bugging the fuck out. Let me go, Trey." She said, trying to remain calm.

They were standing in front of the nail salon and Trey glared at her through the store's front window. He took his arm from around her and backed up, readjusting his weapon.

Diamond, feeling a little embarrassed by the incident, straightened her clothing and then turned around to face him. "What's your problem?" she asked, looking seriously into his hazel eyes.

"Who is this clown you been fucking around with?"

"What?"

Trey stepped closer to her. "Who is this white muthafucka I been seeing you with?"

"Oh, him?" Diamond had to stall to make up some kind of lie.

Trey turned his head to the side and twisted his lips. "Don't play yourself, Diamond."

"OK, first of all, I ain't one of them little tramps you run around with," she said, trying to flip the script on him. "Second, don't forget who you talking to. I'm a grown-ass woman." She pointed her finger at his chest.

Trey chuckled. "Don't try to flip the shit on me. Who is he?"

Diamond smiled. "You got issues. He is gonna be our next come-up, but if you keep acting like this it ain't gonna be no come-up."

"What we need him for? I take care of you."

"I know you do, baby, but I'm telling you, we can't pass this up, and I need you to trust me. I have to be with him to bait him."

"You full of shit!"

Diamond studied Trey's body. She had to admit, Trey was maturing into a sexy thug with each passing day. He turned her on in more than one way, but then there were those immature times. This wasn't one of those times, though. He was turning her on by taking control.

"When did you ever know me to bullshit about money?"

"Never," he said.

"All right, then, what makes you think I would bullshit about it now?"

Trey didn't respond, nor did he stop mean-mugging her, his jaw muscle flexing.

Diamond continued to stare up at him, wishing he would lighten up. She really did have a plan to use Dr. Ricci so they could make some real cash, but she was also enjoying dating him in the process.

"Did you fuck him?"

"Huh?" She frowned. "I tell you about how we gonna use dude to make some real cash, and you talking about me fucking him. How you sound, Trey?"

"Did you fuck?"

"No, Trey, I didn't fuck him. I'm going to get my nails done. I don't have time to play these kid games with you." She turned to leave.

Trey grabbed her by the arm and pulled her close to him. He kissed her passionately before he released her. "Just remember who fucks you good and takes care of your ass." He walked toward his car and got inside.

Diamond was turned on. *I must be crazy letting this little young boy turn me out,* she thought.

✦✦ ✦✦ ✦✦

Later that night, Trey rolled off Diamond and lay panting beside her, while Diamond lay busted up on her back. Trey straight pile-drove into her treasures, until she came over and over again.

"So what kinda game you running on this white cat?"

"Remember I told you about the insurance thing I wanted to put in place?"

"No, I don't remember."

"Come on, Trey. Remember I told you about this insurance thing I wanted to do that we could get paid some real money?"

"No, but go 'head," Trey said, lighting a blunt.

Diamond sat up in the bed and frowned. "Do you have to smoke that now?" She hated the smell of weed.

Trey blew the smoke from his lungs and put the blunt out in the ashtray that sat on the stand next to the bed.

"Thank you," she said, lying back down. "Anyway, Michael is a doctor."

"Michael? It figures." Trey sucked his teeth.

"What do you mean by that?"

"I hate white people, Diamond, and I don't trust them muthafuckas, especially ones named Michael. That's a typical white name."

"This muthafucka that you don't even know is about to fatten your pockets."

"*Psst*, do you think I need him to stack chips? You got me fucked up for the next man. I got the game on lock. How you think you walking around with this expensive shit you rockin'?"

"Trey, you ain't the only one throwing loot my way. Did you forget about the others I get money from?"

"Baby, you can't be serious. Them niggas' flows can't touch mine. Besides, who do you think employs them? Me." Trey was feeling himself extra special.

Diamond lay there looking up at the ceiling. If Trey only knew that in time he wouldn't be able to hold a candle to the type of bread Dr. Ricci was eventually gonna start making. But she didn't want to hurt his feelings, so she just let it go.

"Sure, Trey, you're right." She smiled.

"I know I am, and don't you forget it. You laying up in my shit. Them other niggas don't own two condos. I do. I got two whips." He continued to fuss.

Diamond just lay there and waited for him to calm down.

"Now tell me the rest about Michael, the doctor."

Diamond rolled her eyes. "Like I said before I was interrupted, he is the kind of doctor I was looking for. He's a chiropractor."

"What's that? One of the pussy-feeling doctors?" Trey asked a little louder than Diamond cared to hear it.

"No, Trey." She rolled her eyes up in her head. "That's a gynecologist, fool! Michael is a spine doctor. He works on the back."

"Yeah, OK, he works on the back. How is he gonna bring loot our way?"

"Well, the plan is to get some people who may wanna get down with us and make some extra cash. We gonna have to create a fake car accident and call the police—"

"Aw, naw!" Trey cut her off. "Hold up. Count me out. I ain't dealing with no cops."

"Trey, you don't have to deal with them." She sat up and turned to him.

"A'ight, so tell me why we gotta call them?"

"Because it will be a fake accident, and in order for it to work, we have to call the police to take the report."

"Naw, baby, I ain't with that. I mean, I'll help you in any way I can, but I don't want to be nowhere near the cops. You do remember what I do for a living, right?"

"How can I forget?" She sucked her teeth.

"Well, then I don't need them getting to know my face. I ain't with that. Now if somebody get out of line, or you need some muscle, then I'm your man."

"Well, then you are gonna have to understand that I have to spend a lot of time with him."

"How much time?"

"Trey, I gotta spend a lot of time with him to watch our investment. I need to make sure it's going smoothly."

"Yeah, a'ight." Trey didn't sound convinced.

"You are gonna have to trust me, baby." She leaned over and kissed him on the lips.

"Trust you, huh?" He looked at her sideways.

"Yeah, and speaking of trust, I have been spending a lot of time with you and neglecting the others. You knew the deal with me when we started sleeping together. I gotta pay some attention to the others."

"Yeah, I been meaning to talk to you about that. Them niggas getting paid, so why you gotta fuck with them? Let them get their own broads to fuck."

"I'm not going to go through this with you, Trey. Like I said, you knew the deal from the rip, and I ain't gonna change."

"Oh, really?"

"Yes, really. I'm a grown-ass woman and old enough to be your mother, so let's not forget that. Lately you have been real comfortable with manhandling me and telling me what to do. I ain't that bitch, Trey."

"Whatever, Diamond. Do you." Pouting, he turned his head away from her.

Diamond lay back and turned her back to him.

Within minutes, Trey got comfortable and drifted off to sleep, while Diamond lay there thinking about how much money she was gonna make on the new hustle.

✦✦ ✦✦ FIFTEEN ✦✦ ✦✦

No Time for Me
2001

Dante walked into the apartment and shut the door behind him. The first thing that hit him in the face was the aroma of food cooking in the kitchen. He set his book bag on the floor by the door and pulled out the gun he had begun carrying, which he kept in his waistband. He crept along the floor and peered into the kitchen, his gun raised.

Diamond was standing there looking toward the entrance of the kitchen. She heard him come in and had been waiting for him to come into the kitchen.

"What the hell are you gonna do with that?" She laughed at Dante when she saw him holding the gun.

"I ain't know who was in here." He put the gun away.

"So you really think a robber is gonna cook himself something to eat before he robs you?" Diamond doubled over with laughter.

Dante didn't say a word. He didn't think it was funny.

When Diamond finally recovered from her laughing fit, she noticed Dante's serious expression. "What's wrong with you?" she asked.

"Nothing. You finished laughing at me?" He looked at her with a raised eyebrow.

"Oh, come on, Dante. You can take a joke, right?"

"Sure, I can, if it's funny."

"Stop being like that. I came to cook you a decent meal. I know you haven't had one in a good while." She turned to finish preparing the meal.

"Yeah, I wonder why." Dante turned on his heels and went to his bedroom, shutting the door behind him.

Diamond turned off the pots because the food was finished. She wiped her hands on the dishcloth, walked to his room, and knocked on the door. He didn't answer. She knocked again, and there was still no response.

Diamond opened the door and walked inside. Dante was sitting on his bed, looking in one of his textbooks. He appeared to be reading. He was nineteen and in his second year in community college.

He looked up at her. "What's up?" he asked, exasperation written all over his face.

"No, the question is: What's up with you?" She sat down next to him on the bed.

"I'm straight." He downplayed his mood and buried his head back into his textbook.

"You're definitely not straight, Dante." Diamond pulled the book from his hand and set it on the bed behind them.

Dante sighed, not caring for the interruption. He was trying to study. Diamond sat there staring at him, waiting for him to speak.

He finally noticed her motherly stare. "What?"

"Don't play with me, boy. What's wrong with you?"

"A'ight, since you want to know so bad, I'm gonna tell you. First, you start off sleeping with all my friends and the rest of these young cats around here. I eventually accepted that because I realized that maybe that was your way of staying young. Then I find out you basically pimping these cats and got them running after you, paying your bills and shit."

Diamond tossed her eyes upward.

Dante noticed the look. "OK, so, yeah, you shared the wealth with me, and I know I told you I was OK with it. But, to be honest, it's killing me to know my mother is having sex with dudes my age." Dante stood and walked over to the window, peering outside. "And what really fucked me up was when I found out you and my boy Trey was fucking."

Dante had learned from Al-Malik that his mother was fucking Trey. Although Al-Malik had joined his mother's crew, a.k.a. *the Diamond Syndicate*, he still stopped by to kick it with Dante from time to time, and kept him updated on all the street news. Dante was sick to his stomach when he heard the news about his mother's affair with Trey. For a long time he avoided Trey. He knew that if he saw Trey, the meeting would result in something very violent, and he refused to allow himself to stoop to Trey's level.

"Watch your mouth, boy," she said, ignoring what he'd just said about Trey. Diamond had no idea how he'd found out about her and Trey. She had sworn all the boys from the syndicate to secrecy on that, aware that such knowledge would hurt him more than any of her other exploits.

"You know what? It's stuff like that that pisses me off. You tell me to watch my mouth, but you hang around them niggas all the time, and all they do is talk like that. I ain't a kid anymore, Ma."

"Dante, it's—"

"I'm not finished. You spend all your time with them, never coming home. You don't even know how I'm doing in college. I'm at the top of my class, Ma. Did you know that? Come on, Ma, Trey and them are straight-up in the drug game, so no matter what, if they get got, so do you, whether you sell it or not. Did you think about that?" Trey walked over and stood in front of his mother. "Do you have any idea how I feel when I gotta hear how my moms is running around with a crew of young niggas? Do you know how it makes me feel, when I do kick it with my boys, that I gotta hear about how cool everybody is with you?

They talk about you all the time. They talk about how you got the best pussy and shit. That shit driving me bananas!"

Diamond was about to speak, but Dante stopped her.

"Hold up. You wanted to know what was bothering me, so let me finish. I'm your son. I have done everything you told me to do all my life. I have nothing but respect for you and would do anything for you. We are blood"—He pointed to himself and then to her—"Not them other niggas. I grew up with you hitting on me, punishing me, half the time for no reason, or because you mad at my father." Dante frowned, showing his pain. "Do you know how much I suffered then and now? Do you have any idea how many times I wanted to kill myself because I thought you didn't love me? Why do you think I did whatever you told me to do? Because I thought that would make you love me!" His eyes showed sincerity. "Do you love me the way I love you?"

Diamond was at a loss for words. It wasn't that she didn't love him; she just didn't know how to love. She was raised to think to love was to provide, and when you did wrong, you got beat. She always longed for real love, but since she never got it, she didn't know how to give it.

When she didn't respond to his questions, Dante said, "I thought so."

Snapping out of her stupor, Diamond stood. "First of all, let me tell you something. I raised you, and you will respect me."

"You know what, Ma? I already know that. You raised me by yourself, and I ruined your freedom. I get it. It's in here." He tapped his temple with his index finger.

Diamond could have breathed fire at that moment. For a few moments, she couldn't hear anything that Dante said to her. She wanted to straight slap the shit out of him, but standing there looking up at him, she thought about the last time she'd laid hands on him when she had to pull out her gun because he overpowered her. Plus Dante was a young man now and he could easily overpower her. His physique had definitely developed.

She decided to go another route this time, realizing she was losing the control she had over him. She slowly sat back down on the bed and crossed her legs. "What do you want me to do?" she asked calmly.

Dante shoved his hands into the front pockets of his jeans and shrugged.

"I'm sorry, son. I didn't know you felt that way," she said, pretending to be sincere.

Dante studied her face, trying to make out who she really was. His mother had never been the calm, understanding type. *Maybe she's changed,* he thought. *Naw.* He quickly dismissed the idea. He knew his mother had dual personalities, a bipolar-type attitude.

"You could start by spending more time with me," he said.

"Done. What else?"

"I want you to stop running around with them niggas and stop scheming to get money."

"And do what? Stay on welfare? That ain't gonna happen."

"What about getting a job?"

Diamond laughed out loud. "Doing what, Dante? Bagging groceries out of the store you work at?"

"So you'd rather stay a whore than to be a woman?"

When Dante saw Diamond's facial expression, he wished he hadn't said it.

Diamond jumped up and charged him.

All Dante could do was try and block the many punches that she threw at his face. Anger crept into his body. But he knew he could never put his hands on his mother, so he continued to block her punches, stiff-arming her to keep her at a distance.

Diamond finally tired herself out and stopped swinging on him. She stood there staring at him with daggers in her eyes, while her chest heaved as she tried to catch her breath. Her hands hurt because his body was so tight that when she hit him it felt as if she were punching a steel slab.

Dante stood there looking at his mother, who sat there on the bed, seething.

"You haven't even sent any money over for the rent," he whispered with his head lowered.

Although Diamond hardly ever came home, she made sure the rent was paid. With her still being on welfare, her rent remained two hundred dollars a month. She would send one of the boys to the apartment or by the store to drop off money to Dante, but then that stopped. Dante was too proud to ask his mother for money, so he struggled, trying to make ends meet with the money he made at the grocery store.

"So what have you been doing for money?" She frowned, realizing she hadn't sent money to him for a while. She hoped the guilt wasn't evident on her face, because she had been so caught up in her busy life, she'd forgotten about her only son.

"Trying to pay bills with the money I make from work. I don't make enough to pay for all this stuff by myself."

"No wonder there wasn't any food in here. I had to go back out to the store to pick up some stuff so I could cook for you."

Silence filled the bedroom.

"Yeah, Dante, you're right. You are my son, and if anybody got my back, it's you. You're right, I do trust you the most," she said, finally realizing he was making sense.

"You trust me more than Trey?"

"Of course, I do. What kinda question is that? You're my son. Why would I trust him more?"

"I don't know. Maybe because you two are running around here like a modern-day Bonnie and Clyde?"

Diamond was spent. She sat there trying to figure out who had told him so much about her and Trey. She knew she had a pretty loyal bunch, and not knowing who'd betrayed her was driving her crazy.

"Who told you, Dante?" she asked, defeated.

"That don't matter. But why Trey? It's bad enough you fucking with young boys. I just want to know why my boy—somebody I grew up with? What do you think his mother would say if she knew?"

"First of all, I don't give a shit what anybody has to say. Trey is out on his own and is holding shit down like the next man. Second, I'm sorry you feel the way that you do, but he's much more mature than you know. Just because he's young . . . he's still a man to me."

Dante just stood there looking at the floor.

"Listen, Dante, I'm really sorry you feel the way you do, but Trey takes good care of me, and we click. I can't help it, but we do. I mean, I would've thought that you would at least be more understanding, because it's your friend. You know your friend ain't gonna let nothing happen to me on the strength of you."

"On the strength of me?" Dante laughed. "I ain't got nothing to do with that sick shit."

"Call it what you want, but I'm not gonna change anything about what I'm doing. Now you can still come on board and handle some of the things for me with no problems, but I ain't gonna stop seeing him. If you think this is gonna be a problem for you, or it may cause some problems for us, then maybe you need to reconsider what you want to do."

Dante didn't respond. He didn't know how to respond. What was the point of responding when regardless of how he felt or what he thought, she was still gonna be with Trey?

"Whatever, Ma. I'm done with the situation. Just don't expect me and him to be all cool and shit. It is just business for me, period."

"I need you to do me a favor."

When Dante didn't respond and just looked at her, she took that as a yes.

"I need you to round up a few other people that you know. I need to see if they want to get down on making some money."

"Doing what, Ma?" Dante asked, but he didn't really want to know.

"Insurance claims," she said.

He frowned, not understanding. "Insurance claims? What are you talking about?"

"Auto insurance and health claims. We get people to create false car accidents and set up appointments with a chiropractor to go for therapy. One driver is gonna sue the other driver, and the lawyer is gonna get a big payoff. Everybody gonna get a piece of the cake."

"You always got some kinda hustle going on."

She laughed with him, knowing he was right. "You know how I do it. But, trust, if I didn't have these hustles, we would be struggling on welfare for real."

"Ma, I don't know. That sounds like too many people involved, and it sounds risky to me."

"Dante, people been doing this for a minute, and ain't nobody get caught yet. Listen, ain't you tired of living up in here?" Diamond looked around her room, for emphasis. "I'm tired. I want a house, our very own house. I want a car, our very own car. I just want to get out of this neighborhood, period."

Dante sat there and processed what his mother was saying. He knew if he didn't do what she asked him to do that she would make life hell on earth for him.

Dante also often suffered with depression, unbeknownst to his mother and others. It seemed as if the cycle of life was repeating itself with him the way it had with Diamond. The only difference was. Diamond wasn't abused like she abused Dante.

This was what she saw her father do to her mother and thought it would make him act the way she wanted him to behave.

But Dante wasn't a happy kid most times. He would lie in his room at night wishing on a star, hoping and wishing there was a God.

Someone to save him from his inner sufferings. He wanted to be far away from his mother at times, secretly despising her in moments like this, although he did love her.

His ultimate dream was to finish school, get a job, and move far away from the hood and his mother. He wished he had other relatives he could call on when he felt sad, but his mother revealed nothing to him about other relatives. It was as if she wanted to keep him away from anyone who would possibly show him love.

The thought of being able to buy a house was something that appealed to him. They could get a big enough house so that it would seem as if they each had their own place. He thought about having a huge finished basement that he could turn into his own private apartment. The idea was sounding better and better, the more he thought about it.

"I need you to round up some of your friends to help with this," she said, continuing to make demands, rather than asking for his opinion.

"What? You don't have enough of these niggas around here that would jump for you?"

"They already have their place with me, and I need some new meat on standby, in case I come up with another plan."

"I mean, what am I supposed to tell them, Ma?"

"Shut up, boy!" she yelled. "Just do what I tell you, and let me know who you got in mind before you say anything to them. I need somebody who's trustworthy. Then I'm gonna be the one to talk to them. I'm gonna have Pop and Trey here when I talk to them."

"Seriously, Ma, I ain't tryna go to jail."

Diamond sighed heavily. She had managed to remain patient, trying to be a better mother, but in her mind, Dante wasn't supposed to ask any questions. There was no questioning or talking back as far as she was concerned.

"Boy, you don't worry about all that. Just do like I tell you, and we gonna be all right. We gonna get paid and move. I wasn't supposed to end up like this."

Dante readjusted the gun in the front of the waistband of his jeans.

"By the way, what the hell are you doing with a gun?" Diamond wasn't worried about the gun, because she knew he wouldn't dare try her.

"Ma, ever since you started running with them, I hear a lot of shit out there. I hear how Trey be wildin' out on niggas, shaking them down and shit. I don't know what y'all into out there, so I gotta protect myself in case somebody runs up on me for repercussions because of some shit y'all did."

Diamond was actually proud of Dante for taking the initiative to protect himself. "I understand. Come on, let's eat." Diamond stood and walked out of the room, with Dante on her heels.

Dante hadn't been eating right for months, and was happy as hell that his mother came over and cooked for him.

They walked into the kitchen, and Dante sat down and waited for his mother to fix his plate like she used to do when he was a little boy. She filled his plate with collard greens, yams, baked macaroni and cheese, fried chicken, and corn bread. Diamond sat the piping hot plate in front of Dante, and before she could even fix her plate, he dove in.

For a long moment, they actually behaved like a normal family.

✦✦ ✦✦ SIXTEEN ✦✦ ✦✦

Accidents Happen

Diamond and Dr. Ricci had become quite an item. Although Dr. Ricci's money was tight, he did find ways that they could do things on occasions. At that point Diamond didn't care, since she really enjoyed being with him.

Diamond stepped out of the Jacuzzi-like tub after having sex with Dr. Ricci. She had spent a good hour basking in the tub, soaking her body and swimming in her thoughts after leaving him lying on his back, snoring. She dried her body and wrapped a towel around herself. She walked into the bedroom, got a T-shirt out of his drawer, and put it on. She noticed he was no longer asleep in the bed.

She walked through the house and found him in the kitchen preparing something for them to eat. He turned to see her enter the kitchen and simply smiled at her. She smiled back and took a seat at the kitchen table.

They were both silent while he continued to cook, and she sat watching him move around the kitchen with ease.

After a few moments of silence, he said, "You know, Diamond, I really feel something special for you." He turned to look at her.

Diamond was also enjoying the time she'd spent with Dr. Ricci, even though he wasn't rich. When she was with him, it seemed that a certain calm blanketed her soul. She honestly felt that he genuinely cared for her. That was something that was missing in her life, and she had longed for it for years. She struggled with her inner self often, but this time was different. She really wanted to be with Dr. Ricci. She had even thought of letting everything else go and focusing on building with the doctor. Dante had expressed to her that he didn't like how she was living, and this also played on her mind. But the greedy side of Diamond would not give up.

"You do?" she asked.

Dr. Ricci set a plate of food in front of her, leftovers that he'd warmed up from last night's dinner, and took a seat at the table across from her. "Yes, really. Diamond, there isn't anything I wouldn't do for you. You are a dream come true. I have never had a woman make me feel the way you do. I'm not just talking about the lovemaking either. You are a wonderful woman, and whatever it takes to make you happy, I will do it."

Damn! I really like this man.

Diamond thought about how Trey would take the news if she told him she didn't want to be with him anymore. She knew the others wouldn't have a problem with it, as they were just jump-offs anyway. But Trey actually thought Diamond was his woman and was very overprotective of her, not to mention, he was a beast. Diamond knew it wouldn't be easy to tell him.

She pictured Trey killing Dr. Ricci. She realized she would have to protect Dr. Ricci from Trey. She would just go forward with the plan and then slowly back away from Trey and the others to build a life with Dr. Ricci.

"That is so sweet of you, Michael." Diamond smiled at him. "Now that you mention it, there is something that I do want you to do for me."

"Anything. What is it?"

"No, never mind. You may think it's stupid." She looked down in her plate of food and pushed it around with her fork.

"No. What is it?" Dr. Ricci got up from his chair and sat in the chair next to Diamond. "Don't think anything that you want to say to me is stupid."

"Well, I have an idea that could make your profits double. I mean, it is a little risky, but we can do it a few times and get out of it with no problems."

Dr. Ricci looked into her eyes, waiting to hear more. "What is it, Diamond?"

"I mean, I know you're struggling just like I am. Your ex-wife is trying to send you into the poorhouse, with all the money you have to give her, so I figured this would be a good way to at least get you out of the hole."

"I understand. But what are you trying to tell me?"

Diamond proceeded to tell Dr. Ricci her plan for committing insurance fraud, and he gave her his undivided attention with no interruptions.

"That sounds like a good plan, and yes, it would double my bank account, and I sure can use the extra cash. However, it's illegal, no matter how you dress it up, Diamond. I will lose my license, my livelihood, and all my assets if I get caught in this. I cannot risk that."

"See, I knew you wouldn't go for it. I knew you would say that. It was stupid of me, and I'm so sorry for even asking you to do such a stupid thing." She pouted.

Dr. Ricci looked into her alluring eyes, grabbed her hand and kissed it. "I said it was a good idea, sweetheart. It's just that the risks involved with doing such a thing are too high. I'm no criminal."

Diamond forced tears from her eyes and looked at him, so he would see she was crying. "It's OK, Michael. I'm sorry." She pulled her hand from his and wiped away her forced tears.

"Oh, don't cry." Dr. Ricci was beginning to feel guilty. He had always been a sucker for a woman's tears and hated to see any woman hurt. He moved his chair closer to hers and put his arm around her shoulder, pulling her into his arms.

Diamond continued to play the role. She could have won an Oscar for her performance. While she played the doctor, she did feel somewhat guilty, but she had to move forward with her plans. Money before men.

"Please, babe, just think about it. We'll just do it a couple of times." Diamond looked into his eyes and began to kiss his neck softly.

Chills shot through his body as he enjoyed the attention to one of the more sensitive areas on his body.

"I promise I will take control of everything. I'll be right there to make sure everything goes smoothly," she said as she worked her way to his bare chest and covered it with kisses. She sucked on his nipples and circled her tongue around them.

Diamond kept making her way down to his stomach, leaning her body forward and sticking her tongue in his navel.

Panting, Dr. Ricci lay back on the high-back chair, anticipating where Diamond was going with her kisses.

"Hire me as an office manager, and then I can keep an eye on everything. No one in your office will know. It will be our little secret."

Diamond reached inside his shorts and exposed his semi-hard, pink dick. Then she sucked on it like it was a pacifier, driving Dr. Ricci crazy.

After she released the growing erection from her mouth, she said, "OK, babe, can we just try it a couple of times, and then we can stop?" Before he could answer, Diamond engulfed him again, working her throat muscle on the head.

Dr. Ricci yelled out in ecstasy, "Yes-s-s-s! Yes-s-s-s!"

"Yes, you're gonna do it?" She ran her tongue around the head of his dick.

"Oh . . . yes . . . I'll do it! Ooh!" he said, as Diamond skillfully brought him to an orgasm.

Several hours later Diamond woke up and got out of the bed, leaving a sleeping Dr. Ricci. She went downstairs into the living room and turned on her cell phone. As soon as the phone found reception, voicemails began to flood in. She checked the voicemails one by one. There weren't any emergencies, and most of them were from Trey.

"*Yo, where the fuck you at?*" he yelled. "*I know you ain't still with that cracker muthafucka. Hit me up!*"

She had five more messages just like that one, each one more irate than the previous one. She simply ignored his antics, deciding she'd deal with him later.

One week later, a man in his forties yelled at a woman driver, "What the fuck, man! You can't see?"

The woman had rear-ended the man's Cadillac, and he stood outside the car looking at the damage. A crowd had formed, and everybody was looking to see what had happened.

"Somebody call the fucking cops! This bitch done fucked up my shit!"

The woman never got out of her car. She simply sat there and looked at the man acting a fool.

When the police arrived on the scene, the angry man walked over to the two white officers before they could get out of the squad car.

"This woman rear-ended me for no reason!"

"Calm down, sir," one officer told him. "We will get all the information shortly."

"Is anybody hurt?" the second officer asked.

"Yeah, me and my wife."

The officers looked at each other and shook their heads. If the man was truly hurt, he would have stayed in the car instead of walking around and causing a scene. But the officers had seen it all before. Everyone wanted to shout whiplash and get paid. All they could do was take the report.

"Well, sir, if you're hurt, I suggest you sit down somewhere. Do I need to call an ambulance for your wife?" the first officer asked.

"Yeah, you do."

The second officer radioed in for an ambulance and then walked over to check on the woman in the other car. She wasn't hurt.

The first officer went to check out the damage. "Well, sir, you're lucky. It's not that bad," he said, bending over for a closer look.

"The hell it ain't. They gonna have to replace the whole bumper!"

An hour later the man's wife was carted off to the hospital, and the police had gotten all the information they needed from both drivers. Everyone began to clear the scene, and the police and the woman driver drove off. The man was the last to leave the scene.

Several minutes later he pulled into the parking lot of a supermarket and parked next to a car. He got out of his Caddy and got into the car.

"You are too funny," the woman said.

"What? I had to play it like it was a real accident." He smiled at the woman driver who'd hit the back of his car.

"Yeah, you played it all right. I think you overplayed. You don't know how hard it was for me not to burst out laughing at your dumb ass." The woman laughed.

The man laughed right along with her.

"No, but seriously, you was just supposed to tap my shit, and you really hit me." He looked over at his car.

"Well, it was supposed to look like an accident, so I made it look like one. What you complaining for? We about to get paid."

"Word up!" The man smiled.

SEVENTEEN

Hit and Run
2001

Dante, along with Al-Malik and Pop, were handling all the responsibilities of finding car owners who wanted to get down on the hustle. It had been about a year and it was a smooth operation that Dante and his team executed flawlessly.

The money flowed quite lovely, and everybody involved was eating well. Al-Malik had purchased his first condominium and a whip. He didn't have the time to stand on the corners anymore, and he had completely stopped selling drugs for Trey.

Trey wasn't happy with the transition, but he had no other choice. Dante informed his mother of what was taking place, and she told Trey.

Today Diamond and Dante were moving into their newly purchased home in a quiet neighborhood. She had all of her boys help with the move. During the move, every time Trey and Al-Malik crossed paths, Trey would shoot daggers his way. Al-Malik was starting to feel uncomfortable.

While everyone sat in the house drinking, eating, and laughing, Al-Malik stepped out into the backyard. He stood there and looked at the peaceful surroundings. Not long after, Dante came out into the backyard to join him.

"What's up, man? Why you out here by yourself?" Dante asked.

"I don't feel comfortable in there."

"Why? What's up?"

"Yo, your boy on some shit right now. He grilling me down like I'm some bitch or something."

"Who? Trey?"

"Yeah. It's like, ever since I been down with you and getting mine, he been hatin' on me."

"Man, fuck that nigga!" Dante waved his hand. "He's just jealous, that's all."

"Yeah, but that nigga getting his own loot. Why he gotta hate on me getting mine?"

"Because now he ain't got no control over you. Do you remember when I told you how I always thought Trey was hating on how cool you and I are?"

Al-Malik nodded.

"Well, I know for a fact he is. I'm saying, you used to come to my crib and sleep when you couldn't stay at your mom's crib. You got a job at the store with me. You used to play the game with me. Then, all of a sudden, when he got his crib, he talked you into staying with him, and had you out on the corners banging for him. Just look at it, Malik. I been trying to keep us outta the drug game for a minute, but that nigga always tried to get you to get in it with him. So it has always been about controlling you and keeping us from bonding."

"Yo, you right, man," Al-Malik said.

"I know I'm right, and I always tried to tell you that. But I had to let you find out on your own. Don't worry about him."

"Tae, you don't know him. He has changed, man. Trey is a beast. That nigga don't have a problem putting a bullet in somebody— anybody—and I don't want that to be me. He don't give two shits about popping off."

"Yo, I got you. Didn't I always look out for you?"

"Yeah, but we were kids then."

"And I still look out for you. You my man, and I ain't gonna let nothing happen to you. You ain't got nobody in your corner. I'm more of a brother to you than your own brothers, so like I said, fuck that nigga."

✦✦✦ ✦✦✦ ✦✦✦

Later that night Al-Malik walked into his condo and turned on the lights. Before he could get to his bedroom, someone knocked on the door. He frowned. Looking up at the clock on the living room wall, he saw that it was two am. He didn't have a clue who would be visiting at that hour.

"Who is it?"

"It's me, Trey."

Al-Malik was reluctant to open the door.

"What's up?" Al-Malik said, looking through the peephole at Trey, trying to read his body language.

"Man, open the door! Why you trippin'? We ain't chilled in a minute. I feel like we need to get that back, nah mean?"

Al-Malik opened the door. "What's up, man?" he asked, feeling uneasy.

"What's up?"

They both stood in the doorway.

"You gonna let me in?" Trey finally said.

"Sure." Al-Malik stepped to the side, allowing Trey to enter his condo.

Trey walked in and stood in the middle of the living room. Al-Malik closed the door and hesitated before he walked into the living room.

"What's good, man?" Al-Malik asked.

"You been running your mouth," Trey said, pointing at Al-Malik. Trey's demeanor had changed in an instant.

"Who? Me?"

"Yeah, you, nigga. I don't see nobody else in here but us."

Al-Malik was confused. "I ran my mouth about what, Trey?"

"Some bitch been running her mouth about Diamond fucking with that welfare fraud shit." Trey looked at him.

Al-Malik had no idea what Trey was talking about. "OK, so what the fuck that got to do with me?"

"It got a whole lotta shit to do with you. If Diamond get locked up because you ran your fucking mouth, then it's gonna be some shit."

"But that's what I'm tryna tell you, Trey. I didn't run my mouth to nobody."

Trey was lying about Malik running his mouth. He knew Al-Malik was innocent, but he simply had to get rid of him because he was weak. Trey knew that if enough pressure was applied to Al-Malik, he would fold under that pressure. With the scam business expanding rapidly, someone was bound to get caught, and if that person was Al-Malik, Trey knew he would talk. Trey didn't want that kind of heat coming down on him for having Diamond's back or Diamond. They had a sweet thing going on, and he was gonna do whatever he had to do to keep it that way.

"Yo, kill that noise," Trey said. "You know you did it. Why don't you just fess up, man? I mean, it's cool. All I came by to tell you is that we know. You gotta watch the people you kick it with. Some of these bitches are scandalous, man."

Al-Malik took a seat on the sofa. He put his head in his hands and rubbed his face with both hands. He was so confused, it wasn't funny. He really couldn't understand or remember who would even say such a thing. He also wondered why Trey was the one to come over to his house to confront him about this. Why wouldn't Dante or even Diamond talk to him? He was gonna make sure that he talked to Dante about this as soon as Trey left.

Al-Malik got up off the sofa. "A'ight, man, I appreciate you stopping by," he said. "I'm good. You don't have to worry about me running my mouth to no one."

"As long as you don't," Trey said and turned to walk over to the door.

Al-Malik followed him to lock the door.

Trey stopped walking. "Oh, yeah, I forgot."

"What?"

Trey turned around brandishing a .44. Al-Malik's eyes grew wide. Before he could respond to seeing the gun, Trey bucked off, filling his old friend with lead, and Al-Malik's body jerked backward until he was thrown off his feet and landed in the middle of the glass coffee table, crashing right through it. Trey stood there for a few moments looking at Al-Malik, and then he left the condo, closing the door behind him.

Two Weeks Later

Dante sat in the basement of the new house, which he had made into his own apartment. He still couldn't believe his best friend was gone. He could have kicked himself in the ass, letting something like that happen to his friend. He had always been like a big brother to Al-Malik, and had promised him that he wouldn't let anything happen to him.

The police hadn't found out who murdered Al-Malik as of yet, but they said they were still working on the case. In the meantime, Dante was suffering.

He thought about the possibility of Trey having something to do with it. He remembered the conversation he and Al-Malik had in the backyard on the day he moved to the new house. Al-Malik was acting strange that day, like he was afraid.

Dante wondered why someone would want to kill Al-Malik. He wished he'd never let him drift away from him. He thought about when they were in high school, and the promises he and Al-Malik had made to each other. Dante dropped out of college once he got involved in the insurance hustle, because it took up most of his time. And the money was so good, it made it easy for him to put school on the back burner for the moment. But he really had every intention of finishing college just as soon as the hustle was over. He would take night classes.

Dante's stash was building by the month. He couldn't believe all the loot the scams brought in. But something in his gut told him that he needed to pull out soon.

Just a couple more times and then I'm out, he thought.

✦•✦✦ EIGHTEEN ✦✦ ✦✦

The Doctor's End
2002

The elderly black woman made her way through the front office. The lights had been turned out, because it was after six pm, and the doctor's office was closed for the night. Estelle Brown worked as the office administrator. She had gone home at her regular time of five pm, but when she got home after running several errands, she realized she had left her apartment keys, which she kept separate from the office keys, in her desk drawer at the office. Now she found herself alone in the dark office.

Before she could turn on the lights in the waiting area, she heard a noise coming from inside the doctor's office. She stood still and waited to see if her old mind was playing tricks on her, or if she really did hear something. When there was no other noise, she pushed her tired bones forward through the doors of the waiting room and into the office. She could see a light up ahead in the doctor's main office and clearly heard voices.

Right away she knew it was the doctor. It wasn't odd for him to be in the office late at night. A smile crept across her face when she heard his voice. She figured maybe he was on the phone. She loved the doctor. He was such a joy to work for, not to mention he was young and handsome. He treated her well and often gave her something to daydream about. She often thought that, had she been in her prime, she would have had him wrapped around her finger.

Estelle was a sweet woman and always smelled of flowers, and her warm smile was inviting to everyone who came in contact with her. She had worked for Dr. Ricci for more than five years. After she'd retired, she couldn't sit at home doing nothing, so she opted to find a part-time job to keep herself busy. And that was how she found Dr. Ricci. They got along well, and she handled everything for him.

She walked over to her desk and opened the drawer. She found her keys just where she thought she'd left them. She placed them in her purse and closed the drawer. Then she turned to enter the doctor's office and speak with him before going home.

As she got closer to the door, she heard a woman's voice, piquing her interest. Truth be told, she was a little jealous. Dr. Ricci wasn't married, and every available woman wanted him. Even married women wanted to sex him, and Estelle was no different.

Estelle stood by the door and listened to the conversation the doctor was having with the woman. She assumed the woman was one of his patients. On many occasions Estelle had seen the patients flirt with the doctor. Even the nurses flirted with him, and the office manager Diamond was the most blatant of them all. Estelle despised her, but she tolerated her because Dr. Ricci had asked her to. He always knew what to say to calm her fears and make her feel special.

"Aww, come on, Estelle," Dr. Ricci had said to her on one occasion. "You know you're my favorite."

"I don't like her. She seems sneaky to me." Estelle was serious, wanting to make sure the doctor heard her concerns.

"Who takes good care of me?" Dr. Ricci put his arm around her and looked into her eyes. "You take care of me, Estelle, and nobody can take your place. So don't you worry about her."

Estelle looked into his eyes, and her heart instantly melted. She

truly loved the doctor and would do anything to protect him. "OK."
She smiled up at him.

"Now that's my girl." He kissed her on the forehead.

But Estelle still didn't like Diamond, nor any of the women patients
who came for their appointments wearing next to nothing, so every
chance she got, she made sure to "cock-block," to prevent any hanky-
panky from going on in the office.

Estelle heard the doctor yell, "I don't want to do this anymore,
Diamond!"

This caught her attention, brought her out of her thoughts. She
now knew who the woman was in the office, and it sounded like they
were arguing.

"You don't want to do this anymore?" Diamond's voice was dripping
with sarcasm. She was pissed. After all the money she'd brought into his
office. It was her idea, and it helped him with his financial difficulties,
and to think she was considering a committed relationship with him.
She was more hurt than pissed, and when she got hurt, she did what
she knew how to do best to protect her heart, and that was turn cold.

"Yes, that's what I said. I don't appreciate you coming into my office
with demands, Diamond. You said we would only do this a few times,
and that would be it." He tried to reason with her.

"No, you listen to me, muthafucka! I say when it's over! I ain't
finished yet! You made you a good piece of change off *my* idea, and now
you wanna bounce? Well, to hell with that!"

Diamond stood over the doctor as he sat in his chair behind his
desk. She had brought Dante and Trey with her, sensing the doctor
was gonna be a problem. Dr. Ricci had been hinting to Diamond that
he wanted out of the plan she had concocted to defraud the insurance
industry and make a little money, so when she received the call from
him asking her to meet with him after hours, she knew there was a
problem.

Meanwhile, Estelle had her ear pressed to the door and was practically lying on it, trying to listen.

"Like I said, Diamond, I'm out. I'm gonna ask you and your young friends to leave my office one last time."

"Or what, Michael?"

"Or I will have no other choice but to call the police."

"Oh, so you gonna call the police? What are you going to tell them when they get here, Michael? Did you forget that I work for you?"

"Listen, Diamond, I'm a grown man. I'm not one of your boy toys that you can order around. This has gotten way out of hand, and your greed is making you careless. I'm a professional physician. I'm not going to risk losing my license for you." Dr Ricci was calm as he spoke.

"Careless? I am not careless. What are you afraid of, Michael? Huh?"

"Like I said, I don't want to participate anymore."

"Well, let me tell you something, sweetheart," Diamond said, placing her hand on her hip. "It's too late. You are already in too deep."

Dr. Ricci sat there and thought for a moment. "Well, I'll have no other choice than to report you."

"Report me?" Diamond yelled. "Don't forget I got a lot of dirt on you too, my dear."

"I knew this muthafucka was gonna be a problem. Let me do him?" Trey asked.

"Hold up, Trey! He ain't gonna say nothing. Right, Michael?" she asked him.

Dr. Ricci simply stared into Diamond's eyes.

"He gonna snitch. I see it in his eyes," Trey said. "Word, I don't trust nobody white."

"Yo, ma, let's just go," Dante said, speaking for the first time.

"You're right, Trey. We can't have that," Diamond said, ignoring Dante's request.

Diamond's voice changed in tone, and at that moment Dr. Ricci began to fear for his life. He looked at the three people hovering over him, and especially took note of the demonic look in Trey's eyes.

Estelle also began to fear for the doctor's safety. The first thing that came to her mind was to call the police. As she turned on her heels and began to walk to the phone, her handbag hit the cabinet that sat on the wall right outside the doctor's office. She froze where she stood and looked up at the ceiling. *Oh, Lord!* she silently prayed. *Please, Lord, don't let them have heard that.*

When she didn't hear any movement from the office, she began to walk again, this time securing her handbag over her shoulder. Suddenly the door to the doctor's office swung open, and Estelle stopped walking, too afraid to even turn around.

"Who is it?" Diamond yelled to Trey.

"It's some old bitch!" he yelled back over his shoulder.

"Well, bring her in here," Diamond said with a smirk on her face, already knowing who the "old bitch" was.

Trey snatched Estelle by the arm, yanking her fragile bones into the office. "Get your old ass in here!"

"Well, well, well, lookie here, fellas. Hello, Estelle. What were you doing out there?" Diamond asked.

Estelle didn't say a word. She just looked into Dr. Ricci's eyes with sympathy.

"Estelle, why did you come?" Dr. Ricci wished she wasn't there.

"I-I-I left my keys and I-I came back to get them," she said in a nervous voice.

"Well, you shoulda got your keys and left. But, no, you had to be nosy. Well, now I'm gonna give you something to be nosy about. You're just in time." Diamond smiled a wicked smile.

Dr. Ricci stood. "Let her go, Diamond," he demanded.

"Shut the fuck up!"

Trey lunged forward and punched the doctor square in the nose.

Dr. Ricci fell back into his chair, blood running from his busted up nose. He began to see small specks of light in front of his eyes and moaned and blinked repeatedly, trying to focus.

"You leave him alone!" Estelle yelled.

Dante stopped Estelle from lunging at Trey, stepping in front of her with pleading eyes. He'd always thought Estelle was a nice woman and was trying to save her life. She had no idea what type of person Trey was.

Diamond removed a butcher knife from the big Louis Vuitton bag she carried. "Here." She handed it to Dante.

Dr. Ricci held his nose as blood seeped through his fingers.

"Take care of him, because I don't trust him now," she told Dante.

"Why you got him using a knife? I got my nine," Trey said, revealing the butt end of the gun in his waistband.

"Because that nine of yours is gonna make too much noise," she told him.

Dante took the knife reluctantly and looked at it.

Dr. Ricci tried to stand, but he became light-headed and fell back into the chair.

Dante didn't want to kill the doctor, but then he heard his mother's voice in his head. *"I gave up my life for you! I raised you by myself! You owe me!"*

"You fucked up a good thing, Michael," Diamond said. "What are you doing?" She realized Dante hadn't moved from the spot he stood in. "I told you to kill him!"

Dante stood there staring at the knife. He couldn't move. It wasn't in his heart to be that way.

Diamond turned and stood directly in front of Dante. "You better do what the fuck I tell you to do, or I'll kill you myself," she growled.

Tired of standing by, with a gloved hand Trey snatched the knife out of Dante's hand and then quickly plunged it into the doctor's neck.

It seemed as if time stood still.

Trey pulled the blood-soaked knife out of the doctor's neck, and blood immediately began to pour from the open wound. Dr. Ricci jerked around in his chair, holding his neck where he had been stabbed.

"Again!" Diamond barked.

Trey went into action like an attack dog reacting to a command from his master. He mechanically raised the knife high above his head and plunged it down into the flesh of the doctor. This time the razor-sharp knife dug deep into the doctor's esophagus.

Gurgling sounds echoed in the office as the doctor began to choke on his own blood.

"You're making a fucking mess!" Diamond snatched the knife from Trey's hands and commenced to stabbing the doctor ten times in his stomach. She didn't do much better in creating less of a mess, but the doctor was surely dead.

Breathing heavily, she wiped her forehead with the back of her hand and then remembered Estelle was standing there. She whipped her head around and stared at her.

Estelle jumped. Too afraid to turn and run, she simply stood there, her mouth gaping open in shock. Through the whole ordeal Estelle was numb with fear and hadn't screamed or made a sound.

Diamond walked over to her. She snatched the woman's arm and yanked her over to the doctor's body, and Estelle nearly fell to the floor. "You are one nosy bitch! I have said it before, and I knew you would be a problem! You wanted to see so bad, so look!" She grabbed Estelle by the back of her head and forced her to look at the dead doctor.

Blood soaked through his physician's coat, turning the white fabric a deep shade of crimson. Estelle could feel vomit traveling its way up her throat and into her mouth. Forcing it back down, she swallowed hard. Tears continued to fall from her eyes, and she could hear her heart racing in her chest.

Diamond took her gloved hand and forced the knife into Estelle's hand, then rammed it into the doctor's stomach another time.

This time Estelle screamed.

"Now you're involved in this murder, so you better think twice before you go running off to call the police," Diamond said to her. Then she said to her boys, "Get the money out of the safe and make sure he's dead."

Trey busied himself with Diamond's instructions and was cussing Dante out for not having Diamond's back. Dante, slow to help him get the office in order, stood there watching him.

Diamond and Estelle stood at the back door of the doctor's office while the boys wiped away any evidence of them being there. Once everything was done, they all left out of the back door that led into the parking lot behind the mini mall.

Diamond grabbed Estelle by her shirt and pulled her close. "Remember what I said," she told her. "Just remember you participated in this thing too. If you so much as open your mouth, I got witnesses that saw you take a stab at the good doctor."

Estelle wanted to lie down and die.

Part Two

✦·✦ NINETEEN ✦·✦

Caught
2002

"Freeze!" the police officers yelled, their service revolvers aimed at the suspect.

The suspect held his hands high in the air. He and two of his friends were standing on the corner when three police vehicles screeched to a stop, and the officers jumped out of their vehicles with their guns raised. The suspect looked at his friends and then back at the officers, whose facial expressions were controlled and confident.

"Slowly put your hands behind your head and interlock your fingers!" one officer yelled.

The three men did as they were told.

Hiding behind a house in the bushes across the street was Dante Reed, an associate of the men now being searched, and the perpetrator the officers thought they were arresting. Dante had switched clothes with one of the men when he got word that the police had arrested his mother. Apparently she went out fighting the police like they were from the streets. His boys had told him that his mother had knocked one of the female officers' unconscious with a right hook.

Dante knew he was next to be arrested, so he wasted no time switching clothes with one of his associates. Dante stood six feet three inches with a slim build. The jeans he wore didn't reach his ankles, and the sleeves on the jacket barely stretched past his elbows, since he was taller than the person he'd switched with, who happened to be the taller than the other two.

After Dante's friends were searched and placed into the squad car, the officers began to talk amongst themselves.

"I don't know, Ed," the young black officer said to his partner. "I don't think this is the guy."

Ed, the white officer, responded, "He fits the description, Jerry. He's wearing the clothes the dispatcher said he was last seen wearing."

"But his physical description doesn't quite match. OK, I agree he's wearing the right clothes, but did you look at them closely? Those clothes he's wearing swallow the boy whole. Besides, I've seen Dante Reed one time before, and I don't remember him being short."

"This is the guy," Ed said, pointing a finger at Jerry, "and you know it. And if he isn't the right guy, then the call should have been more specific. If you ask me, they all look alike anyway."

Jerry took a deep breath. He'd heard comments like that quite often from Ed. The racial slurs flew from his mouth with no regard for Jerry or other black officers.

"We're talking about murder," Jerry said. "If we're wrong on this one, then you know the captain is gonna have our heads for it. We've made three false arrests in the last month. Talk around the station is starting to build against us in a negative way."

"To hell with what those assholes think! Not one of these officers out here seems to think we got the wrong murder suspect, and they have the same description we do."

Ed walked away and got into the driver's seat of the squad car. Jerry reluctantly followed, and the squad cars all pulled off in different directions, lights flashing.

After the police cars disappeared into the night, Dante relaxed his tense body and sat on the grass. He breathed a sigh of relief, but he knew this was only temporary relief. It was only a matter of time before the cops realized they had the wrong person. What he needed to do was change his clothes and get the money he'd stashed in the hollow statue that stood on top of the water fountain in the backyard of his house. Then he planned to go back to the old neighborhood where he and his mother used to live to see if anybody knew anything about what was going on. His friends from the old neighborhood always seemed to know what was going on in the streets.

He carefully looked around to make sure the coast was clear and then walked out of the front yard of the house where he'd been hiding. As he walked home, he constantly looked around, making sure no one was tailing him. It was well after midnight, and he was paranoid and uneasy. A dog ran up to a fence, barking loudly and startling him. Sweat surfaced on his forehead and ran down the sides of his face. Realizing that being outside was like a circus elephant walking down the middle of the street, he decided to hail a cab.

Ten minutes later, Dante had the cab driver drop him off a few blocks away from the new home his mother had recently purchased. Making his way carefully up the street toward his house, he surveyed it before walking to the back of his neighbor's home so he could check out his backyard.

From the neighbor's backyard, he carefully studied the house he and his mother lived in—a quaint four-bedroom colonial they'd purchased together, with a large backyard that had an in-ground pool and a water fountain. The statue in the middle of the fountain was an African queen that stood tall and erect, wearing native African garb. Dante had made sure the commissioned custom statue was hollow, so he could stash the money he and his mother made from their illegal enterprises there in a secret compartment located under the water.

Before approaching the fountain, Dante sat still, patiently waiting to see if police were watching the house. He was sure they would set up some kind of a stakeout to capture him if he returned.

After about fifteen minutes of observing the inside and outside of his house, Dante scaled his neighbor's tall picket fence with ease. He had done this a million times. Once he jumped to the ground, he crouched low and didn't move a muscle. Finally, after nothing seemed out of the ordinary, he proceeded.

He was thankful his mother had turned off the fountain for the night. He slithered over to the fountain, pulled the lever to the secret latch, and the hidden bottom door to the statue popped open. He reached inside and pulled out the duffel bag. He unzipped the bag and saw it was just as he'd left it—seven bundles of bills, each bundle holding five thousand dollars. He removed the .45 that sat at the bottom of the bag. He chambered a bullet and placed the gun in a side pocket of the duffel bag.

He closed the bag and draped it across his shoulders. After taking one last look around the yard, he made his way toward the back door of his house to change his clothes. He thought about just squashing the idea of changing clothes, but just as quickly as the idea came, it disappeared from his mind.

Taking deep breaths, Dante prepared to go inside the dark house. He carefully opened the back screen door and stayed close to the ground as he slid through the back door and onto the porch. He crawled over to the door that led to the inside of the house. He reached up and turned the handle. The door was open, so he quietly made his way into the dark kitchen.

He thought he heard something and immediately pressed his body against a wall in the kitchen. He stood still, trying not to breathe, and listened intently. *I should have just grabbed the loot and bounced!*

After hearing nothing else for several seconds, he decided that leaving was a better option than trying to change his clothes.

Just as he started to turn around, he heard a creaking sound coming from the adjacent room. He removed the .45 from the duffel bag and waited for his eyes to adjust to the darkness. Looking through a mirror that hung on the wall in the kitchen, he saw a shadow creeping along the wall, and his heart sped up to twice its normal speed. Sweat ran down his neck and down the middle of his back. He placed both hands around the gun, gripping it tightly, and watched the shadow approach. Dante had no idea who the intruder was, but at this point he didn't care. It was do or die.

As the intruder tried to make his way into the kitchen, he knocked the leg of the dinette set chair, sending out a scratching noise.

That was Dante's cue. He stepped out into the open and squeezed the trigger repeatedly, flares of light sparking from the barrel of the gun as each bullet exited. When return fire whizzed into the kitchen, Dante dashed out of the back door and escaped the same way he'd come, leaving gunfire echoing behind him as he traveled through each yard.

Finally he slowed his pace when he realized no one was chasing him. Then he stopped and took in deep breaths, trying to control his breathing. He switched the duffel bag to his other shoulder, readjusted the straps, and began to walk down the street.

About twenty minutes later he arrived at Trey's apartment, a new townhouse he'd purchased in the Society Hill section of Newark, New Jersey. He could smell the weed coming from inside, so he reasoned Trey was still awake. He knocked on the door and waited. Then he heard rustling behind the door, and then footsteps.

"Yo, it's me, Trey," Dante said in a loud whisper, so his friend could hear him, but not loud enough to wake the neighbors.

Trey unlocked the door and peeled it back slowly, and Dante dashed inside.

"Yo, what's up with you?" Trey asked, barely awake.

"My bad for waking you up, man, but the cops are after me. Man, they got my moms, and they was at the crib waiting for me when I got there. I had to shoot my way outta that muthafucka," Dante said, exhausted.

Trey stood there looking confused. "They got your moms?"

"Yeah, they got her, and now they after me. Listen, man, I need to stash this loot here until I can figure out what to do."

"Until you can figure out what to do? How you sound, nigga? Them muthafuckas locked yo' mother up. You need to be trying to get her up outta there."

"They after me too!"

Trey didn't comment. He sat down and placed his hand over his face. "Do you think they coming for me too?"

"If they was coming for you, you'd be got already. Yo, let me get a change of clothes or something. I'm gonna go see if I can find out anything."

"Why don't you just chill? I'll go out and see what the streets are talking about."

"Naw, man, I ain't gonna be able to sit up in here," Dante told him. "I need to be out there." He went into Trey's bedroom to find a change of clothes.

Trey walked into his room and found Dante inside the walk-in closet. He walked over to the door and watched Dante look for a pair of pants that would fit him. Although Trey and Dante were the about the same height, Trey was much stockier than Dante, so Dante had to be careful about which pants he chose.

"Yo, man, for real, let me hit the turf to see what I can find out 'bout my babe."

Dante, stress written on his face, turned and looked at Trey. "Do me a favor, man. Don't call my mother that to my face. That's your name for her. I don't want to hear it." He turned and continued to look for something to wear.

Dante put some jeans against himself to measure the fit, but they were too wide. Frustrated, he threw the jeans against the floor and punched the wall behind him.

"Yo, Tae, man, I got you. Chill out here. There's a belt in the drawer."

Dante sat on the floor and laid his head against the wall he'd just punched. Pain shot through his knuckles, but he didn't care.

"I'm out, Tae. Yo!"

Dante looked up at Trey with red eyes.

"Stay here," Trey said in a firm tone.

An hour later, there still was no word from Trey. Dante got up off the sofa he'd been sitting on for the past hour, picked up Trey's house phone, and called his cell, but Trey didn't answer. He went back into Trey's closet and found a pair of sweat pants that basically fit. The length wasn't the way he normally wore his pants, but he no longer cared. He needed to get out.

Dante found himself back in his old neighborhood. While walking up the street, he pulled his fitted cap way down over his eyes to try to disguise his identity. As he walked up the street toward his old apartment building, where he knew he could talk to some of the dudes that hung out there, a cruiser bent the corner and drove up the street. A lump formed in his throat making it hard for him to swallow and his heart began to race. He could feel his body temperature heat up. When the cop car passed Dante and continued up the street, he relaxed his shoulders from being tense and he exhaled through his nose, after holding his breath. Relief almost instantly began to invade his body.

"Yo, who that?" one of the dudes at the apartment building asked as he tried to see who was coming up the street.

"I dunno," his friend said, looking intently and then placing his hand on the butt of his weapon.

"Oh, I know who that is," the first dude said after Dante got closer. "Yo, what up, Tae? What you doing over this way?" He held out his hand to shake Dante's.

Dante slapped hands with both men. "Yo, anybody out here talking?" he asked, looking around.

"Naw, man," the first guy said. "Trey just left here not too long ago asking the same shit. What's up? Y'all in some shit?"

Before Dante could even answer his question, a siren from a squad car sounded off again. One of the police officers said as he exited the car, "All right, fellas, you know the routine."

Dante could have shitted bricks at that very moment. He was tempted to make a run for it, but he knew that would be suicide.

The officers began to search them. When one officer found a gun on one of the males, he immediately handcuffed him and sat him on the curb. While that officer stood watch over the handcuffed male, the other officer searched them one by one. He took off the next man's hat and felt around the inside to make sure there were no drugs stashed there.

When he felt around the man's crotch, he felt a bulge. With his gun drawn, not sure what was hidden, the cop made the guy remove what was in his pants. "Nice and easy, son," the cop said, keeping a steady hand on his gun. "All right, now toss it over there."

The bag was tossed near the other cop, who unwrapped it and found a glassine bag full of crack vials. The man was then handcuffed and placed on the curb.

"Looks like it's gonna be a good night," the cop said. "Now let's see what's behind door number three."

Now it was Dante's turn to be searched. He was sweating bullets, and his stomach did flip-flops. He tried to control his breathing and remain cool, but his heart was racing in his chest so hard, it hurt.

He was frisked, and then his hat was removed and searched as well.

While his hat was off, he held his head low, not wanting to make eye contact with the cop.

The cop noticed how much Dante was sweating. "What's wrong with you, man? What, you high or something? Why you sweating so much? What are you nervous about?" He grabbed Dante by the arm, trying to turn him around to face him so he could look in his face, but Dante kept his head low and wouldn't look the man in the eyes.

Just then the police radios went off with an all-points bulletin—*"All units, the murder suspect is still at large. The earlier capture was a false arrest. I repeat, the suspect is still at large and believed to be armed and dangerous. Police are now at the suspect's home, where shots were fired earlier. Shooter unknown but suspected to be the suspect, Dante Reed."*

Dante's friends stared at him when they heard his name announced over the police radio. Of course, they didn't say a word. Now they were wondering how things were gonna play out.

Dante held his breath, trying not to shake from nervousness.

"What's your name, man?" the cop asked.

"Brian James," Dante responded, saying the first thing that came to his mind.

The police officers decided to take all three men down to the station and book them on the gun charge, and drug possession with intent to distribute.

Down at the police station Dante sat tapping his foot on the floor nervously, while sweat seemed to pour from his forehead. He was terrified that they would find out who he was. He was handcuffed to the table and was waiting for someone to come into the room.

In the other two rooms the police were interrogating the boys about the drugs. They offered to exchange a lesser sentence for the gun and drugs charges with any information they could get from them. This was a tactic that most police officers used when they wanted to come up on a big score of some sort.

After about two hours of manhandling and interrogating the two boys, they finally broke down and snitched. They informed the cops that the third guy they'd picked up was Dante Reed.

✦ ✦✦ **TWENTY** ✦✦ ✦

The State versus Reed and Reed
2003

"The said defendants Diamond and Dante Reed are being charged with two counts of murder, conspiracy to commit murder, welfare fraud, insurance fraud, extortion, bribery . . ." The court clerk announced the long list of charges filed against mother and son.

The Newark, New Jersey courtroom was filled to capacity. This was the first day of the big trial. The media was stirred to a frenzy when news of the Reeds' arrests went public.

After the clerk was finished, Judge Lewis D. Fritz asked, "Are counselors ready for opening statements?"

The attorneys for the state and the defense lawyers both nodded in agreement, shuffling papers.

"Proceed," Judge Fritz said to the prosecutor's table.

At the prosecutor's table sat three attorneys for the state—two men and one woman—all handling different aspects of the case. The courtroom was so quiet, the atmosphere was eerie.

The female lead prosecutor stood, preparing to give her opening statement. Her stiletto pumps echoed as they hit the hardwood floor. Attorney Christine Swartz walked over to the jury box, her hands clasped behind her back. She was deep in thought, as she organized her opening remarks.

Prosecutor Swartz's sandy-colored hair with streaked blond highlights lay perfectly about her shoulders, not a strand out of place. She'd carefully placed the loose hairs behind her ear, revealing her smooth, olive-colored cheek. She'd inherited her ocean-blue eyes and pointy nose from her white father.

Once in front of the jury box, she placed her hands on the railing. A warm smile spread across her small, pouty, rose-colored lips. She had a small black mole on the right corner of her mouth just above her full lips, just like her Spanish mother.

Watching her intently were twelve jurors that she, her team and the defense had selected: five Caucasian women and seven men, five black and two white, all ranging from thirty years old to fifty. They stared at Prosecutor Swartz, not moving a muscle as they waited patiently to hear her opening statement.

"Good morning," she began. "Your Honor, ladies and gentlemen of the jury, I am prepared today to prove to you that Diamond and Dante Reed are guilty of the charges that were read to you only moments ago. It is my duty, not only as an attorney for the state, but as a tax-paying citizen of the United States, to make sure the two defendants are convicted of the heinous acts they committed against innocent people. Ladies and gentlemen of the jury, these two have committed crimes against you as well. Yes, you too are tax-paying citizens. We all work hard to earn a living, and criminals like these two have robbed us of our hard-earned money." She pointed toward the defense table. "Our tax dollars are providing funds for citizens on welfare, Medicaid, and Medicare. But"— She walked away from the jury box and stood in front of the defense table—"Diamond and Dante Reed have illegally taken money from you, creating false insurance claims, several welfare claims under aliases, and even resorted to murder to hide their fraud. They have used the system and they have used you.

"On top of all that, they have committed first degree, pre-meditated, coldblooded murder! But, ladies and gentlemen, it stops here today. I will present you with facts and hard evidence during this trial, and I promise you that you will hear evidence of a brutal execution-style murder and countless thoughtless acts committed by the defendants with no regard for the law. The evidence will show you that Diamond and Dante Reed are guilty of everything they are being charged with today. I only ask one thing of you." Prosecutor Swartz stood still and made eye contact with the jurors. "Help me put an end to these types of crimes by setting an example to others who may think they can end a human life and get away with our hard-earned money. Don't sit back and allow these two defendants to insult you by letting them off. Let's show the other criminals of this country that we will not stand for their behavior, and let's start with Diamond and Dante Reed!"

While the prosecutor gave her opening argument, the attorneys for the defendants sat quietly listening. They had instructed their clients to do the same. The defense attorneys were Kyle and Kendall Boris, two handsome black brothers who had been practicing as defense attorneys for more than ten years, although they were only in their early thirties. Their expensive, tailor-made suits hung perfectly on their muscular six-feet-plus bodies. They sported thin mustaches and low, faded haircuts. Their almond-colored eyes and long eyelashes sat underneath bushy eyebrows. These men were more than just handsome, and in their presence every woman did a double take.

The Reeds both sat at the table with the Boris brothers. Diamond was fifty-three years old, but even after spending two months in a women's prison, she still didn't look a day over thirty. Diamond was that chick. At five feet seven with pecan-colored skin and a thick hourglass shape, she resembled the legendary Josephine Baker.

Her son and co-defendant Dante Reed sat next to her. He had the same pecan-colored skin as his mother. At twenty-one, he was a handsome young man, taking after his mother in looks.

Diamond sat in the courtroom exuding confidence while watching Prosecutor Swartz give her opening argument. She refused to listen to the allegations the prosecutor spewed, trying to incriminate her and her son.

Unlike his mother, Dante wasn't feeling confident at all. He kept thinking he would have never been in this position had it not been for his mother. He never wanted the type of lifestyle his mother bestowed upon him because of her greed. After spending two months in jail, he couldn't imagine spending twenty-five to life in prison, which was what he was facing if convicted. He hoped his attorneys, who were raping them of their huge stash of cash with their high fees, could do their job well and get him and his mother off.

"Counselors," Judge Fritz said to the defense attorneys, prompting them to begin their opening argument.

Kendall, the elder of the two brothers, stood and buttoned his suit jacket. He stepped around the table and stood directly in front of the jury. "Your Honor, ladies and gentlemen of the jury, I am Attorney Kendall Boris," he began. "Today my brother and I are representing the defendants. You have heard the opening statement from the prosecutor, and I'd like to add that it was a great performance. However, my team and I are prepared to show you that everything the prosecutor stated is false.

"My clients are anything but thieves. They have not robbed you or the system of anything. My clients were obviously set up. I will prove to you during the course of this case that murder was not premeditated. Self-defense plays a key part here. All the allegations my clients are accused of are false. Diamond Reed is a loving, caring mother who raised her son alone. Neither of my clients has a criminal record. So, you tell me, how can these two defendants with squeaky-clean records be accused of the alleged crimes that have been announced today? I will show you that they are a product of misconceptions. My team has hard evidence showing that Diamond and Dante Reed are not only innocent, but were blackmailed, blackmailed by people that you and I trust every day—doctors and city and government officials. What choice did they have?" Kendall paced in front of the jury box, making sure he made eye contact with each juror, especially the women. "So, I say this to say to you. You were not robbed by my clients. How can you make an example out of two people who have been used and taken advantage of? We intend to prove that the prosecution's evidence is purely circumstantial, and that Diamond and Dante Reed are not guilty."

With that, Kendall walked back over to the defense table, unbuttoned his suit jacket, and took his seat. The trial of the year had begun.

✦ ✦ ✦ TWENTY-ONE ✦ ✦ ✦

The State versus Reed and Reed

"Counselor, are you prepared to call your first witness for the state?" Judge Fritz looked over the top of his gold wire-framed glasses at Prosecutor Swartz.

"Yes, Your Honor. The state would like to call Ms. Estelle Brown to the stand."

Reporters lined the first two rows on both sides of the courtroom. No camera flashes were allowed, but the reporters wrote furiously on their notepads. Most people in the courtroom were outsiders who just wanted to be a part of the big case after hearing about it in the news.

Within the fifth row Estelle stood. Her skin bore a few wrinkles, but other than that, it was dark and smooth, and her hair was completely white, her prescription glasses clinging to the edge of her nose. She eased her way past the others who sat in the same row.

The men stood, giving her more room to pass by.

Once in the aisle, Estelle pushed her glasses up onto her nose. A gold, black, and white flowered dress draped her slightly overweight figure as she carefully walked down the aisle sporting low-heeled, black-and-gold patent leather shoes.

The bailiff held her hand and helped her climb the three steps up to the witness stand. Once seated, she was sworn in. She sat there and began to wring her hands, her face clearly showing her discomfort.

Prosecutor Swartz finally stood after reviewing some papers in front of her. She walked over to the witness stand, her hands clasped behind her back. "Hello, Ms. Brown." She gave Estelle a warm smile, trying to make her feel comfortable.

Estelle gave a half-smile and simply nodded in acknowledgment.

"Ms. Brown, you worked for Dr. Michael Ricci. Correct?"

"Yes."

"How long did you work for the doctor?"

"For five years."

Estelle wondered why Prosecutor Swartz was asking her questions she already knew the answers to. In their brief encounter, she'd openly told Ms. Swartz that she would cooperate because she didn't want to be involved in the allegations against Diamond and Dante. She felt she did the right thing by calling the police and just wanted to go on her merry way.

"So you knew the doctor pretty well, huh?"

"Yes, ma'am." Estelle lowered her head, thinking about the awful state in which she'd last seen him.

Prosecutor Swartz noticed Estelle wringing her hands. "Relax, Ms. Brown. It's OK," she whispered to her.

Estelle took a deep breath in an attempt to calm herself. She pushed her glasses up on her nose again.

"So you pretty much handled everything in the office, huh?"

"Objection!" Kyle interrupted. "She's leading the witness, Your Honor."

"Overruled."

Prosecutor Swartz rephrased the question, to appease defense counsel. "What were your duties in the office, Ms. Brown?"

"I handled all the paperwork for the doctor, all the important phone calls, and the books."

"Dr. Ricci must have really trusted you to handle his bookkeeping?"

"Yes, ma'am."

"Would you say Dr. Ricci was a good doctor?"

"Yes."

"What type of medicine did the doctor practice, Ms. Brown?"

"He was a chiropractor."

"How did the doctor's patients feel about him?" Prosecutor Swartz walked back over to the table and faced Estelle.

"Everybody loved him."

"Did he have many patients?"

"Yes, ma'am."

"How many would you say?"

"I . . ." Estelle hesitated as she tried to gather a number in her head. "I don't rightfully know."

"You kept the doctor's books and handled all of his important paperwork, and you don't know how many patients he had? OK, just give me a figure off the top of your head. It doesn't have to be exact."

"OK. Um . . . maybe about sixty."

Prosecutor Swartz picked up a piece of paper and looked at it. She then looked at Estelle. "Dr. Ricci had ninety-three patients, according to the files confiscated from his office."

There was a buzz in the courtroom, and reporters continued to jot down notes on their pads.

Estelle was nervous. She'd known the number of patients the doctor had. She just couldn't think right. She looked around at the sea of faces in the courtroom and became giddy. She looked into Diamond's face for the first time and suddenly felt like she no longer wanted to testify. She remembered Diamond's threat.

"With that number of patients, I would say the doctor was well liked. Would you say that the doctor deserved to lose his life?"

"Objection, Your—!"

"Sustained!" Judge Fritz said before Kyle could give his reason for the objection.

Judge Fritz knew Prosecutor Swartz well. He was on a couple of court cases with her before and knew how she operated.

"How did you feel when Diamond Reed came to work for Dr. Ricci?" Prosecutor Swartz asked.

"I felt fine."

"Did you like her?"

"I didn't have any reason not to like her."

"When did you first realize that illegal activities were taking place in the doctor's office?"

"I didn't."

"So are you stating that you never told anyone that you had a feeling something wrong was going on and that you didn't trust Diamond Reed?"

"No, ma'am." Estelle shook her head.

"Ms. Brown, are you telling me that you didn't give a statement to the police stating such?"

"I never said that."

Prosecutor Swartz walked over to the table and shuffled through a few papers. After finding the papers she needed, she approached the bench.

"Your Honor, I hold in my hand a police transcript from Ms. Brown signed by her. I would like to submit this into evidence as Exhibit A. I'd also like to ask Ms. Brown to read from page three, section B of the statement."

She handed the papers over to the defense attorneys, who both looked at the papers and then handed them back to her. Prosecutor Swartz then handed the papers over to the judge, who looked them over, nodded, and handed them back to her.

"Ms. Brown, I'm asking you to please read from the statement that you gave to the police department when you were brought in for questioning. Please, if you will, read section B of this page." She handed the papers to Ms. Brown.

Estelle took the papers, pushed her glasses up on her nose, and began to read. While she read, Prosecutor Swartz paced in front of the jury.

"Question by Officer Blake: Ms. Brown, were you aware that Dr. Ricci and Ms. Reed were committing insurance fraud?

"Answer by Ms. Estelle Brown: I knew something was going on with those two, but I couldn't quite put my finger on it. But I believed it to be illegal. I never trusted her."

"That's enough, Ms. Brown." Prosecutor Swartz took the papers from Ms. Brown and continued to pace, letting Ms. Brown's words sink in.

Estelle lowered her head. She'd forgotten about the statement she'd given to the police. She was so nervous that night, she could've said anything.

"So after reading the statement, do you remember saying this?" Prosecutor Swartz asked.

"No, I don't remember saying that," she responded sincerely. "Someone must have added that in."

What puzzled Estelle when Diamond came to work at the office was, Diamond had no prior medical office experience. She often wondered how the woman was able to obtain a job with such a limited resume. After working beside her and finding small amounts of evidence, she figured out that Diamond and Dr. Ricci were up to something illegal, and it made her uncomfortable. Now she was on a witness stand trying to pretend that she never had an inkling illegal activity was going on.

"Ms. Brown, you just read a statement given by you and signed by you," Prosecutor Swartz said, snapping Estelle out of her thoughts.

"I understand that, but I don't remember saying that." Estelle began to wring her hands again. She wanted to tell the truth badly, but she was afraid for her life.

Low whispers and murmurs could be heard throughout the courtroom.

Prosecutor Swartz stopped pacing and faced Estelle. "Maybe this will help your memory." She walked over to a covered easel and began to drag it over, but one of the bailiffs came over to assist her and placed it where she indicated.

"Thank you," Prosecutor Swartz said to the bailiff. "I want the court, jurors, and Ms. Brown to see what these defendants did to Dr. Ricci." She pulled the cloth off the easel to reveal a blown-up picture of the dead Dr. Ricci, courtesy of the coroner's office, for all to see.

The spectators in the courtroom gasped at the picture of Dr. Ricci lying on the metal table in the coroner's office. His chest was bare, and every stab wound inflicted on him was visible. The skin was spread apart around each stab wound. Blood seeped from the wounds, and the flesh looked swollen around the wound sites. Some of the jurors covered their faces; others simply turned green with sickness.

Estelle turned her head and began to cry.

"Do you remember now?" Prosecutor Swartz asked her.

Estelle could only remember that day at the office.

"Ms. Brown," Prosecutor Swartz called out to her.

"Yes?"

"Ms. Brown, were you at the doctor's office when Dr. Ricci was killed?"

"I told the police that I left my house keys at the office, and when I came back to get them, that's when I found him dead. I called the police, and that was it."

"Was there a murder weapon on the scene?"

"I don't know. I ran out of the office when I saw him dead." She lowered her head, remembering the sight of Dr. Ricci bleeding.

"Did you give that statement in the police report?"

"No." Estelle looked at the attorney with unfocused eyes. It was clear she was giving conflicting answers.

"Sounds like you said exactly that, Ms. Brown. You do know that you were sworn in to tell the truth and nothing but the truth? Do you know the penalty for perjury in this state?"

Judge Fritz looked over at Estelle and could tell she was clearly upset. She began to breathe heavily from the pressure Prosecutor Swartz was applying. "Counselor . . ."

"OK, let me redirect the question. So do you admit that you didn't trust the defendant, Diamond Reed?" Prosecutor Swartz asked as she stood directly in front of Estelle.

"Yes," Estelle answered nervously. She was now unable to see the defense table because Prosecutor Swartz had positioned herself directly in front of them.

Prosecutor Swartz placed her perfectly manicured hands onto the ledge of the witness stand where Estelle sat. "Did you know that the defendants killed Dr. Ricci?" She tried to give Estelle confidence with her eyes.

"No!" Estelle yelled.

"Objection! What kind of questioning is this?" Kyle asked the judge.

"Sustained!" Judge Fritz looked at Prosecutor Swartz over the top of his glasses. "One more question," Prosecutor Swartz said, looking straight into the eyes of Estelle Brown. "Was your life threatened for testifying today?" She had a feeling that was the reason for Estelle's conflicting answers.

"No," Estelle said, shaking her head from side to side.

"Were you involved in the murder of Dr. Ricci?"

"Oh, for heaven's sake, no!" Estelle placed her hand over her chest. Her brows furrowed, and her mouth gaped slightly open, as she stared back into the eyes of Prosecutor Swartz, hoping and praying she would stop questioning her. Estelle couldn't understand what Prosecutor

Swartz was doing. She felt like she was the one on trial for murder.

Diamond leaned forward in her chair, so she could see Estelle. She sat there and stared at her with threatening eyes. She wanted to remind Estelle of her threat, to make sure she didn't say anything that would further incriminate her and her son.

Diamond was concerned that the older woman would spill her guts in front of the jury. She realized that she should have gotten rid of her a long time ago. She'd tried to tell the good ol' doctor that Estelle would only be in the way, not to mention Diamond already had a gut feeling that Estelle was the one who'd turned dime on them in the first place.

Dante sat slouched in the chair next to his mother, thinking back on how he should have done things differently. He regretted having gone into the house the night he was captured. Now he was facing additional charges on attempted manslaughter and attempted murder of a police officer.

There were two police officers in the house the night he'd returned. They were placed there as lookouts, anticipating Dante's return. But what they didn't expect was gunfire.

Dante knew they were going to try to throw the book at him, if not seek the death penalty. At the age of twenty, his life was definitely over. He thought about how he'd allowed his mother to manipulate him and his friends. She only dated young men Dante's age and sometimes younger, depending on her mood, turning them out with her experienced sex game and then making them take care of her.

As Dante sat there he wondered if his mother hadn't set him up to take the fall. She wasn't facing nearly as much time as he was. His mind was speaking to him in ways he'd never allowed in the past.

"So who are you protecting, Ms. Brown?" Prosecutor Swartz yelled, bringing everyone out of their thoughts and back to the present.

"No one!"

"These people are murderers! You said you would cooperate with the state!"

"Objection!" Kyle hollered.

Swartz ignored him. "Were you present when the defendants killed Dr. Ricci?"

Estelle's eyes widened. "No!"

"Objection!" the defense attorneys yelled in unison.

"Sustained!" the Judge finally interjected.

"What are you trying to hide? Are you afraid of someone? Tell me! You can tell me! Why are you taking up for these coldblooded murderers? Have they threatened you?" Prosecutor Swartz pointed behind her to the defense table.

"Objection, Your Honor!"

The defense attorneys had stood by now, and the judge was banging his gavel against the sounding block, but it fell on deaf ears as Prosecutor Swartz continued to try to scare answers out of Estelle.

The judge banged his gavel with venom seeping from his voice. "Sustained!" You could see the fury in his eyes as he burned a hole through Prosecutor Swartz. "Prosecutor Swartz, you are way out of line. The next stunt you pull like this, I will fine you for contempt of court and have you thrown in jail so fast, you won't know what hit you. Do you understand, counselor?" He pointed a finger at her as his lips quivered.

Prosecutor Swartz was good at what she did, and she was hard-hitting. She would test any judge to see how much she could get away with. She was the type of attorney who would turn on her witnesses if she wasn't getting the responses she needed, and as far as she was concerned, Estelle was no different from anyone else. But Judge Fritz was also a tough cookie, and he wasn't going to have any of that nonsense in his courtroom.

"No more questions, Your Honor," Prosecutor Swartz said in a calm, yet firm tone. She sashayed back to her table and sat down in her chair, crossing her legs at the knee and exposing her smooth, muscular legs.

"What are you doing?" one of her partners whispered to her.

"I'm trying to win a case," she whispered back.

"But you turned on our witness."

Prosecutor Swartz looked at him like he had a lot of nerve to question her. "I'm the lead prosecutor for the state. I will win this case for the state the best way I know how. No witness is trustworthy, and I don't trust Ms. Estelle Brown. She is in on it, and I intend to prove it. Her story was shaky from the beginning." She turned to look back at Estelle.

"Counselors, your witness," the judge said to the brothers.

Kyle stood and walked over to the witness stand. He could clearly see that Estelle was about to have a breakdown. So far she hadn't said anything to incriminate his defendants. He decided to get on her good side and hopefully get some information out of her that would help his case. He smiled a warm smile at her. "Are you OK?"

She nodded.

"Would you like something to drink?"

"No, I'm OK," she whispered, wiping away a tear on her cheek.

"Good. Ms. Brown, the prosecutor for the state had you read a statement that you now say someone allegedly fabricated. Correct?"

"Yes."

"Why do you think someone would do that?"

"I don't know. I know I didn't say those things."

"What about the signature?" Kyle walked over to the evidence table, picked up the statement, and brought it over to Estelle. "Would you say that this is your signature?" He handed her the paper.

She looked at it. "Yes, that's it," she said and then returned the papers.

"Do you think Prosecutor Swartz may have switched the wording around on the statement?"

"Objection!" Prosecutor Swartz yelled.

"Sustained."

"OK, Ms Brown, were you involved in the death of Dr. Ricci?"

"No!" she yelled, clearly getting upset.

"I understand, Ms. Brown. I apologize for my line of questioning, but I am simply trying to make a point that the state is trying to falsely accuse not only you, but also my clients."

Estelle wiped away the tears that had started to stream down her face again. She sniffled and continued to wipe her eyes. As God is her witness, she tried to live her life in a Christian manner. She didn't approve of crime, nor did she like to lie. She was at a loss for words because her conscience was faithful. She didn't know what to do.

She looked up into the eyes of Diamond, who was scowling at her, and suddenly she began to shake uncontrollably, bawling and having difficulty breathing.

Prosecutor Swartz was heated.

Attorney Kyle felt sorry for the older woman. "Your Honor, I'd like to ask for a recess so the witness can get herself together before I continue my questioning."

"We will take a recess." Judge Fritz looked at his watch. "We will meet back here in two hours." He banged his gavel before standing and shuffling out of the courtroom.

TWENTY-TWO

Recess

"It don't look like y'all doing much out there to me," Diamond said to her two attorneys as they all sat in a conference room discussing the case.

"We're just getting started, Ms. Reed. Give us a chance," Kyle said.

Diamond sat there while the brothers looked through folders and shuffled papers. She ran her tongue across her perfect lips, envisioning a threesome with the two brothers. They weren't as young as the men she normally dated, but they were definitely inviting.

"OK, Ms. Reed—"

"Call me Diamond," she said, cutting Kyle off.

"OK, Diamond," he said, tugging at his tie. "I know we've asked you and Dante a million questions thus far. However, is there anything that the two of you have not told us?" He looked from one to the other.

Kendall stopped shuffling papers and looked up at them as well.

Dante looked over at his mother, noticed the lust in her eyes, and simply shook his head. After the brothers were recommended by a friend of the family, Dante jumped at the offer. He was facing a lot more time than his mother because of the shootout in their house with the police. They were trying to pin attempted murder charges against him, and he knew he needed a good attorney.

He wanted Kyle and Kendall to concentrate more on his case, but

Diamond wasn't letting that happen. Not only was she controlling, she was extremely selfish. She wanted what she wanted, and she made sure she got it. So, without question, Dante knew Diamond was going to have their attorneys put most of their energy into getting her the least amount of time in jail.

As Dante sat there staring at his mother, his recent premonitions were starting to become reality. With the lustful stares from his mother, Dante knew she would get one of the men, if not both. She just had that effect on men.

But Dante held an ace. His mother hadn't been totally honest with the brothers, which might play to his advantage later.

"Of course not, baby," Diamond finally answered. "I've told you all you need to know to get me outta this hellhole."

To get her *out?* Dante wondered. *I guess that doesn't include me.*

"What about any other witnesses that would testify on your behalf? Is there anyone at all we could contact to help with the case?" Kyle asked.

"No. I gave you everybody who I know that would help me out."

Both brothers went back to shuffling papers.

Diamond would've loved to have Trey on the stand, but he was dead set against being a part of the case. Involved in too many illegal activities, he didn't care for the authorities to get used to his name or his face.

Dante just wanted to get back to his cell. Although he hated being locked up, he had become cellmates with an elderly man named Preacher, who had been talking to him, enlightening him on his situation. Preacher was trying to help him keep a level head, and Dante had found comfort listening to the old man speak.

Dante had been doing a lot of thinking lately about how this whole situation would play out, and bitter feelings started to invade his mind more and more. But he loved his mother unconditionally. Or did he? She had been the only person who'd been there for him and cared for him all his life, never mind the beatings. Sure, she was controlling, but he knew she loved him.

What about the father Dante never met? Was there such a man? Whenever he asked about him, Diamond would flip her wig.

Dante once asked her, "So, Ma, do you even know who my father is?"

Diamond turned her head slowly, like it was being controlled by a remote. "What the hell did I tell you before? Don't ask me about that piece-of-shit of a man that I don't even consider a father! Don't worry about who or where he is! I'm here, and that's all you need to know!"

◆✦˙ ◆✦˙ ◆✦˙

"Dante!" Diamond yelled now, snapping him out of his memories. "You don't hear Kyle talking to you? What is wrong with you? You better get your mind right, boy." She rolled her eyes at him.

"My bad."

"Do you have anything you want to say, or anyone you know that may be a good witness in assisting us in this case?" Kyle asked again.

Looking down at the table, his handcuffed hands resting in his lap, Dante so desperately wanted to tell all, but he shook his head. He couldn't betray his mother. Diamond was never close to her mother's or father's side of the family. Once Betty left, it seemed as if Betty's family never existed. Chester didn't have a good relationship with his side of the family, and his parents had died before he met Betty. Chester was all that Diamond knew and he was her world.

So it seemed as if history was repeating itself. Now Diamond was all that Dante knew and he knew his mother was his life.

While the attorneys and Diamond continued to talk about the case, Dante looked down at his handcuffs, and the reflecting light caused him to squint because of the brightness. He drifted off, thinking about how he was going to get out of this situation without losing the only family he had.

⁺⁺ ⁺⁺ **TWENTY-THREE** ⁺⁺ ⁺⁺

The Prosecutor's Meeting

Prosecutor Swartz walked into the break room at her office, which was within walking distance of the courthouse in downtown Newark. She welcomed the two-hour recess. It gave her a chance to get some coffee, go over the case, and prepare for the next witness. She was beat and hadn't gotten much sleep the night before. Working on this case and raising two boys was taking its toll on her.

Prosecutor Swartz had placed the empty coffee pot in the sink and turned on the water to fill it for a fresh pot of coffee when she drifted off.

"Christine, are you all right?" Susan, her secretary, asked.

"Oh yeah, I'm fine," she said.

"Fine is hardly what I would say you are," She gave Prosecutor Swartz a light shove to move her out of the way.

"What are you doing?" she asked the secretary, irritated.

"Look." Her secretary pointed to the overflowing coffee pot. Not only was the coffee pot overflowing with water, but the sink had filled up and was now overflowing all over the counter.

"Shit!"

"That case must really have your brain fried."

"Susan, you have no idea. But it's not just from the case." She sat back down at the table.

"Anything I can do to help?" Susan asked while she cleaned up the mess Prosecutor Swartz had made.

"Yeah. Do you want a part-time nanny job?" Prosecutor Swartz laughed.

"Excuse me?"

Prosecutor Swartz waved her hand. "Never mind. Don't pay me any attention."

Peter, a young prosecutor assigned to the case with Prosecutor Swartz, walked into the break room and pulled up a chair. He had a smile on his face.

Prosecutor Swartz looked at the goofy grin on the young man's face and frowned. "What the hell are you smiling about?" she asked as she shook her head and pecked away on her laptop.

"I just got a new star witness," he said, still smiling. Peter's yellow skin was shiny from perspiration, having just come in from the heat, and his brown eyes danced in his head.

Prosecutor Swartz stopped typing and looked at him. "What did you say, Peter?"

Peter was new to the firm and fresh out of college, but he was sharp. He didn't have the experience yet for the DA's office to make him lead counsel, but he worked on a lot of the cases with other established attorneys. With the information he now had, he hoped it would show his superiors that he could be the lead on his own case.

"I got us a new star witness," he said, making his eyebrows go up and down.

"I thought that's what you said. Who do you have?" Prosecutor Swartz leaned forward, eager to hear what Peter had to say.

He went into his briefcase and pulled out a small notepad. He set the notepad on the table and slid it over to Prosecutor Swartz.

She read what was written on the pad, and a smile quickly spread across her face. "Good job, Peter. You're going to be a great prosecutor." She patted him on the shoulder. "Maybe you should have been a detective."

Peter laughed. "No way. That's something I never wanted to do."

"Oh, by the way, what's going on with the witness that turned over on this crew?" Prosecutor Swartz asked about the person who snitched on Diamond, ending her whole operation.

"The police can't find him." Peter shrugged.

The witness who could put the nail in the coffin had come up missing. This person was subpoenaed to come in and testify against the whole crew

"All right. Well, let's get ready to go back to court and show them what we got."

TWENTY-FOUR

The State versus Reed and Reed

"Your Honor, the state calls Tammy Starks."

Diamond looked up from the pad she had been drawing circles on. When she heard Tammy's name called, all kinds of thoughts went through her mind. She never thought the state would question Tammy. She hadn't considered it, because Tammy was her friend, or so she'd thought.

She turned around to see if it was really Tammy they'd called. Sure enough, an officer opened the court doors in the back of the courtroom, and Tammy came rolling in. Diamond rolled her eyes and sighed.

Kyle looked over at Diamond when he heard the sigh and saw a distraught look on her face. He leaned over to her. "Are you OK?"

She simply nodded. She couldn't believe Tammy was there to testify against her. After the night Diamond called her a cripple, their friendship hadn't been the same. She still went down and sat with Tammy, but not as often. Diamond apologized to her for calling her that name, but they were never again as close as they used to be.

Diamond saw Tammy even less once she bought the house and moved out of the complex. The last time she saw Tammy was a year earlier, but she still couldn't understand why Tammy would be there to testify against her, especially since she'd given Tammy money on several occasions.

"By the look on your face, I'm guessing that this witness could be trouble. You didn't tell me about her, Diamond. Who is she?" Kyle asked.

Diamond huffed and rolled her eyes. "She's supposed to be my friend."

"Is she gonna be a problem?"

"I don't know." Diamond rolled her eyes again.

Tammy had finally reached the front of the courtroom and rolled right past the defense table without making any eye contact with Diamond or Dante. Modern-day courtroom accessibility allowed Tammy to be able to sit in the witness stand. With the aid of the bailiff, Tammy was wheeled into the box. She was then sworn in, and Prosecutor Swartz proceeded to question her.

"How are you today, Ms. Starks?" Prosecutor Swartz asked from behind the table.

"I'm fine." Tammy leaned forward and spoke into the microphone, making her voice sound very loud.

"How do you know the defendant, Diamond Reed?"

"She used to live in the same building I live in."

"Would you consider the two of you good friends?"

"I wouldn't say good friends. I would say we were neighbors. We spoke to each other because we lived in the same building."

Diamond's eyes grew large. She couldn't believe Tammy was sitting in the witness stand lying. Diamond really had considered Tammy a friend. In fact, Tammy was the only person who had gotten that close to her as a friend. Diamond wasn't exactly the friend of the month. She couldn't keep friends because of her selfish and arrogant ways, not to mention her horrible disposition and angry temper. So if Diamond did manage to make a friend, they would always stop messing with her because of the way she treated them. Tammy was the only person she felt comfortable opening up to. So hearing Tammy say they weren't friends hurt her to the core. After all, she'd helped Tammy out when she needed it, and Diamond told Tammy all of her secrets. So, of course, Diamond began to get angry and began to handle her hurt the only way she knew how—by trying to hurt the other person. Diamond knew that Tammy was gonna be a problem.

"Cripple bitch," she said under her breath.

Kyle heard. "What's wrong?" He looked alarmed. No witness had gotten under Diamond's skin this way yet.

Diamond whispered to him, "She's gonna be a problem."

Kyle's frowned and then leaned over and whispered the news to his brother. Kendall leaned forward and looked over at Diamond with an ice grill. Diamond just rolled her eyes at the brothers and sat back in her chair while she ice-grilled Tammy.

Tammy had yet to make eye contact with Diamond, and the way Diamond saw it, Tammy was doing her damnedest to avoid her.

"OK, so you're cordial to each other," Prosecutor Swartz said. "Tell the court what you know about the defendant Diamond Reed."

Prosecutor Swartz sat down in her chair, a smirk of confidence on her face. She knew exactly what Tammy knew, and considered her the star witness. She could tell Tammy was ready and willing to testify against Diamond, and wouldn't back down. The other two witnesses were dead ends, but she felt relieved that Tammy hadn't turned on her. This meant Diamond either didn't have a chance to get to her, or she never thought Tammy would testify against her.

"What is she gonna tell them?" Kyle whispered to Diamond.

"Probably something you don't want them to know," Diamond responded, referring to the jury.

Kyle stood before Tammy could begin to speak. "Your Honor!"

Prosecutor Swartz threw daggers his way.

"May I please approach the bench?" he asked.

The judge waved his hand, giving Kyle permission, and Prosecutor Swartz jumped to her feet, trailing Kyle.

Judge Fritz leaned forward to hear what Kyle had to say.

"Your Honor, pardon my interruption," Kyle whispered. "But I have no knowledge of this witness, not to mention, Prosecutor Swartz didn't have this witness on her list of witnesses provided to me."

Judge Fritz narrowed his eyes at Prosecutor Swartz.

Prosecutor Swartz feigned innocence, although she had purposely tried to surprise defense counsel. "I'm sorry, Your Honor. I failed to let the counselor know about this witness because she just contacted me, and there wasn't enough time. But I'm happy to give the defense any information on the witness that he requires."

Kyle looked disgusted, and his eyes showed it. "Your Honor," he said, "I'd like to ask for time to complete my findings on this witness."

Judge Fritz said, "Permission granted. Ms. Swartz, you make sure you cooperate and give the counselor any information he requests."

Both attorneys returned to their respective seats.

"Ladies and gentlemen of the court, at this time court will be adjourned for further investigation," Judge Fritz said. "We will proceed one week from today at eight am!" Judge Fritz banged his gavel against the sounding block.

Diamond and Dante both stood and awaited the two officers who would escort them back to jail. Diamond looked over her shoulder into the crowded room and locked eyes with Trey, who loved her more than her own son did at the moment, and would do anything for her. It was a look only the two of them understood, since they had a bond that made words unnecessary at times.

And, just like that, Trey knew what he had to do.

✦ ✦✦ **TWENTY-FIVE** ✦✦ ✦

2003

Diamond stood in line in jail waiting to use the payphone. She was getting a little frustrated because the girl had been on the phone longer than the time allotted. Each phone call was timed, and each inmate received the same amount of time to use the phone, unless someone else gave up their phone privilege time. Well, that was exactly what happened here. Two of this inmate's friends allowed her to use their time.

Diamond wouldn't have been so pissed if her phone call wasn't urgent. Time wasn't on her side, and she needed to act quickly. She huffed, showing her impatience. There were two women in front of her. She folded her arms across her chest and huffed again, trying to get her message across.

"OK, to hell with this," Diamond said, leaving the line.

As she walked up on the girl, she could hear the girl wasn't talking about anything Diamond felt was important. From what Diamond could tell, she may have been talking to a boyfriend. Diamond tapped her on the shoulder.

The girl turned around. "What?" she asked with much attitude.

Diamond was shocked by the small girl's forwardness. The girl looked to be all of eighteen years old, was very short, and had a petite frame. The jumpsuit swallowed her whole. She had a bandana tied around her head, cornrows hanging out the back.

"Listen, little girl, there are other people who want to use the damn phone, so have some common courtesy and get off the phone so somebody else can use it," Diamond said in a motherly way.

"Bitch, please! You better go wait in line like the rest of them." She pointed to the others in line and turned her back on Diamond.

Diamond looked over at the two women leaning against the wall, watching events unfold before them. The two women simply shrugged.

Diamond tapped the young girl on her shoulder, interrupting her again.

"Hold on a minute!" the young girl said into the phone. She placed the handset on top of the telephone box and whipped around to face Diamond. She yelled, "Bitch, what is your problem? You can't understand English?"

Diamond simply curled her lips into a sarcastic smile and planted a power fist into the bridge of the young girl's nose. Blackness enveloped the young girl as her body dropped in slow motion to the floor, where she lay spread-eagled.

The other two women waiting in line stared, awestruck by what Diamond had done.

"Did you see that shit?" one woman asked.

"Damn! That bitch ain't no joke! That punch must have lifted that chick two feet off the floor," the other woman said.

Diamond stepped over the girl's body and grabbed the phone receiver from off the top of the phone box.

"Hello?"

"Who dis?" the male on the other end of the phone asked.

"This is Diamond."

"Who you? Where is Michelle?"

"Oh, she's out right now. She will have to call you back. Bye-bye."

Diamond disconnected the call and proceeded to make a call of her own.

"Yes, collect from Diamond," she told the operator who came on the line. Diamond kept her eyes on the young girl lying on the floor, still out cold.

It seemed as if no one cared or wanted any part of Diamond after witnessing the sick right hook she'd landed on the girl.

The party accepted the call.

"What's up?" Diamond asked.

"What up, Diamond? I'm on it," Trey said.

"I just wanted to make sure you were."

"Come on, don't insult my intelligence like that."

"That's not my intention. I just wanted you to know we ain't got much time. Be clean about it."

"No doubt. Always." Trey disconnected the call.

Diamond hung up and looked around at the girls who still stood in line. She looked down at the girl that she had put on her back and saw that she was starting to come to. Diamond stepped over the young girl and walked back to her cell, content now that her business was handled.

Tammy was wheeling herself down a hill, but the wheelchair got away from her, and she couldn't control it as it barreled down the hill at a high speed. She knew she was going to die because every time she tried to place her hands on the rubber part of the wheel to steer it or stop it, the rubber would burn the inside of her hands.

Finally she reached the bottom of the hill, and to her surprise, she came rolling to a stop. She breathed a sigh of relief and looked around at her surroundings. She noticed Diamond and Dante were running toward her. They both carried guns and began to fire at her. She grabbed the wheels of the wheelchair and began to push with all her might, trying to escape.

Bullets whizzed past her head, causing her to scream. She headed for the same hill she had just come down because that was the only place to go. She pushed and pushed up the hill, with no progress. She looked behind her, and they were closing in on her. The more she pushed up the hill, the more her wheelchair rolled backward.

"You snitch!" Diamond yelled behind her and fired more bullets.

Tammy woke up screaming. She knew she wouldn't get back to sleep anytime soon, so she decided to get some ice cream and pound cake. She was gonna sit in front of the TV and watch old movies until she fell asleep.

She sat in front of the TV trying to focus on the movie, but her mind kept wandering as she thought about the testimony she was going to give against her old friend that Monday. Tammy fought with herself about testifying, but a visit from the young prosecutor changed her mind. Peter advised her that, if she knew anything about Diamond's illegal actions, she too would serve time in jail as an accomplice, unless she agreed to testify against Diamond.

Tammy was terrified of going to jail. She knew she didn't do anything wrong, so going to jail wasn't an option for her. She prayed on it and decided testifying would be the best thing to do as a Christian.

She nodded off periodically while sitting in front of the television. Then she thought she heard a noise coming from her bedroom. She listened intently for a moment, but heard nothing else. She put her empty bowl on the coffee table and readjusted herself in her chair. She refocused on the movie that played on the television.

A few minutes later, she was in a deep sleep, her chin resting on her chest.

The male figure emerged from her bedroom and crept along the linoleum floor. As Tammy snored lightly, the light from the TV illuminated the living room. He stood directly behind Tammy and watched her sleep. In one swift movement, the gunman put a pillow to her head and pulled the trigger. Down from the pillow mixed with blood and brain fragments splattered everywhere as Tammy sat there slumped in her wheelchair, the back of her head missing.

In a flash, the intruder left Tammy's apartment the same way he'd come in—through the bedroom window.

✦ ✦ **TWENTY-SIX** ✦ ✦

Preacher

Dante lay on his cot looking up at the ceiling, his hands resting behind his head.

His roommate, Preacher, was reading a book. He looked over the top of the book at Dante. The older man, sporting a long salt-and-pepper beard with long salt-and-pepper dreads, scratched the top of his head and put down his book. "Tell me what's on your mind, young brother," Preacher said.

Dante looked over at the man and then back at the ceiling, not saying a word.

"OK." Preacher then picked up his book and resumed reading.

"I think they gonna throw the book at me," Dante said, not looking at him.

Preacher looked over the book at him. He lowered the book again, placing it on his lap. He waited patiently before speaking, in case Dante had more to say, but Dante remained silent.

"Why do you think they're gonna throw the book at you?"

"Because I know my mother."

"What do you mean? Your mother is being charged with murder too."

"Somebody can testify and say I did it."

"Dante, they have to prove that you committed the murder before they can convict you."

"Yeah, I hear you." Dante placed his hands over his face. It just seemed as if everything was against him, and he felt alone.

"Have some faith in your attorneys, young brother."

"You don't understand. They've been working on my mother's part of the case."

"OK. So what are you worried about? I'm not understanding you."

Dante sat up and swung his feet to the floor. He rested his elbows on his knees and looked at the floor. "My mother is gonna make sure that they get her off. She has no concern for me and what I'm facing," he said, finally looking over at Preacher.

Preacher leaned forward and placed his elbows on his knees as well. "Listen, young brother, what you need to do is be honest with the attorneys you got. Tell them everything that happened, tell them everything you didn't tell them. They don't need any secrets. You have to trust them. After all, you're paying them to defend you."

"My mother would lose it if I told them everything."

Preacher studied Dante's face and could see a young man holding on to a lot of stress. He knew from experience what that look was all about. He too held on to stress, but was working on releasing it through reading and meditating.

Preacher was from the old school and grew up in a time when racism was at its finest. He wasn't a violent man but was in and out of jail most of his life because he had a problem with the way authorities threw their weight around and bullied the innocent. He always found himself in handcuffs because he believed in freedom of speech. It just so happened that, every time he used his right to free speech, it was at the wrong time and the wrong place, causing him to get arrested for petty misdemeanors here and there.

This time was no different. He'd organized a rally against police brutality in front of the police station in downtown Newark. He was cited and warned on several occasions during his demonstration for not having a permit. Finally the police arrested him, and the judge, having had enough of seeing his face, gave him six months in county. Doing time came easy for Preacher because it gave him more time to read and meditate on his next project.

He liked talking to Dante. It was a way of putting his mentoring and teaching skills to use. Soon after first talking to Dante, he realized that Diamond had a strong hold on his mind, something he challenged himself to break.

"Let me break it down to you, son," Preacher said as he got up and sat next to Dante on his cot.

He held a letter in his hand that he had received from his father many, many years ago. The paper had turned yellow from age. Carefully he unfolded the delicate, tattered letter and held it out in front of him, so Dante could read along with him. He had two sentences underlined in the letter.

"A mother can only nurse you and show you unconditional love. But showing you how to be a man can only come from a man, your father," Preacher read out loud.

"You never really got a chance to know your father," Preacher said, "so your mother had to be your father and your mother, but that does not make her capable of showing you how to be a man. From what I see, your mother has been successful in turning you into her slave."

Dante looked at Preacher with hate-filled eyes.

"Hold on now, young brother. Hear me out before you get on the defense for your mother." Preacher held up his hand. "I know that's your mother, and she has been the only person to raise you and care for you, but I want you to take a look at your life and reflect on how it has gone up until now."

Dante lowered his head and thought. He had so many things running through his mind, he didn't know what to think anymore.

"Your mother loves you, but your mother is controlling. Just the small amount that you have told me about her since you've been here led me to believe that. Your mother has always been controlling of men, and you are no different." He stood and sat back down on his cot across from Dante. "Tell me about your case."

Dante looked at him with unsure eyes.

"I'm gonna help you, young brother," Preacher assured him.

"How? You're not a lawyer."

"I know, but I do a lot of reading about the law. I'm gonna do the best I can in giving you advice."

The two talked for hours about what really went down the night of Dr. Ricci's murder. They also talked about Diamond. At first Dante didn't want to tell Preacher anything. He didn't trust telling his business to a stranger, especially since his lawyers had told him on several occasions not to speak to anyone but them about the case. But Preacher was such an easy dude to talk to, and the knowledge he held helped to make Dante feel comfortable talking with him.

"So you see what I'm saying? I'm gonna do a lot of time, man." Dante shook his head.

Preacher lay on his back, looking up at the same ceiling Dante had been staring at earlier. "Yeah, I see what you're saying, but let me tell you this. You need to call your lawyers and have a private conversation with them to let them know what really happened. Listen, young brother, you got yourself a chance to get away with minimal time."

Dante looked over at him. "How you figure?"

"Simple." Preacher turned on his side and rose up on his elbow, looking at Dante. "Your mother had complete control over a minor. She premeditated the murder and manipulated you."

"But I ain't no minor."

"Not now you aren't, but your mother has manipulated, controlled, and trained you to be her personal slave since you were a child. She used you for her personal gain. Son, you can plead insanity and get off with a lot less time than what you're facing now."

Dante let Preacher's words process in his mind. He battled with himself. He thought about the love and loyalty he had for his mother. His mother wouldn't do that to him. She had raised him by herself, and besides the abuse, she did a good job giving him the things he always wanted. Even though they were on welfare at one point, it didn't seem as if they were, because Diamond made sure he had what he needed. So to his knowledge, they lived well. His mother always seemed to have more money than the average single mother raising children on welfare did. Although she only attended his games, his plays, and anything else they had at school while he was growing up to flirt with men in the school, she was still there. She wouldn't betray him, would she?

But, then again, maybe she would. There was that other side of her that he had to deal with. The side that always told him what to do, even though he was old enough to make his own decisions and do for himself. That side where she always rode his back about how he'd ruined her single life by coming into the world, and that if he wasn't there, she would be rich and living the good life.

Then there was the physical abuse side of her. He thought about how she controlled him and his friends, making them do things that they sometimes didn't want to do. He realized that she always got the biggest part of the cut on anything they did, even though he and his friends were the ones doing all the legwork while she lay back and counted the dough.

Dante decided he would arrange a meeting with his attorneys in the morning to go over the case again in a different light. Trey was the one still handling all of their money and taking care of business while they were locked down, but he wasn't so sure if he would give Dante any money for his own attorney without telling his mother. So, talking to the brother attorneys would be his only option.

"Yeah, man, you're right," Dante said to Preacher. "I think I'm gonna call them cats in the morning and set up a meeting."

When Preacher didn't respond, Dante looked over at him and could hear him snoring lightly. He went back to staring at the ceiling, processing his thoughts about how he was gonna present the information he had to the attorneys.

TWENTY-SEVEN

The Meeting

Dante sat in a waiting room handcuffed to the metal ring attached to the table. He was waiting for his attorneys to arrive. It was Friday, and they would all be back in court on Monday.

The doors opened, and a police officer led in Kendall.

Kendall looked distraught, and Kyle wasn't with him.

Dante watched as the handsome attorney set his briefcase on the table and sat in the chair in front of him. Kendall kept his gaze on Dante as he folded his hands in front of him.

Dante started to feel uncomfortable. He couldn't understand why Kendall seemed so upset.

"What's up, Dante?" Kendall said in a monotone voice.

"What's up? Where your brother?"

"He doesn't need to be here. I can relay to him anything that we discuss."

"Yo, what's up with you?" Dante asked.

"A'ight, let's cut the shit. Please tell me you didn't have anything to do with Tammy Starks being murdered."

"What?" Dante sat forward in shock. "What the fuck you tryna say?"

"I just said it."

"Hell no! Yo, what kinda shit is that?"

"Tammy Starks was murdered, and it's just mighty funny that after your mother told me how Tammy may have known something that could hurt the case, the woman turned up dead. What's even stranger was that she was supposed to finish testifying for the state on Monday, not to mention, my brother had an appointment to question her this weekend." Kendall sat back in his chair.

"Yo, that's some foul shit! You need to be asking my mother that question, not me. I ain't have shit to do with that chick getting slumped."

Dante couldn't believe his ears. He didn't even think Tammy knew anything. He was pissed that Kendall would come at him the way he did, because if anybody was capable of pulling off something like that, it would be his mother. This news was enough to really give Dante the go-ahead to free himself from his mother. It was definitely time to detach himself from his mother's tittie.

Kendall sat back and observed Dante for a few moments. Trained to read people, he saw no indication that Dante was lying.

"So what's on your mind then, kid? Why'd you call me down here?"

"See, it's shit like that is why I called you to come see me, because I really need to talk to you."

"Shit like what?"

"My mother. I don't think I want to be represented in a shared case with her anymore. I want one of y'all to represent me, and the other one to represent her."

"That's what we're doing, Dante."

"Naw, y'all are not representing us separately," Dante said seriously. "I want to be represented on what I tell you today."

Kendall now saw the concern on Dante's face. "What's the problem?"

Dante took a deep breath and proceeded to tell Kendall as much of the truth as time allowed.

Kendall took notes on his legal pad. When Dante was done talking, he had filled six sheets of paper from top to bottom.

"Why tell me the truth now?"

"Because you saw how my mother is. She did all the talking. She told me what to say. I did what she told me to do. I can't do it anymore. I've done what she's told me to do all my life. I'm my own man now, and from what I see, she is for self."

"I understand that, but why change now and go against what she told you to do?"

"Because I ain't taking the fall for everything while she gets off without doing any time."

Kendall tapped the pen on the table. "Listen, Dante, let me talk to my brother about this. Now we're gonna have to take another approach to this matter, and what pisses me off is, we only got two days to rearrange shit."

"I mean, so what you think? Do you think I can get some of my time reduced?"

"Well, I'm gonna see what I can do."

"Come on, man. Damn!" Dante laid his head on the table.

"Hold up, Dante. You didn't let me finish. I'll review everything, and I may have enough to go on right now. But I'm damn sure gonna try like hell to get that sentence reduced."

Dante lifted his head. "Word?"

"Yeah, I believe so. See, what you're not seeing is that we're gonna have to let your mother know that you told me the truth."

"So what, man? She gonna find out anyway, and you representing me don't have jack to do with her. Your brother can represent her."

"Yeah, but it's a touchy situation. We don't need her doing anything stupid to jeopardize either of your cases."

Dante nodded.

"So don't say anything to her, and leave the rest up to me and my brother."

"A'ight, but I hope my mother don't fuck this up."

"Listen, Dante, we're gonna have to make your mother understand how serious this is. My brother and I have an undefeated record, and I ain't tryna let her fuck that up for either of us. So if we can't make her understand, then she's gonna have to get herself another lawyer. My brother may be sweet on her, but I ain't the one." Kendall began to pack his briefcase.

From Kendall's last statement, Dante knew his mother had gotten next to Kyle. He hoped her vindictive ways wouldn't cause dissension between the two brothers, because, from what he could tell already, Kendall obviously didn't agree with his brother being sweet on Diamond.

After Kendall finished packing his briefcase, he picked up the legal pad and looked at the first page. "This is some shit right here." He shook his head. "Are there any more secrets or tricks pulling rabbit's outta hats that you need to be telling me?" He tossed the legal pad in the briefcase and shut it.

"Naw, man, that's it from me on all that I know. But maybe y'all better check your girl again," Dante said, referring to his mother.

"Oh, trust, she will be checked," Kendall said as he stood.

Dante shook his head. Kendall had no idea who he was about to go up against.

✦✧ ✦ TWENTY-EIGHT ✦✧ ✦✧

The State versus Reed and Reed

2003

On Monday morning the courtroom began to fill as the reporters and spectators took their seats. As the attorneys for both the defense and the state walked into the courtroom, reporters clicked photos on their flashless cameras, making the attorneys look like celebrities walking down the red carpet. One by one they marched down the aisle to their respective tables and began to set up, removing paperwork from their briefcases.

Prosecutor Swartz was the last to enter the courtroom. Once seated, she looked over at the two defense attorneys and gave them a slight nod. Both brothers returned the pleasantry before huddling together to discuss their strategy.

Ten minutes passed, and the courtroom still buzzed with anticipation. When the bailiff came out of the side door, he held the door open, and two uniformed officers walked in holding the arms of Diamond and Dante.

Once the two defendants were seated, the bailiff went through his ritual of announcing the judge. "All rise! The Honorable Judge Fritz presiding!"

Everyone stood and waited for the judge to exit his chambers.

Judge Fritz walked into the courtroom and made himself

comfortable in his seat. "You may be seated," he said and banged his gavel.

Once everyone was seated and all movement ceased, Judge Fritz removed his glasses. He folded his hands and studied the spectators.

Everyone started looking around at each other, wondering why the judge was not proceeding with court.

"I don't know what has happened to our country," Judge Fritz said. "But I do know that I am fed up!"

Kyle and Kendall looked at each other and slouched their shoulders, sitting back in their chairs, defeated. From past experiences with Judge Fritz, the brothers knew it wasn't going to be a good day in court when he was pissed. They both knew why Judge Fritz was pissed. All the attorneys had a meeting with him before coming into court, and they all got an earful from him.

"There has been a change to the case over the week-long recess," the judge said. "I am praying that it had nothing to do with this case. God help those who are involved, and God help anyone here today that had anything to do with the reason for this change in the case!"

Everyone in the room began to murmur, trying to figure out what the judge was talking about.

"I am not at liberty to reveal details, but we will proceed with this case." He banged his gavel. Judge Fritz was aware of Tammy Starks's murder and had worked closely with the police department to keep the murder out of the newspapers and away from the jury until the case was completed. The jurors had been sequestered in a hotel and had no outside contact. The spectators in the courtroom began to talk amongst themselves, wondering what the judge was talking about.

Judge Fritz banged his gavel. "Order!" he yelled.

Everyone settled down and became quiet, waiting to hear what else he had to say.

Prosecutor Swartz listened to Judge Fritz's announcement with a blank expression on her face. When she got the phone call about Tammy Starks's murder, she knew deep down inside that the Reeds had something to do with it. Although Tammy was now dead, and she was the star witness for the prosecution, Prosecutor Swartz felt confident enough in her case and the witnesses she had left that she still felt she had a good chance of winning.

"Counselor, since you aren't able to finish questioning with the prior witness, you can call your next witness," Judge Fritz said while putting his glasses back on.

"Yes, Your Honor." Prosecutor Swartz stood. "I would like to call Karen Odums to the stand."

Karen stood when her name was called. She was another nurse that worked for Dr. Ricci. Karen and Diamond got along for the sake of the job, but Karen was closer than anyone else to Ms. Brown.

Karen was tall and slender. She wasn't the most attractive flower in the bouquet, but she was a pleasant person. She tried to keep to herself at the office, and she didn't get in the middle of confrontations that would often break out between Diamond and other staff members.

Karen's five-feet, eleven-inch frame glided down the aisle and up into the witness box. After she was sworn in, she took her seat. She glanced over at Diamond. Diamond looked back at her and smiled. Karen gave a slight smile.

While Karen waited for Prosecutor Swartz to begin questioning her, she thought about how never in a million years would she have imagined herself sitting on the witness stand testifying at the trial concerning Dr. Ricci's murder. She, like all the other women who worked there or came through the office, was in love with Dr. Ricci. And now here she was sitting on the witness stand ready to testify against the person she believed murdered the good Dr. Ricci.

Prosecutor Swartz made her way over to the witness stand. "Hi, Karen," she said.

Karen was nervous. "Hello."

"How do you know the defendant Diamond Reed?"

"We worked together."

"Worked together where?"

"We worked for the late Dr. Ricci."

"How did you like working at the doctor's office?" Prosecutor Swartz walked over to the witness box.

"I loved it."

"How long did you work there?"

"Three years."

"How did you feel when you found out the doctor was murdered?"

"I cried." Karen lowered her head, remembering what had happened.

"It must have really hurt to hear that Dr. Ricci had been murdered."

Karen nodded, her eyes watering.

"Tell me about the defendant Diamond Reed."

"What do you want to know?"

"How well do you know the defendant?"

"I don't know her that well."

"You worked with her though, correct?"

"Yes, but we barely talked."

"Why did you barely talk to her when you worked with her?"

"Because I didn't trust her."

"What was it that you didn't trust about her?"

"She just seemed sneaky to me."

"Objection, Your Honor!" Kyle said. "That's merely the witness's own opinion."

"Sustained."

"OK. Well, was there anything that she did that made you feel uncomfortable?"

"Besides her complaining about not having money? Everything. I learned to tune her out."

"She complained about money?"

"She always complained about money . . . how she didn't have enough to live like she wanted to live."

"Objection, Your Honor! The witness is speculating."

"Overruled."

"Do you think she killed Dr. Ricci?"

"Objection!" Kyle said.

"Sustained."

"Allegedly, the defendant murdered Dr. Ricci. From your experience working with the defendant, did she give any indication that she didn't like Dr. Ricci?"

"No. They were actually really close."

"Close, huh? What do mean by really close?" Prosecutor Swartz moved closer to Karen.

"Um . . . I mean . . . it wasn't a secret to any of us that they were having an affair."

"Objection, Your Honor!" Kyle shouted. "That's speculation."

"Sustained!"

"What made you think that they were allegedly having an affair?"

"She told me."

"Who? The defendant?"

"Yes. Plus, I walked in on them kissing one night."

"OK, now we're getting somewhere. So you actually saw the two of them engaging in a kiss?"

"Yes, I did."

"How did you feel when Diamond told you she was having an affair with the doctor?"

"It didn't make me feel like anything. I mean, to each her own."

"Did it ever occur to you how Diamond had gotten the job there when she had no experience?"

"No, because when I went to work, I minded my own business."

"Ms. Odums, please tell the court what you did know about Dr. Ricci and Diamond Reed."

Karen looked over at Diamond, who was now leaning forward in her chair, wondering what Karen had to tell. She didn't think Karen knew anything.

"They were involved in insurance fraud."

The courtroom began to buzz again, and Judge Fritz banged his gavel to quiet the court.

"Insurance fraud?" Prosecutor Swartz asked.

The defense attorneys began to whisper to each other.

"Ms. Odums, please explain to the court what you are talking about."

Kyle stood. "Objection, Your Honor! The witness is speculating,"

"Overruled. Continue, young lady," Judge Fritz told Karen, interested in what she had to say.

"Diamond would bring in fake accident patients. They would come to Dr. Ricci for weekly visits. And Dr. Ricci would file the claim and get paid for each visit, although the patients had no injuries."

"So let me get this straight. These patients who came into the doctor's office were not real patients?"

"No."

"Dr. Ricci would set up fraudulent claims to collect money on each patient's visit?"

"Yes."

"Go on," Prosecutor Swartz said, taking her seat and crossing her legs.

"Well, apparently the patients would set up fake car accidents which really weren't that bad, but they would say they were injured. They would come to Dr. Ricci's office, although they didn't really need treatment. He would bill the auto insurance company for the treatment, and then each client would file suit against the other driver who hit them. With Dr. Ricci documenting the person's injuries, the cases usually settled, and everyone got a cut of the claim, including the lawyer."

"Wow! So the doctor and the defendant had a little fraud operation going on, huh?" Prosecutor Swartz looked over at the defense table.

"Objection, Your Honor!" Kyle said yet again. "There is no proof of any of these accusations. This witness is purely speculating."

"Your Honor, there is proof." Prosecutor Swartz snatched up several pieces of paper from the table and marched them over to the judge. "Your Honor, in my hand I hold a signed statement given to the police department by the witness Karen Odums."

Judge Fritz looked at the statement and then handed it back to Prosecutor Swartz.

Prosecutor Swartz walked over to Karen and handed her the statement. "Ms. Odums, is this the actual fraudulent case and file on a patient that you turned into the police?"

Karen looked at the papers and then handed them back to the attorney. "Yes, it is."

"Your Honor, I also hold in my hand the arrest records of several patients involved, as well as the accused attorney for the case." She then turned to Karen. "Why don't you explain to the court what your statement says." She walked over to the jury to show them the documents.

"Well, I found out about the fraud cases when I stayed late one night. I overheard a conversation that Diamond was having on the telephone with someone. She was in Dr. Ricci's office using his phone. She told the person on the phone that if they didn't keep up with their therapy, they weren't going to get that much money when they sued. I heard her call the person's name out, and I took the liberty to make a mental note of the name I heard."

"Objection, Your Honor!"

"Overruled."

Prosecutor Swartz said, "Go on, Ms. Odums."

"Well, when Diamond hung up the phone, she and Dr. Ricci began to discuss the telephone conversation. I heard the two of them talk about new accident cases that hadn't even happened yet. I heard Diamond tell him that she had some guy friends of hers that were going to set up the fake accidents. I remembered one particular scheme because she said the street where the accident was gonna take place, and that is the street where my mother lives.

"I waited until new patients came to the office several days later for therapy, and sure enough, the young man who had the accident on my mother's street was there for therapy. I looked up the other name I had heard her talk to on the phone and I found two people with the same first name, Derrick. But one of those Derricks I knew as a longtime patient because he has a herniated disk in his back and had been coming to the office for over a year. The other Derrick was a brand-new patient, and yes, his file was created three weeks prior, and he had only come for one treatment."

Conversations erupted in the courtroom.

Bang! Bang!

"Order in the court!" Judge Fritz yelled.

After the courtroom settled down, Prosecutor Swartz then asked, "Ms. Odums, do you know the other defendant, Dante Reed?"

Karen looked over at Dante, who wasn't giving her any contact. "I don't know him personally, but I know that he is Diamond's son," she said, looking back to Prosecutor Swartz.

"OK. So tell me what you do know about him."

"Well, I know he came to the office a few times, and that's about it."

"Do you know if he was involved with insurance fraud as well?"

"Well, yeah, I knew he was doing that."

"How did you know this?"

"Because I heard her tell him one time on a telephone conversation she was having that he had better find more people to set up for the fake accidents."

"Objection!" Kendall said. "Hearsay, Your Honor."

"Overruled!"

"So you say that the defendant Dante Reed actually went out and found people to create the false accidents?"

"Yes."

"No further questions, Your Honor." Prosecutor Swartz smiled a winning smile at Kyle and Kendall before she sat down.

"Counselors, your witness," Judge Fritz told the brothers.

Kyle stood and buttoned his suit jacket. He took another look at his notes and then walked toward the witness stand. "Ms. Odums, you and the defendant weren't friends, correct?"

"Correct."

"Are you trying to tell the court that you worked with someone for three years and you didn't become acquaintances with her?"

"I didn't work with her for three years. I said I worked for Dr. Ricci for three years. Diamond came during my last year working at the doctor's office."

"So you worked with her for a year, let's say."

Karen nodded. "Yes, it was a little over a year."

"So you worked with the defendant for a year, and the two of you managed to stay out of each other's way?"

"Yes, pretty much."

Kyle walked over to the jury box and faced the jury. "How is it that you know so much about insurance fraud?" he asked, never turning to look at Karen.

"Because I-I ran across some of the cases, like I told the prosecutor." Karen began to break down under Kyle's badgering.

Karen had been sleeping with one of Diamond's boy toys, and that was how she knew so much about the insurance scam, but she didn't want to admit that in court.

"But that does not make my client the mastermind." Kyle turned around to face Karen. "You knew didn't you?"

"I didn't ... I—"

"You knew illegal activity was taking place in a professional establishment, and you didn't go to the police with it right away? There had to be a reason you kept your mouth shut. What was it?!"

"But ..." The tears began to form as Karen tried to give an accurate answer and not incriminate herself. She didn't think that testifying was going to go this way. Prosecutor Swartz had asked her if she was telling her everything when she had her interview, and had tested her on the type of questioning that was going to take place in court to see if she could endure it, but it seemed totally different coming from Kyle.

Karen looked over at Prosecutor Swartz through her water-filled eyes for some help or guidance. Prosecutor Swartz felt at that moment that Karen hadn't been totally honest with her and was damaging the case she had against Diamond.

At that moment Karen wished she'd just kept her mouth shut, but like most, she wanted Diamond nailed to the wall, and now it seemed as if it was backfiring against her.

"Ms. Odums, you could be just as guilty of committing the crime that the state is trying to accuse my client of committing. How do we know you weren't the one who ran these illegal insurance fraud claims? How do we know you aren't trying to pin this charge on my client?" He stood directly in front of Karen, waiting for her answer.

Prosecutor Swartz and her co-counsel both stood together and yelled together, "Objection, Your Honor!"

Judge Fritz looked over at the prosecutor's table. "Overruled."

The young attorney whispered to Prosecutor Swartz, "What is he doing?"

"I don't know, but this is pissing me off!"

"I didn't kill him!" Karen yelled.

"I never said you killed the doctor. Now that you bring that up, did you?" Kyle leaned into the witness box.

"No!"

"Were you in on the alleged insurance fraud, Ms. Odums?"

"No!"

"Oh, come on, you had to have been in on it. The good doctor must have been getting a pretty good penny off of each case. I'm sure he gave you some of it."

"Objection!" Prosecutor Swartz yelled.

"Sustained."

Prosecutor Swartz sat back down and whispered, "It's about time."

"Counselor rephrase your question," the judge ordered Kyle.

"Ms. Odums, did you have anything to do with the murder of Dr. Ricci?"

"No, I had nothing to do with it. That's why I quit!" Karen blurted out hysterically, crying now.

"Why did you quit, Ms. Odums? Because the doctor cut you out of the deal?"

"No!"

"Why didn't you go to the police when you quit?"

"Because I didn't want to have nothing to do with what was going on in that office. You have no idea what went on!" Karen yelled back through snot and tears.

"Ms. Odums, you knew about the illegal activity, and you didn't report it to the proper authorities. Why should the jury believe you?"

Karen broke down in tears, unable to answer.

"Order in the court!" Judge Fritz yelled as the court murmurs grew louder. "We will take a thirty-minute recess, so the witness can get herself together."

✦✧ ✦✧ **TWENTY-NINE** ✦✧ ✦✧

"All rise! All rise and greet the Honorable Judge Lewis D. Fritz!" Judge Fritz walked into the courtroom and took his seat. "You may be seated," he said.

Karen Odums was escorted back to the witness stand to continue with her testimony.

The judge said to Kyle. "Counselor, you were questioning the witness before recess. Would you like to continue?"

"No, Your Honor. I have no further questions of this witness on behalf of Diamond Reed."

The judge said to Kendall, "Counselor, your witness."

Kendall stood and looked over at Diamond, who was looking at him like he was crazy.

At that moment, Diamond found out that the brothers were now representing each of them separately.

Kyle, Kendall, and Prosecutor Swartz had had a private meeting with Judge Fritz about Kyle and Kendall representing the defendants separately. Prosecutor Swartz and her team didn't have a problem with the change, nor did Judge Fritz.

Kyle had told Kendall he was going to tell Diamond about the change, but by the look on Diamond's face now, it didn't appear as if Kyle had told her yet.

"What the hell is he doing?" Diamond asked Kyle.

"I'll tell you about it later," Kyle whispered.

"How are you doing, Ms. Odums?" Kendall asked.

"I'm OK."

"Good. I'm not here to make you feel uncomfortable. I just have a few questions. I'm representing Dante Reed. He is Diamond Reed's son. My questions will only pertain to Dante Reed, OK?"

"OK." She sniffled.

"Do you know the reason Dante would come to the office?"

"Yes. He would usually come to talk to Diamond."

"Do you have any idea what they talked about?"

"Well, the few times I saw him there, he would wait in the waiting room, and then she would go into the waiting room to talk to him."

"So he's never been inside the office, to your knowledge?"

"Not to my knowledge. I've never seen him come past the waiting room."

"How long would you say their conversations lasted?"

"Not long. Usually about ten minutes." Karen began to feel comfortable talking with Kendall. Although she thought Kyle was the cuter of the two, she was intimidated by him, but Kendall made her relax.

"OK, Ms. Odums, so you say you never saw Dante Reed enter the office past the waiting room, and defendant Diamond Reed would only talk to him for ten minutes or so the few times that you know he came by the office, correct?"

"Yes."

"Has Diamond Reed ever discussed anything about her son Dante with you?"

"No. Well, one time she complained that if she hadn't had Dante her life would have been different."

"Did it seem as if she was angry when she made that statement?"

"No. I guess she was just venting."

"Was that all she said?"

"I mean, she talked about him, but most times I wasn't listening, so I really couldn't give you examples of complete conversations."

"Ms. Odums, from what you recall, did it seem like Diamond was very possessive of her son?"

"Well, I'm not sure. Like I said, I rarely listened to her when she talked."

"Ms. Odums, do you believe Dante Reed had any involvement with the murder of Dr. Ricci?"

"No."

"Objection!" Kyle stood.

"Sustained!"

"Scratch that last answer from the transcripts," Judge Fritz said.

"Ms. Odums, you said that Dante Reed was involved with insurance fraud?"

"Yes."

"You said you overheard the defendant Diamond Reed talking on the phone with Dante about insurance fraud?"

"Yes."

"What made you think she was talking to Dante on the phone?"

"Because I heard the way she talked to him, like a mother would talk to her child, and she said his name once or twice."

"So you were eavesdropping on her personal conversation?"

Karen held her head low. "Yes."

"Where was the defendant Diamond when she was allegedly talking to her son on the phone?"

"She was in the doctor's office."

"Was the door opened or closed?"

"It was closed."

"So you eavesdropped on a personal conversation Diamond Reed was on allegedly with her son Dante Reed, and you listened through a closed door?" he asked her, looking directly into her eyes.

"Yes."

"Couldn't it have been possible that, with the muffled voices, you may have heard incorrectly?"

"No. I knew she was talking to him."

"How?"

"I heard her say his name, and she was kinda scolding him."

"What did you hear?"

"She said something like, 'Boy, you better do what the hell I tell you before you regret it. I am your mother, Dante, and I said round up some more people so we can get this paper from the fake accidents.'"

"Objection!" Kyle said.

"Overruled."

"Was there anyone else there that heard what you heard?"

"No."

"So, in other words, you want me to go by your word because you eavesdropped on a conversation that you overheard through a closed door?"

"Yes."

"Is that all the evidence you have against my client Dante Reed on insurance fraud? An overheard telephone conversation?"

"Yes."

"Is there any paperwork, or have you actually seen him commit the crime?"

"No."

"Thank you, Ms. Odums. No further questions, Your Honor."

While Kendall walked back over to the table to take his seat, Diamond ice-grilled him the entire time. "What the hell do you think you're doing?" she asked him.

"Diamond, calm down," Kyle said.

"To hell with that! What is going on? Dante, what is going on?" she asked him, noticing Dante hadn't made eye contact with her the entire time they'd been in court.

Judge Fritz looked over the top of his glasses. "Counselor, is there a problem?"

"No, Your Honor," Kyle responded.

"To hell it ain't! I want to know what y'all are doing." Diamond was getting louder.

Kyle continued to try to calm her.

"Counselor, if you don't get control of your client, I will have her removed from the courtroom."

"Diamond, calm down before you get thrown out of court." Kyle looked deep into her eyes, letting her know he was serious.

Diamond looked around Kyle and over at Kendall and Dante, who were now whispering to each other. Envy and betrayal filled her heart. She had no control of this situation. She whispered to Kyle, "When this is over today, I want to see you alone, ASAP!"

Kyle simply nodded and looked over at his brother, who had a smirk on his face. Kyle rolled his eyes and shook his head in disgust.

✦✶ ✦✶ **THIRTY** ✶✦ ✶✦

Brotherly Love

Once court was adjourned, Kyle and Kendall walked out of the courthouse together. Neither uttered a word on the walk to the car. Kendall hit the automatic locks on his Benz, and they both got inside. Before he put the key in the ignition, he looked over at his brother, who was looking straight ahead.

"Talk to me. What's up, Kyle?"

Kyle didn't say a word. He continued to sit there, his jaws flexing.

"OK, cool. Keep it to yourself." Kendall shrugged and put the key in the ignition.

"What the fuck was that today, man?" Kyle blurted out.

"What was what, Kyle?" Kendall took his hand off the key and sat back, looking at Kyle.

"What kind of questioning were you doing in there today?"

"I'm still not understanding your question," Kendall said calmly.

"Don't fucking play games with me! You know damn well what I'm talking about!"

"No, I don't, and I suggest you calm the fuck down, doing all that yelling."

"Or what?"

Kyle and Kendall were always close. They grew up in a two-parent household in the suburbs. Their father was a history teacher, and their mother worked as a nurse. Raised in a loving environment, they always got what they wanted. When Kyle was just eleven and Kendall was thirteen, their fairy-tale lives took a turn for the worse when their father was arrested and convicted of child molestation on one of his students.

Their mother went into a state of shock from the ordeal. She eventually gave up on life because of it, losing her job due to the time she took off. She couldn't stand that the hospital staff constantly talked about her husband. When the community in which they lived turned on their family as well, she sank into a deep depression and began to neglect her motherly duties, and both boys became objects of ridicule from their classmates.

Finally their mother was admitted into a mental hospital, and the boys were carted off to spend the rest of their childhood with their alcoholic aunt. Unaccustomed to the mean streets of Newark, New Jersey, they had to adjust quickly. And living in their new environment only brought them closer to each other. Kendall made sure he protected his younger brother at all costs.

Kyle and Kendall decided to be lawyers, so they could represent people like their father, who they knew was wrongly convicted.

As they grew older, Kyle became competitive with Kendall. Anything Kendall did, Kyle wanted to do it better. Kendall never minded his younger brother being so competitive, because he thought it was a great way to keep him focused. But now, as adults, Kendall didn't think Kyle's competitiveness was so cute anymore. In fact, it was now becoming annoying and distracting to what they were building as a team.

Kendall also thought that Kyle was hardheaded and thought he knew everything.

"Why don't you just keep it funky and say what the fuck is your problem?" Kendall asked.

"We are supposed to be a team! We are supposed to be brothers. How could you go against me in this case?"

"Kyle, I am representing Dante. I gotta do what I gotta do to keep that boy from going to jail for life."

"And I don't have a problem with that. But you're going against me, and everything we worked on for this case in the beginning."

"How you figure, Kyle?"

"Come on, man! If you gonna defend Dante, then defend him. You know good and gotdamn well the questions we prepared to ask the witnesses. Don't override what I'm doing by using the witness to incriminate Diamond on Dante's behalf."

"Oh." Kendall threw back his head. "Now I see where this is going." Now Kyle was confused. "What are you talking about?"

"You know what I'm talking about. Don't play me for stupid. You sweet on Diamond, and you know it."

"Man, fuck you! Ain't nobody *sweet* on her. I'm working for her. I represent her, and you getting paid too. In fact, at one point you were representing her too." Kyle looked at Kendall sideways.

"You know what's funny to me, Kyle?"

"No. What's funny to you?" Kyle asked sarcastically.

"It's funny how you always allow pussy to interfere with our cases."

"Bullshit!"

Kendall was right, though. Kyle was indeed a ladies' man. He loved the ladies, and the ladies loved him. Sometimes he would allow a beautiful woman to cloud his brain when working on a case. Kendall would always pull his coattail, and the two would get into a heated argument over it. In the end, Kyle would still end up having sex with the client.

"Naw, no bullshit, brother. You always let pussy be your downfall."

"Fuck you, Kendall! I got an undefeated record on my cases! No amount of pussy in the world is gonna cloud my judgment. Remember, I'm the lead attorney in this case."

Kendall simply laughed. "Don't forget, you didn't get that undefeated record by yourself."

"Fuck you, Kendall!" Kyle turned and looked out the window.

"A'ight, all jokes aside, I'm your brother, Kyle, and I love you, but I'm gonna do what I gotta do to make sure that boy gets the best representation I can give him. And if that affects your case, I'm sorry. But just know I'm not going to do anything to intentionally jeopardize your track record. It's a sticky situation, and it may even seem like we're going against each other in court, but they're facing a lot of charges that they share. We just may bump heads and cross paths during the case, but just know that I have nothing but love for you, baby boy."

"Man, fuck you!" Kyle waved his hand at him. "Stay the fuck outta my way, or you gonna wish you had."

"Are you threatening me, Kyle?" a surprised Kendall asked.

"You heard what I said."

"Oh, it's like that? You don't have love for me? What happened to brotherly love?"

"You just fucked that up by going up against blood. Man, just start the car and take me back to the office so I can get my own car."

✦✦✦ ✦✦✦ ✦✦✦

Diamond paced in the interrogation room as she waited anxiously for Kyle to arrive. "So they think I'm stupid," she said out loud. "Something is going on, and I ain't the one for the game. They got the right bitch." She huffed.

Several minutes later, Kyle walked through the doors.

Diamond rushed over to him. "It's about damn time you got here!"

"Hold on, Diamond." Kyle threw his hand up to stop her from

getting up in his face. He gently grabbed her arm and ushered her over to the table, where he laid his briefcase.

Diamond yanked away from his grip and whirled around to face him. "You better tell me what the fuck is going on, and I want to know now!" she said through gritted teeth.

Kyle sat in the chair and leaned back. He gazed at Diamond as she stood there with her hand on her shapely hips. Even with the prison jumpsuit on, he could still see her hourglass figure.

Kyle and Diamond had had plenty of conversations over the phone and in person about the case. Most times he came to see her alone and then relayed any information about the case to his brother. Dante never knew this. This was Diamond's way of keeping control over the situation. She knew Kyle was the stronger lawyer and smarter brother and acted as lead counsel in most of their cases.

Kyle shook his head at her. He liked her feistiness. Under any other circumstances, he knew he would have fucked her, but he had to keep his head level and concentrate on the subject at hand.

"Diamond, sit down, please," he said, extending his hand toward the empty chair.

"I don't want to sit down. I want to know what's going on, Kyle!"

"I will tell you if you just calm down and have a seat."

"I said I don't want to sit down," she said, pronouncing every word clearly.

Kyle didn't say a word. He just continued to gaze at her, and the two of them engaged in a staring match.

Diamond's mood began to soften, but she was stubborn and didn't want to be the one to give in first.

I know what she needs, Kyle thought. He stood and walked over to her.

She never took her eyes off him, and he never took his eyes off her.

Kyle stood inches away from Diamond, staring down at her. He gently grabbed her hand and led her over to the chair.

Diamond felt like she was floating on a cloud.

Kyle helped her sit down and then walked back to his seat. He smiled at the way he'd tamed the wild beast.

Kyle had to make sure he chose his words wisely. Diamond was like a time bomb. He knew if he didn't relay the situation to her in just the right way, she would blow.

"It is easier for my brother to represent your son, and me to represent you," he said, giving her a sexy grin. "This way I can focus more on you."

Diamond was all in, and wanted to do him right there on the table. She licked her lips and exhaled. "Why does my son need to have representation? I mean, both of you are representing both of us anyway, so why can't y'all keep us together?"

"Diamond, you just said it yourself. My brother and I are representing the two of you anyway. So it doesn't make any difference whether I represent you and my brother represents Dante. Besides, you and I have been meeting on this case alone for quite some time anyway."

"Yeah, I guess you're right. But why didn't somebody tell me this? It made it look like y'all was being sneaky."

"I know what it looked like, but there was no time to tell you. My brother and I discussed the matter ahead of time and decided in court. Dante was told just before my brother stood to question the witness."

Diamond thought about what Kyle had told her. She wasn't quite sure if he was gaming her. She would just have to keep a close eye on the brothers for now.

"Do you understand now?"

She looked at him with mischief in her eyes. "I guess I do."

✦✦ ✦✦ THIRTY-ONE ✦✦ ✦✦

The State versus Reed and Reed

"If there are no further questions, then, counselor, you're up," Judge Fritz said to Prosecutor Swartz.

"Your Honor, I'd like to call Shakeeda Bingham to the stand," Prosecutor Swartz said as she glanced at the paper with the young lady's name written on it. She wanted to make sure she pronounced it right. She looked into the audience to see if Shakeeda was coming.

At the rear of the courtroom in the last row, Shakeeda stood. Prosecutor Swartz rolled her eyes when she saw Shakeeda's bright red hair.

Shakeeda was a key witness for the state, because she was Diamond's caseworker down at the Department of Health's welfare assistance program. She wore tight-fitting, straight-leg jeans with a low rise and a fitted shirt that showed tons of cleavage. Her eyes were shaded with heavy blue eye shadow and her lipstick cast a bluish-colored. As she pranced down the aisle in her six-inch glass-heeled stilettos, her cleavage jumped with each step. She had a swooped bang, and her red hair was pulled up into a neat ponytail on top of her head. The added weave extensions flowed down to the middle of her back.

As she made her way past Prosecutor Swartz, she gave a small smile and climbed into the witness stand. The room buzzed at her appearance, and the judge banged his gavel for silence.

As soon as the room was silent, Prosecutor Swartz walked over to the table and flipped through her notepad. She then clasped her hands behind her back and stepped over to the witness stand.

The bailiff began to swear Shakeeda in. "Raise your right hand," he told her. "Do you solemnly swear to tell the truth, the whole truth, and nothing but the truth, so help you God?"

"Yes."

"State your full name for the court."

"Shakeeda Dawn Bingham."

"You may be seated," Judge Fritz told Shakeeda.

"Ms. Bingham, do you know the defendants, Diamond and Dante Reed?"

"I know her, but not him."

"Is she a friend of yours?"

"No."

"How do you know the defendant?"

Shakeeda huffed because she thought the line of questioning was irrelevant. "I was her caseworker."

"Ms. Bingham, where do you work?"

"I work for welfare."

"In what city?"

"In Newark. Don't you know that already?" Shakeeda, nervous as hell, couldn't understand why Prosecutor Swartz was asking her questions she already knew the answers to.

Judge Fritz looked down at Shakeeda over the top of his glasses. "Just answer the questions, young lady."

Shakeeda sat back in her chair and slouched. Worried that her involvement in the welfare fraud might come out, she didn't want to come to court in the first place. After a couple of years had passed without her seeing Diamond, she thought it was over, but when she received a subpoena in the mail, she really didn't have a choice. She showed her supervisor, Joe, the notice, and he advised her it would be best to cooperate with the courts. Afraid she could lose her job if she didn't cooperate, she was now in court answering questions she preferred not to answer.

Shakeeda looked up at the judge. She was so nervous, she could hardly keep still.

"When was the first time you noticed the defendant was committing welfare fraud?" Prosecutor Swartz asked.

"I don't remember the exact date."

"OK, so can you give an estimated time frame?"

Shakeeda looked into the courtroom and into the face of her supervisor and friend. Joe narrowed his eyes at her and scowled, an indication to Shakeeda that she had better cooperate with the court system. She looked away from him. "I guess about two or three years ago." Shakeeda was obviously avoiding eye contact with Diamond and looked everywhere but at her.

"What was it about Diamond Reed's case that alarmed you and made you aware that she may have been committing fraud?" Prosecutor Swartz stopped and stood in front of the jury.

Shakeeda sat up straight in her seat. She avoided eye contact with Diamond, but she could feel Diamond staring at her. "Well, I got a call from the fraud department about a lot of doctor bills coming in for the client."

"Are you referring to Dr. Ricci?" Prosecutor Swartz asked.

"Yes."

"Go on. What did they notice about the doctor's bills?"

"Well, just that it was an unusual amount of bill flowing in from the same doctor's office. Plus, she told me at our last appointment—"

"Who told you? The defendant Diamond Reed?"

"Yes."

"Continue."

"Ms. Reed and I had a scheduled appointment to review her file and recertify her benefits. She told me at that time that she'd met a man she really liked, and thought that they might start going out."

"OK." Prosecutor Swartz leaned back onto the jury box and folded her arms across her chest.

"I remember congratulating her and asking her what his name was."

"Did you know then that she was referring to Dr. Ricci?"

"No, because—"

"Objection!" Kyle interrupted. "She's leading the witness."

"Sustained."

"What was the name of the man she said that she was dating?"

"She told me his name was Michael."

"As in Dr. Michael Ricci?" Prosecutor Swartz shot a sarcastic smirk at the defense attorneys.

"Objection, Your Honor!"

"Sustained." Judge Fritz warned Prosecutor Swartz with his eyes.

"OK, so you said the defendant told you she started dating a man whose name was Michael. So what did she tell you about Michael?"

Shakeeda remembered the day Diamond did indeed tell her about the doctor she'd met.

Diamond had showed up at the welfare office for an unscheduled visit. When Shakeeda got out to the lobby and saw her, her heart dropped into her panties. She was sure Diamond was there to kill her. She had dropped two of the claims without telling her.

When Diamond saw Shakeeda standing there, she got up and walked over to her. Shakeeda was trying to read her face, but couldn't.

"Can we talk?" Diamond asked as she walked past Shakeeda and into the offices.

Shakeeda followed behind her, and then Diamond let her get in front of her so that Shakeeda could find an empty cubicle. They both sat down once inside the cubicle.

"So what's up?" Shakeeda asked nervously.

"It's all good."

"Oh, that's good. What do you need today?" Shakeeda tried to sound professional, but she was scared out of her mind.

"I just wanted to let you know you can close those claims, because I got me a man that I'm working for who pays me well."

"Really?" Shakeeda was shocked and relieved all at the same time.

"Yup. I don't need them bullshit cases no more. He's a doctor, and he's good to me."

"Wow! That's a good look."

"Yeah, he's a chiropractor, girl, and his business is rolling in dough."

Which wasn't true. Dr. Ricci didn't have many clients, and he was still paying off student loans, and alimony so he was doing average for himself.

"What's his name?"

"Michael."

"Where did you meet him?" Shakeeda continued to delete the other claims from the system as fast as she could.

"I met him down in Atlantic City," she said, playing with the rings she wore on three of her fingers.

Shakeeda saw the rings in her peripheral vision, but never gave Diamond the satisfaction of asking about them. "Well, I'm happy for you, Diamond."

"Oh, yeah, leave my claim up there. I need it for something," she told her.

"Oh, I thought you wanted to delete it because you got a man to take care of you."

"Well, you thought wrong. That's why you and I didn't click when I tried to do business with you. You thought too much when it wasn't required from you," Diamond said sarcastically. "Leave the claim."

Shakeeda looked away and finished off what she was doing, but she made sure she kept Diamond's original claim. "OK, it's all done, Diamond."

"That's what's up." Diamond stood. "Take care of yourself." She walked away, leaving Shakeeda sitting there.

Shakeeda sighed with relief, thinking everything with Diamond was finally over.

"Well, at that meeting she didn't tell me much," Shakeeda said now. "But when I started working with the department on bills and she told me that she had been going to Dr. Ricci's office regularly, I started to think something wasn't right."

"What do you mean by something wasn't right?" Prosecutor Swartz walked over to the witness stand.

"Well, I was assigned to her case five years ago, and during that time, neither she nor her son had gone to the doctor that much, especially not this doctor."

"When collaborating with the fraud department on these doctor bills, what made you think something wasn't right, especially since the defendant had several illnesses?"

Shakeeda began to shake her leg out of nervousness. She knew she was telling a half-truth. "Well . . ."

"Go on, Ms. Bingham, it's OK," Prosecutor Swartz said, trying to calm her. She really needed Shakeeda to help nail the fraud case, since none of her other witnesses had panned out.

"It just seemed funny that, soon after she told me about the doctor she was dating, I was contacted about the bills from a doctor's office, and she now had this back problem."

Some of the courtroom spectators moaned.

"Objection!" Kyle said. "The witness is voicing her opinion."

"Sustained."

"So, Dr. Ricci's office was sending bills for the defendant Diamond Reed to you on a regular basis. Did you think she had a back problem?"

Kyle stood. "Objection, Your Honor! Neither Prosecutor Swartz nor the witness is a licensed physician, so they can't possibly know why the defendant had to see a chiropractor."

"Sustained."

"So what did you do?" Prosecutor Swartz asked.

"Well, I tried to contact Ms. Reed to set up another appointment for her to come in, but she never came. I did talk to her on the phone and tried to find out if this doctor was the same man she was dating."

"So you began to do some investigative work on your own?"

"Well, kinda, yes. Our procedure is to work with the fraud department and submit any suspicious activities as well."

"So what did you do?"

"Well, I didn't do anything else because my supervisor told me to turn everything over to our investigator at the fraud department."

"So after the fraud department continued with the case file, is that when you found out that the Michael the defendant was seeing was indeed Dr. Michael Ricci?"

"Yes."

"No more questions, Your Honor." Prosecutor Swartz took her seat.

Judge Fritz looked over at the defense table. "Your witness."

Kyle stood and walked over to the witness stand. He faced Shakeeda and gave her a warm, inviting smile.

Shakeeda stared into his beautiful eyes and almost melted right there on the witness stand.

"Ms. Bingham, would you say that you and the defendant were somewhat cool with each other?"

"Um . . . yes."

"So you and her were friends, right?"

"No, not friends."

"Come on, Ms. Bingham, being cool with her means that you and her were more like friends than just her caseworker. You know, sister girls, right?" He smiled.

Shakeeda smiled back. "Well, yeah, something like that."

"OK, good. So whenever you had to meet with her, the two of you would talk like old girlfriends, right?"

"Yeah."

"What did you talk about?"

"About men, being a single mother, clothes, shoes, things like that."

"Yeah, I know, girlfriend type stuff."

"Yes." Shakeeda started to feel more relaxed talking to Kyle. He didn't demand answers from, or put pressure on her like she thought he would.

"So you said the two of you talked about men, huh?"

"Yes." Shakeeda blushed a little.

"Would you say that Diamond had good luck in dating?" Kyle smiled at her.

"Oh, yes, Diamond could get any man she wanted." Shakeeda smiled, thinking of some of the crazy stories Diamond had told her.

"Do you have a boyfriend, Ms. Bingham?"

"Objection! Not relevant to the case, Your Honor," Prosecutor Swartz said.

"Your Honor, the questions I'm asking are necessary to lead up to my point."

"Overruled," Judge Fritz said. "Answer the question, young lady."

Shakeeda lowered her head. "No, I don't have a boyfriend."

"So when Diamond came into the office to see you, it was exciting to hear all of the stories about her and the men she dated, right?"

"Yes."

"Would you say the defendant was an easy person to talk to?"

"Yes."

"Has she ever given you advice before?"

"Yes."

"What about tips on how to get a man?" Kyle leaned on the witness stand.

"Objection!"

"Sustained."

"Have you and the defendant gone out together?"

"Huh?" Shakeeda was puzzled by the question. In her mind she was thinking Kyle meant some type of lesbian activity.

"Have you and the defendant gone out to party together?"

"Well, not really partying."

Kyle continued to stare into Shakeeda's eyes. "Well, what would you call it?"

"Well, sometimes when I would go out, I would see her, and we would talk," she lied.

"So the defendant frequented the same establishments you went to?"

"Yes, sometimes."

"Would you and the defendant have a few drinks together and talk like you do when she came into the office?"

"Yeah."

"Would you say that Diamond was a woman who had it going on?"

"Yes."

"Did you wish you could be like her?"

"Sometimes."

"So when she told you that the new man of the month was a doctor named Michael, you were in fact thrilled to hear about the stories because you thought about having a Prince Charming as well, correct?"

Prosecutor Swartz stood. "Objection, Your Honor!"

"Overruled." Judge Fritz eyed her.

Prosecutor Swartz huffed and plopped back down into her seat.

Shakeeda looked at the judge, who nodded for her to proceed.

"I wouldn't say I fantasized."

"I didn't say you fantasized. I asked you if you were thrilled to hear her stories. Did you look forward to talking with her?"

"Yes."

"Did you on more than one occasion meet with the defendant after work at a bar and grill for drinks?"

Shakeeda was at a loss for words. When she looked over at her boss, his face showed shock. She didn't want to admit to that. She finally looked over at Diamond and saw that Diamond was looking right through her. She knew she was in trouble now.

"Ms. Bingham, answer the question, please," Judge Fritz said.

Prosecutor Swartz sat forward in her seat, a look of contempt on her face.

"Yes, we did."

"So, back to my original question. Would you say you and the defendant Diamond Reed were friends?"

"Yes." Shakeeda was ready to scream.

"Ms. Bingham, did you or did you not ask the defendant if she wanted to help you with setting up some fraudulent claims because you were struggling?"

"No," she said, shocked that they would try to flip this around on her.

"Sure, you did. In fact, didn't you have a false claim going to your sister's house to cover up what you were doing?"

"No!" Shakeeda shouted.

"Didn't you know all along that Diamond was seeing Dr. Ricci, and you, in fact, didn't report anything to the fraud department until Diamond no longer returned your calls or contacted you?"

"No! That's a lie."

"Did you tell the defendant she should submit false claims so that the money could be split between the two of you, since she worked for

Dr. Ricci?"

"No!"

Diamond shouted. "You're lying!"

"Order in the court!" Judge Fritz said. "Ms. Reed, another outburst and you're gone!"

Kendall placed his hand on Diamond's arm to calm her.

"Get off me!" Diamond snatched away her arm.

"You knew Diamond was ignoring your calls, and it made you angry that she was keeping all of the money," Kyle continued. "You were jealous, so you threatened her by telling her that you would make up a story, saying that she wanted to submit false claims because she wouldn't do it for you, right?" Kyle reported what Diamond had told him about Shakeeda.

"No, that's not true!"

Kyle, his hands clasped in front of him, walked back over to the table and faced Shakeeda.

"No more questions, Your Honor."

"Ms. Swartz, redirect?" the judge asked.

"No, Your Honor."

Prosecutor Swartz shot Shakeeda an evil stare as she walked back to her seat in the courtroom. She'd interviewed Shakeeda before subpoenaing her to testify for the state, but Shakeeda hadn't revealed any of the information that Kyle got out of her. She didn't know if she could trust questioning any more employees from the welfare department. Now she would have to do some rearranging of her witnesses.

THIRTY-TWO

Prosecutor Swartz prepared to question her next witness.

Peter sat down next to her. He had just come from out in the hall, where he returned a phone call from his contact down at the police station. "I found our witness," he said, referring to the witness the police had been looking for.

Prosecutor Swartz looked at him with enthusiasm, until she saw the look in his eyes. "What?" she whispered.

"They found him dead," Peter whispered back.

"Shit!" Prosecutor Swartz said under her breath and hung her head. She was really counting on the special witness. She took a deep breath to try to get herself together.

Tyquan was their star witness along with Tammy, and they were both now dead. Tyquan rolled over on Diamond and her crew because he was still pissed off at the way she embarrassed him that day in front of her building. He knew he would never be able to get next to her again as long as she had Trey and the crew surrounding her at all times, so he decided to get back in good with her and infiltrate from the inside. He'd made good money with the crew in the process, but it was a big pill he had to swallow, to stay in good with everybody until he was ready to put them on blast.

But when he told the police about the whole operation, he had no idea he would have to testify in court against them, which he didn't want to do. Not to mention, if he did testify, he would've had to turn his own sister in for getting the social security cards for the welfare fraud cases. So Tyquan went on the run, staying off the streets during the day, and selling drugs by night, until he got into a confrontation with a drug rival and was shot and killed.

"Prosecutor, your next witness," the judge said, interrupting Prosecutor Swartz's thoughts.

"Yes, Your Honor, I'd like to call Chief Inspector Robert Lippe, Special Services of the Welfare Fraud and Investigative Unit of New Jersey," Prosecutor Swartz said, looking through her papers.

Robert Lippe had been with the Special Services for seventeen years. He was transferred to the Newark, New Jersey division three years earlier. Since then, he had solved dozens of fraud cases, but the number of welfare fraud cases was still climbing.

Robert Lippe wasn't liked by many, but he did his job well. He was a dweeb with a cocky and arrogant demeanor. He stepped up into the witness stand and stood at attention with his hand held up, waiting to be sworn in.

Some people in the courtroom snickered. Most who knew him disliked him because he looked down on people. When it came to doing his job, he would sometimes treat the employees for the state as if they were the criminals, creating tension within the department.

"Please state your full name for the court," the bailiff told Robert after he was sworn in.

"Robert Daniel Lippe," he said in his signature nasal voice.

"You may be seated," Judge Fritz said.

"Mr. Lippe, where do you work?" Prosecutor Swartz asked from her seat behind the table.

"I work for the Special Services of the Welfare Fraud and Investigative Unit," he said with confidence.

"What is your title?"

"I am chief inspector," he said as if he were the president of the United States.

"Mr. Lippe, do you take your job seriously?"

"You damn right, I do! I have a perfect record."

Prosecutor Swartz smiled. "Mr. Lippe, can you please tell the court your findings on the defendant Diamond Reed's case?"

"Why, of course. On October nineteenth two thousand two, I made a call to Shakaya, the caseworker," he said, pronouncing her name wrong. "I proceeded to tell her of my suspicions. I advised her to send me all the information and the case file on the defendant Diamond Reed. My findings were simple. Diamond Reed had one false claim open from what I could tell."

"Mr. Lippe, how did you know this claim was fraudulent?"

"Well, when investigating, it is a delicate matter," he said, adjusting his suit jacket and crossing his legs. "I dug deep into this case. I found out that the social security number used for the claim was fake. I also discovered that the people on the claim didn't live at the address where money was being sent. I also discovered that Diamond Reed had connections to the address where the welfare check was being sent each month." He sat back as if waiting for applause for his efforts.

"OK, Mr. Lippe, is that all?"

"Jeez, no. Not only did she have the false claim, she had tons of doctor bills coming in for Medicaid."

"Well, she did have a back problem. What made you think that the doctor's bills weren't legit?"

"Well, you see, Prosecutor Swartz, I have a substantial amount of education. I have some medical knowledge."

Prosecutor Swartz had to hold in her laughter. "Go on, Mr. Lippe." She thought he was a character, and enjoyed listening to him talk.

"I reviewed the medical bills and the diagnosis of the patient. It appeared to me that the patient had an acute back problem. And for that type of problem, her doctor's bills were for far more visits than what would be normal for that condition."

"Objection, Your Honor!" Kyle said. "Mr. Lippe is not a licensed physician."

"Sustained. The jury will disregard that last statement," Judge Fritz said to the jurors.

"How much were the doctor's bills for Diamond Reed?"

"I went back for two years, and my findings showed that her medical bills totaled in the hundreds of thousands."

"Hundreds of thousands?"

"Yes."

"What else did you find out?"

"Well, I set up surveillance and found out that the doctor's office had been processing quite a few false claims."

"OK, Mr. Lippe, thank you," Prosecutor Swartz said, deciding she had gotten enough out of this witness.

Kyle began his questioning before Judge Fritz gave him permission. "Mr. Lippe, you stated that the amount of doctor's bills for the defendant exceeded the normal amount for her condition. Correct?"

"Uh, yeah, that would be correct."

"Mr. Lippe, did you take into consideration or even notice that the defendant had many hospital treatments for her condition?"

"Well, yeah, I saw some of those bills too and put them in my report."

"So, when reviewing the bills, did you notice the costs of therapy?" Kyle looked at his notes.

"You see, there is a certain—"

Kyle cut him off. "Answer the question, Mr. Lippe. Yes or no?"

"Well, yes." Mr. Lippe fiddled with his tie.

"You state that the cost for a chiropractic visit was listed at eight thousand, when in fact, that is not the normal rate. Correct?"

"Well, yeah, it is, I saw the bills, and they were way overpriced."

"Overpriced? That's your opinion, Mr. Lippe. Your Honor, I hold here in my hand price lists from other chiropractic offices showing what they charge for the same type of treatment Diamond Reed received, and they were nowhere near the amount that Mr. Lippe put in his report. In fact the sessions were only a few hundred. I offer this as an exhibit." Kyle got up from his seat, showed the exhibit to Prosecutor Swartz, and then to the judge.

After the judge approved the exhibit, Kyle handed the papers to Mr. Lippe. After looking closely at the price lists, he handed them back to Kyle.

"So, did these offices charge more than Dr. Ricci for the same services, Mr. Lippe?" Kyle asked.

"I suppose."

"So am I correct in saying that your statement about Dr. Ricci overcharging for treatment in order to make money off the system is false?"

"For crying out loud, no! The bills were bogus!"

"Mr. Lippe, how would you know that?"

"Because I watched her every day for three weeks, and she didn't look like a woman who had a chronic back problem. She walked around in those . . . those stilts. Anyone with that type of a condition could barely stand up straight."

People in the courtroom began to mumble, and Judge Fritz banged his gavel for silence.

"Mr. Lippe, do you have pictures, film, or anything else that will back up your findings?" Kyle asked.

"Why, no. I am the chief—"

"We know your position, Mr. Lippe. Thank you for reminding us. So you have no physical proof, and you expect the jurors to believe you because you are the chief inspector for the welfare fraud department?"

"This is bullshit! I have never lost a case in any of my years of investigating fraud."

"And I haven't lost a case since I became a lawyer, but neither my track record nor yours is in question here today. Are you trying to tell me that you went to East Orange, New Jersey and sat in the ghetto on Main Street and watched the activity going on around the doctor's office?"

"Objection, Your Honor!"

"What's your reason for the objection?" Judge Fritz asked Prosecutor Swartz.

"He's badgering the witness."

"Sustained."

By now Mr. Lippe was furious because Kyle would not allow him to shine like he'd done with Prosecutor Swartz. Not only that, Kyle was twisting his words, and that made him even more frustrated.

"So, in other words, Mr. Lippe, you have no proof, besides your word?"

Mr. Lippe squinted so hard at Kyle, it looked like he would burst a blood vessel in his eyes. "My word is more than enough solid proof," he said through clenched teeth.

"No further questions, Your Honor." Kyle simply walked away.

"Counselor, would you like to question the witness?" Judge Fritz asked Kendall.

"No questions at this time, Your Honor," Kendall felt the witness only knew about Diamond and had nothing on Dante.

Diamond smiled at Kyle when he sat down, showing him her approval.

"You may step down, Mr. Lippe," Judge Fritz told him, and that quickly, the inspector's moment of fame was over.

✦✦✦ THIRTY-THREE ✦✦✦

The State versus Reed and Reed
2003

It had been a grueling two months, and all the attorneys were tired. Both teams of attorneys had pulled out all the stops questioning several witnesses, but there hadn't been a spectacular breakthrough in the case.

Kyle had questioned two young boys from the crew that Diamond had given them. The boys gave good statements and surprising didn't supply Prosecutor Swartz's team with any information that could be held against the defendants. Kendall questioned Dante's old boss from the Extra supermarket he used to work at, and several teachers from his high school, including his basketball coach. They were all credible witnesses for the defense and had nothing but good things to say, but their statements weren't strong enough for what the state had against the Reeds to relieve them of the harsh charges.

Prosecutor Swartz and her team sat at their table and waited patiently for court to begin. The spectators were still outside, so it gave her some much-needed peace to meditate before the trial began. She was still seething over the main witnesses that were killed.

It was the last day of trial, and the jury would be sent out for deliberations. She rubbed her temples while the two members of her team softly talked amongst themselves. Peter, the youngest attorney on her team, was missing. She hadn't heard from him since the night before but wasn't worried, since she didn't need him for the last day.

The defense attorneys weren't feeling as peaceful. With the way the case had been going, it seemed as if they were competing against each other, instead of working as a team. Each time a brother questioned a witness, he would badger the witness to testify against the other defendant. So Kendall and Kyle sat there with stoic expressions, not speaking to one another.

The courtroom doors opened, and in walked Peter. He made his way down the aisle at a quick pace. He plopped down in the chair next to Prosecutor Swartz and smiled. "Guess what?"

"What?" she asked, looking at him like he was crazy.

"I got a surprise witness. Plus, I got one of the witnesses who testified already to come back."

"No." She sat up in her chair.

"Yes, I do."

"Who is it?" She was eager to hear who he'd gotten. He'd come up with a good surprise witness, but she'd been murdered.

Peter pulled a paper from his inside pocket and unfolded it. He laid it on the table in front of them.

Prosecutor Swartz's eyes lit up after reading the name of the surprise witness and the information written below it. "OK, I know this one." A frown on her face, she pointed to the name on the paper. "But who is this one?"

"Somebody who contacted our office. Just trust me on this one." Peter was ecstatic. He didn't reveal the information to Prosecutor Swartz like he knew he was supposed to because he really wanted to prove to her that he could do the job.

Prosecutor Swartz wasn't too happy about the whole thing, but decided to play along and trust Peter's judgment.

Finally the bailiffs began to let the spectators into the courtroom.

The room filled quickly. Once the courtroom was filled to capacity, the side door opened, and Dante and Diamond were escorted in, the way they had been since the trial started.

Judge Fritz was then introduced, and he banged his gavel to start court.

"Have all the listed witnesses been questioned?" he asked the attorneys.

"Yes, Your Honor," Prosecutor Swartz said.

"Yes, Your Honor," Kyle said.

"Yes, Your Honor," Kendall also said.

"Are there any witnesses that either of you would like to recall, or are there any last-minute witnesses?"

"Yes, Your Honor," Prosecutor Swartz said as she stood. "First, I'd like to recall Shakeeda Bingham to the stand."

Kyle and Kendall looked at each other, wondering why she was being called back.

Shakeeda made her way down the aisle and back into the witness stand.

"You are still under oath, young lady," Judge Fritz told her.

Shakeeda nodded, letting Judge Fritz know she understood.

Diamond sat forward in her seat. She was filled with anger, and it showed on her face. Diamond didn't think about what effect her expression would have on the jurors, who had been studying her closely during the trial. She was desperately trying to get Shakeeda's attention, so she could try to instill fear in her.

Shakeeda never gave Diamond eye contact, knowing she would try to intimidate her.

"Ms. Bingham, you were called back because you spoke with one of the attorneys on my staff, and you said you were ready to cooperate. Correct?" Prosecutor Swartz asked.

Kyle looked over at Diamond, her gaze locked on Shakeeda, and thought he saw a glimmer of fear in her eyes.

Diamond sat there thinking how her life had turned out. She was indeed afraid. Afraid of what might come of the time she had left on this earth. She thought that if she'd just accepted the doctor's love and not allowed her greed to get in the way, she would've been happy.

She battled with her two minds, as she often did. She wanted to curl up in a ball and cry for her mother. Why did she do the things she did? Her father always told her that she shouldn't let people take advantage of her, and she'd always lived that way. Because she protected her heart, people still tried to hurt her. Why?

As she sat and thought about those things and listened to Shakeeda's testimony, she began to do what she did best—protect her heart and not let anyone know she was in pain.

"Yes," Shakeeda answered.

"Go ahead and tell the court what you want to say." Prosecutor Swartz took her seat and crossed her legs.

"Well, Diamond Reed came to me and asked me if I would create a couple of false claims so that she could get some extra money."

"Are you talking about welfare claims?" Prosecutor Swartz asked her.

"Yes."

"She's lying!" Diamond yelled.

Kyle grabbed Diamond's arm, to calm her.

Judge Fritz banged his gavel. "Order! Ms. Reed, I've already warned you once. Don't let it happen again. Counselor, either control your client or she will be removed from my courtroom. Go on, young lady," he said to Shakeeda.

Shakeeda still avoided looking over at Diamond. She put her head down, ashamed and afraid at the same time. She knew that she too would be facing criminal charges for her involvement. She'd struggled with that thought for a long time.

But it was also driving her crazy that she would have to look over her shoulder forever, fearing that Diamond had someone watching her and at any moment she would lose her life.

Her sister had told her before that she needed to confess. She also told Shakeeda that if by chance she had to go to jail, that she would be there for her. But Shakeeda was dead set on not confessing at that time.

She went to church to confess to the pastor, who prayed with her and spoke to her regularly. He taught her how to deal with the demons she held within herself. He helped her to accept God and taught her how to repent. Once she began to heal, she realized there was only one thing she had to do in order to lift the burden she carried around. Her pastor also hired a lawyer for her and got everything prepared for what she was facing once she confessed.

Shakeeda had moved several times because of her fear of Diamond and her crew. But once she testified she could rest easy because she would be under protective custody. She'd made a plea bargain and would get five years probation, but depending on her testimony today, the state could still press charges and take her to trial.

"I created the claims. I didn't want to create the claims, but Diamond is a ruthless woman, and she has a team of ruthless men behind her."

"Objection, Your Honor!" Kyle shouted. "The witness is speculating."

"Sustained," Judge Fritz said.

"She's a lying bitch," Diamond whispered to Kyle.

Shakeeda kept her head turned toward Prosecutor Swartz, so that she didn't have to look at Diamond.

"You *better* look away," Diamond muttered.

"Do you honestly think acting this way in front of the judge and jury is gonna help your chances of getting out of jail?" Kyle whispered to her through gritted teeth.

"That bitch is lying!" Diamond stood, no longer able to contain her anger.

The two bailiffs in the courtroom prepared to restrain Diamond, but Kyle stood and forced her back down in her seat.

"Do something!" she yelled at Kyle. "You just gonna let this bitch sit there and lie on me?"

"Calm down, Diamond!"

Bang! Bang!

"Counselor!" Judge Fritz yelled. "If you don't get control of your client, I will have her removed from my courtroom!" Judge Fritz could have removed Diamond a long time ago but he intentionally didn't. He knew her antics wouldn't sit well with the jury and whether she knew it or not, he knew that she was putting the noose around her own neck by acting a fool in his courtroom.

Diamond sat back down, ice-grilling Shakeeda.

When the room became quiet again, Prosecutor Swartz continued her questioning. "Did you feel your life would be threatened if you didn't create the claims?"

"Yes. In fact, in so many words, it was."

"So what else happened?"

"Ooh!" Diamond said loudly, ready to blow a gasket. "You better burn this bitch when you get up there," she told Kyle.

He simply stared at his client, telling her to be quiet with his eyes. Judge Fritz was also looking over at the defense table, showing his disapproval of the defendant's behavior.

"Well, she told me that she would give me some of the claim money and food stamps if I helped."

"Did you use them?"

"Yes, I did, but then she cut me off."

"So what did you do?"

"I went to speak with her about it, and she threatened me. I was scared for both my life and the lives of my children. She made it clear that if I stirred up any trouble I would be handled. So I never said anything."

"You dumb bitch! Tell the truth! You was just jealous because I had it going on and you didn't! You wanted to be like me!" Diamond screamed. "I'm that bitch!"

Diamond suddenly jumped over the table, and neither Kyle nor Kendall could control her.

Dante sat back calmly and coolly, watching as his mother made a spectacle of herself.

The two bailiffs ran over just in time to grab Diamond and tackle her to the floor as she kicked and screamed.

"You better watch your back, bitch!" Diamond yelled.

"Diamond!" Kyle yelled in a last attempt to get control over her.

Shakeeda, who was now standing and looking at Diamond, clearly showed fear on her face as tears welled in her eyes.

"I want her out of my courtroom!" Judge Fritz yelled.

Diamond was still fighting with the bailiffs, trying to get to Shakeeda, spitting obscenities at her all the way out the door. The courtroom was in a buzz. The spectators stood, and the reporters took pictures and wrote quickly on their notepads.

It took ten minutes before Judge Fritz could finally get the courtroom under control. When the room settled down and everyone was quiet, he gave Prosecutor Swartz a nod to continue.

Dante turned around, looked into the faces of the spectators, and locked eyes with Trey. He could see fire in Trey's eyes and knew Trey was pissed. He turned back around and continued to slouch in his chair.

Prosecutor Swartz walked over to the witness stand. "Are you OK?" she asked Shakeeda.

Shakeeda nodded and wiped the tears from her eyes, letting Prosecutor Swartz know she was OK to continue.

"Are you sure? Do you want to take a recess?" Prosecutor Swartz whispered to her.

"No, I'm all right."

"OK, Ms. Bingham. Why didn't you say anything the first time you were questioned here?"

"Because Diamond sent a message that she could still reach me."

"So she threatened you from behind the walls of the prison?"

"Yes."

"No further questions, Your Honor."

"Your witness counselor," Judge Fritz told Kyle.

Kyle stood. "Tell me why you didn't tell the truth before."

"I told you I feared for my life."

"So you were afraid for your life. What makes you so fearless now?"

"Because I've committed myself to God."

"Come on, Ms. Bingham. You committed yourself to God? All of a sudden, you became holier-than-thou, when just a few weeks ago you were sitting here in the stands lying through your teeth. You were lying then, and you're lying now!"

"No, I'm not lying now. It's the truth!"

"Ms. Bingham, you are like the little boy that cried wolf. Do you honestly think because you bring God into this that it will make us believe you?"

"No!" Shakeeda was finding it hard to keep a handle on herself.

"Were you in fact jealous of my client, Diamond Reed?"

"No!"

"Yes, you were, Ms. Bingham! Don't you remember, when you first took the stand, you told me you wanted to be like her?"

"No, that's not what I meant." She cried.

"Yes, it is! You said you wished you could dress like her and get the men that she got! Don't you remember? Or is it because you've become religious that you forgot?"

"I-I-I—"

"Ms. Bingham, you were jealous of my client, and because she allegedly cut you off, as you say, it made you angry. So now you're back on the stand trying to sabotage my client."

"No, I'm not!" Shakeeda yelled, tears streaming down her face.

"Yes, Ms. Bingham. You are as guilty as you try to claim my client is, and you're trying to bring my client down with you with these unbelievable lies!"

Prosecutor Swartz stood. "Objection, Your Honor! The counselor is badgering the witness!"

"Sustained!" Counselor, you are out of line!" Judge Fritz had been wondering when Prosecutor Swartz was going to object. He didn't like the way Kyle was making accusations against the witness.

"No more questions, Your Honor!" Kyle walked back to his seat.

Kendall stood and approached the witness. "Ms. Bingham, was my client, Dante Reed, involved with this alleged welfare fraud?"

"No." Shakeeda was still crying. She wiped her eyes with a tissue that one of the bailiffs handed to her.

"Have you ever seen him around Diamond and her so-called henchmen?"

"No."

"Ms. Bingham, do you know if my client Dante Reed is or was involved with any illegal doings with Diamond Reed?"

"No."

"Thank you, Ms. Bingham. No more questions, Your Honor." Kendall walked back to his seat. He glanced at his brother and could see the stress all over his face.

Kyle wanted to crawl under a rock. This was major. The witness had revealed that she herself was involved with the crimes Diamond was being tried for, so she made a very credible witness for the state. Diamond had caused a scene in the courtroom, which didn't look good for her at all, and he had run out of witnesses. All he could do was ride it out on a wing and a prayer.

Kendall, however, was confident that he could plead temporary insanity for his client on the murder charge and get Dante off with minimal years.

THIRTY-FOUR

Surprise Witness

"Counselor, do you have another witness?"

"Yes, Your Honor." Prosecutor Swartz looked down at her legal pad. "I'd like to call Waheed Akbar Dupree to the stand," she said, mispronouncing his name terribly. She then looked into the audience, as she herself had never met the witness.

Kyle and Kendall looked around the courtroom, but when no one stood, the two men looked at each other, perplexed.

Dante also turned around in his chair and looked back into the faces of those who sat behind them. He had no idea who the witness was either.

Seconds later, the side door to the courtroom opened, and a man, escorted by two guards, walked in, dressed in prison khaki pants and shirt, his hands cuffed in front of him. His dreads were pulled back into a thick ponytail at the nape of his neck.

Prosecutor Swartz looked over at Peter, who looked at her and winked his eye at her. He seemed to be gloating over the witness. Dante who had been slouching in the chair was now sitting erect. He couldn't believe his eyes. It was his cellmate, Preacher.

Kendall looked over at Dante. He leaned and whispered to him, "You know this cat?"

"Yeah, he's my cellie."

"Why would your cellie be here testifying for the state?"

Dante simply shrugged his shoulders.

Kyle leaned in to listen to their conversation when he saw them conversing. "Please don't tell me that you told this man anything."

Dante didn't say a word. He kept his focus on Preacher, who was being sworn in by the deputy. Once sworn in, Preacher took his seat and then looked over at Dante. He winked his eye at him. Dante relaxed his shoulders. The gesture by Preacher was an indication that he wasn't there to fry him.

Prosecutor Swartz approached the witness stand. "Hello. Can you state your name once more for the court?" Prosecutor Swartz asked.

"Certainly. My name is Waheed Akbar Dupree," he said with confidence. "But I am known to most as Preacher."

Kyle and Kendall looked at each other and then rolled their eyes up in their head with disapproval.

"OK, Mr. Dupree, how do you know the defendants?"

"Well, I only know one of the defendants."

"Which defendant?" Prosecutor Swartz looked back at the defense table and noticed they were just as confused as she was.

"I know Dante Reed."

Kendall looked over at Dante, but Dante never returned the look.

"Again, how do you know the defendant?"

"He is my cellmate," Preacher said into the microphone.

The spectators whispered amongst themselves.

Prosecutor Swartz leaned against the jury box. "And what information do you have against the defendant?"

"I plan to reveal that the defendant Dante Reed is innocent of all charges and was brainwashed by his mother, Diamond Reed."

"Objection, Your Honor. This witness is in no way qualified to make such an accusation.

"Sustained."

"This is bullshit!" Kyle whispered to his brother.

Prosecutor Swartz asked, "Mr. Dupree, do you have any information on the murder of Dr. Michael Ricci?"

"Yes, I do."

"Please proceed." Prosecutor Swartz held her hand out, giving him the floor.

"Diamond Reed planned to kill Dr. Ricci when he refused to cooperate with her on insurance fraud."

"Objection, Your Honor," Kyle said. "This is hearsay, or speculation."

"Overruled."

Kyle was indeed pissed, because this only made Dante look good, but put all kinds of pressure on him, in reference to Diamond. Fuming, he leaned back in his chair.

"Go on, Mr. Dupree," Prosecutor Swartz egged him on, eager to hear what he had to say.

Preacher proceeded to reveal all that Dante had told him about that day in the doctor's office. Preacher never said who did the killing; he merely stated that the doctor was "desecrated" that day due to the argument. Preacher went into specific details, as Dante had told him, revealing the welfare claims and insurance fraud claims.

"Mr. Dupree, so you're saying that the defendant Dante Reed stated he had nothing to do with the crimes committed?"

"What I am saying, miss, is that the young brother was a product of a form of black slavery. His mind was enslaved by his nurturer. As she nurtured him, she calculated and dictated the life he would live by her hands."

"Objection, Your Honor." Kyle stood. "This is garbage. This witness is merely stating an opinion, not fact!"

"Sustained."

"Did the defendant reveal who actually killed Dr. Ricci?"

Preacher looked over at the defense table and into the eyes of Dante, as if waiting for approval.

Dante was sick to his stomach. He didn't want to serve time for crimes he didn't commit, but it was as if he would be the one to put his mother in jail because of what he'd told Preacher. He lowered his head.

Kyle was fuming and looked back and forth between Dante and Preacher, trying to read any body language between the two.

"Yes," Preacher said.

Mumbles and whispers filled the courtroom, but not loud enough that the judge interfered. He simply looked on, awaiting Prosecutor Swartz's next question.

"Who was it that killed Dr. Ricci?"

"The question is: How *many* killed the doctor? Because no one will really know which blow actually killed him."

Kyle threw his hands up in the air. Kendall simply looked on in confusion.

Dante kept his head lowered. "What do you mean by that?"

"Well, miss, I believe that we as black people are a product of this hostile environment in which the devil roams freely. The judicial system makes it hard for an innocent man to speak freely and be recognized for his ability to contribute to this world."

"Huh?" Kyle said louder than he thought he did. "Objection, Your Honor. This witness is clearly confused and cannot answer the question because he does not know the answer. I make a motion that he be removed from the stand and his testimony be stricken from the record."

"Overruled," Judge Fritz told him, and added, "I will make the motions as I see fit, counselor. Answer the question, Mr. Dupree."

"I can tell you who didn't kill Dr. Ricci, and that was Dante Reed."

"Who did kill the doctor?" Prosecutor Swartz persisted.

"Objection, Your Honor. This man was not on the scene of the crime, so how could he know?"

"Overruled."

"Do you know who killed Dr. Ricci?"

"I will tell you that there were other people present, including Diamond Reed, but Dante Reed wasn't present when the doctor was killed."

A shocked Kendall looked over at Dante because he knew Dante was present the day of the killing. Dante was in awe and looking at Preacher.

Prosecutor Swartz was quite surprised at the testimony of Preacher and asked him several more questions pertaining to the murder, and Preacher was adamant with his answers. Kyle objected so many times during her questioning, it let her know that he was losing his cool and would blow the case himself with his behavior. The noose was already around Diamond's neck, so Prosecutor Swartz decided to let Kyle push the chair out from under her feet, hanging her himself.

"No more questions, Your Honor."

Kyle jumped to his feet before he was even given permission to question the witness. "Mr. Dupree, what are you? Some kind of revolutionary?"

"You could say that. I am an activist who speaks out against hate crimes and police brutality," he said, looking over at the court officer who stood off to the side.

"OK, so you are a public speaker for which organization?" Kyle was having a hard time remaining calm.

"Me, Myself, and I, young brother."

"I'm not your brother."

"We are all brothers, my brother."

"Yeah, OK. Black power to the people. What are you currently incarcerated for?"

"Public disorderly conduct."

"So you created a disturbance and were arrested?'

"Yes."

"How many times have you been arrested?"

"Brother, I have been ridiculed and disrespected by the man for many years."

"Answer the question please."

"I've been imprisoned at least twenty-five times during the course of my life."

"Twenty-five times? You've gone to jail twenty-five different times for breaking the law, and you come here in court and tell lies on my client and expect the court to believe you?"

"Objection, Your Honor. Mr. Dupree is not on trial here."

"Sustained."

Kyle was pissed. "Mr. Dupree, how is it possible for you to know who actually killed Dr. Ricci if you were not present?"

"My brother, I told you that Dante was not present, but your client was." Preacher sat back and crossed his legs.

"How could you know such a thing? Did Dante Reed tell you this? That makes no sense."

"It's like I said. Diamond brainwashed the young brother into being her personal slave. She taught him to obey her every command."

"That's your opinion, Mr. Dupree, and your opinion holds no weight in this courtroom. You are a criminal and have been for most of your life, and you expect the jury to believe that you have information on a murder that you know nothing about."

"I beg to differ, young brother."

"How can two people kill one person?"

"Well, as I was told, they did, and Dante Reed was not there."

"Who told you that?" Kyle was ready to strangle the black man.

"I am not at liberty to say," Preacher simply told him.

"Then your testimony means nothing here, unless you reveal your sources, so they too can be questioned."

"Unfortunately, that wouldn't be possible. Just let the powers that be handle this, my brother."

"Oh, please spare me the power-to-the-people crap. You have no proof and no evidence against my client. Your Honor, I am done with this witness. They have not proven anything!" Kyle marched back to his seat, pouting like a child.

Kendall stood. "Mr. Dupree, what else did my client, Dante Reed, tell you about his mother, Diamond Reed?"

"That she abused him physically and mentally for as far back into childhood as he could remember. The boy is scarred, counselor, and he has not thought or made decisions for himself his whole life."

Prosecutor Swartz interrupted. "Objection! This sounds like hearsay Your Honor." Although the testimony hurt Diamond, it was also giving Dante a defense and Prosecutor Swartz didn't like that at all.

Preacher looked up at the judge.

"Overruled," Judge Fritz said, looking down at Preacher.

"What do you know?" Kendall asked.

"I shared a cell with that young brother, and he told me about things that were done to him that I wouldn't do to a dog. His mother abused him physically and mentally for so many years that he doesn't know if he is coming or going. She has threatened his life to get him to do what she wanted him to do once he became a teen. I can assure you that I've been on this earth for long enough to know a scarred person, and that kid is damaged."

Kyle was so exhausted with anger, he didn't even make an attempt to object. It was like he was throwing in the towel.

Kendall nodded and said, "Mr. Dupree, thank you. No more questions, Your Honor."

Preacher was then escorted out of the witness stand. When he walked past the defense table, he locked eyes with Dante and held up his fist. "Stay strong, young brother," he said as he was escorted out of the courtroom.

Judge Fritz released the courtroom for recess so the attorneys could prepare their closing arguments. It was time to hand this case over to the jury.

✦•✦ ✦✦ **THIRTY-FIVE** ✦✦ ✦•✦

Closing Arguments

"Counselor for the prosecution, are you ready to make your closing argument?" Judge Fritz asked.

"Yes, Your Honor, we are." Prosecutor Swartz stood and took one last glance at her papers. She walked over to the jury and stood in front of them. "Ladies and gentlemen of the jury, it has been a very intense and exhausting trial. You have been kept from your families and the outside world because of this case. I know you all want to get back to your families and your normal lives.

"My team and I have presented to you the actual facts on this case, and I hope that you will look at the facts presented to you to help you come to a guilty verdict against the defendants. You have heard from credible witnesses who have revealed to you that Diamond and Dante Reed committed horrible crimes. Don't let these criminals get away with murder, extortion, and fraud. Do the right thing and put them away for life," she said and walked back over to her seat.

Kyle stood and straightened his tie. "Ladies and gentlemen of the jury, you heard from the prosecution and its witnesses. However, I've sat here with you in the same courtroom and have heard the witnesses' testimony. I have to be honest with you. I didn't hear anything that would suggest that my client actually murdered Dr. Ricci. I also have not heard solid evidence that my client committed insurance fraud or welfare fraud. All that has been said in the last two months has been hearsay, speculation, or accusations against my client, Diamond Reed. Yes, she had an outburst in court; however, if someone was trying to frame you or tell untruths about you, wouldn't you get frustrated as well? I apologize for her behavior, and so does she. But my point to you, ladies and gentlemen of the jury, is that there was no hard evidence presented during this trial to convict my client. I have confidence in you and know that you will make the best and right decision based on the lack of evidence presented during the trial by finding Diamond Reed not guilty." Kyle walked back over to his table and sat down.

Finally Kendall stood and faced his brother. Kyle stood and they shook hands before Kendall made his way over to the jury.

"Ladies and gentleman of the jury, my closing argument will be brief. I know you want to get to your deliberations. My client, Dante Reed, has been accused of being guilty by association. He is the son of Diamond Reed, so naturally, he would be pulled into this matter. My client is innocent of all the charges brought against him. He was raised by his mother and brainwashed. Diamond Reed raised him to respect her as well as worship her. She constantly put into his head that he owed her for having to give up her life because she gave birth to him.

"There is no police evidence, and there were no witnesses that could testify against my client. Please make the right decision. You and I both know Dante Reed is innocent." Kendall took his seat next to Dante and gave him a pat on the back.

Judge Fritz removed his glasses and turned to face the jury. "I want each of you to go into deliberations and take as long as you like to make your decision. I want you to study the facts and only the facts on this case. I know you will make the right decision." He looked over at the jury. Judge Fritz banged his gavel and dismissed the jurors and the courtroom.

Everyone began to file out, talking amongst themselves.

Prosecutor Swartz walked over to the defense attorneys and

extended her hand for a shake. "I think you guys did a great job. You gave me a hell of a run." She smiled at them as if she had already won.

Kyle chuckled as he shook her hand. "Don't count your chickens before the eggs have hatched."

Kendall simply shook her hand and prepared his briefcase to leave.

"So what do you think?" Kyle asked Kendall once they were in the car.

Kendall looked over at him in shock. "You talking to me?"

"Yeah. Who you think I'm talking to?"

"Oh, I didn't know, since you haven't said more than two words to me at one time lately."

"*Pssh*! Come on, man, just answer the question." Kyle frowned.

"I don't know about Diamond. That last witness and Shakeeda threw a monkey wrench in your program, little brother."

"Yeah, I know. I was pissed off with that bullshit!"

"Yeah, me and everybody else in the courtroom could tell. You lost your cool, and that ain't never good," Kendall said, schooling him.

Kyle looked out the window while Kendall drove. "You did a good job with Dante's part of the case."

"Thank you. I mean, really, they didn't have anything on the kid concerning the murder. Whether he did it or not, they couldn't provide any evidence."

"Do you think he did it?" Kyle looked over at him.

"Naw, I know he didn't do it. But he was there and it was Diamond's master plan. She got that boy so well trained to jump on her command that if he did testify on his own behalf that he didn't do it, she probably would have had him killed. I don't know where this Waheed character came from, but by him putting out there that Dante wasn't at the scene of the crime is surely gonna help my case."

"Yeah, I feel you. Diamond is a piece of work. All I can say is, if she ever had a chance, she fucked it up by tripping out in court." Kyle sighed.

"So you're throwing in the towel?"

Kyle didn't say a word. He continued to look out the window while he bit on his thumbnail.

"Uh-oh, you're biting your nails. You're really concerned about this one, huh?"

"I never lost a case," Kyle said.

"Little brother, it's not always about the kill, the *W*. Sometimes you gotta take the *L* for the team. You focus so much on the win, you lose focus on what's important."

Kyle nodded. For once, he listened to his older brother, instead of thinking that he knew it all.

"Don't worry about it, bruh. Just let the chips fall where they may. You are still the best damn attorney I have ever seen."

"Better than you?" Kyle looked at him, a smile on his face.

Kendall smiled back. "Yeah, little brother, better than me."

✦✦✦ THIRTY-SIX ✦✦✦

The Verdict

It had been one week since the jury went out for deliberations. Prosecutor Swartz was at home when she got the call that the jury was back. She called her partners and got herself together to go to the courthouse.

Kyle and Kendall were already at the courthouse on another case they were investigating, which was scheduled to start in two months. They made their way to the courtroom to hear the verdict.

One hour later, everyone began to fill the courtroom. The attorneys were already sitting at their tables when Dante and Diamond were escorted back into the courtroom for the verdict.

Diamond looked around for Trey, but didn't see him. She had been in lockup since her courtroom outburst and had no phone privileges due to her behavior. She was pissed because she desperately wanted to get in touch with Trey so he could get rid of Shakeeda for testifying against her. But she didn't know that Trey was sitting in jail while she sat in court.

The police had raided Trey's townhouse and found drugs, money, and an arsenal of guns. The police had had him on surveillance for several months. He had gotten too big and was pulling in a lot of money.

Trey was always careful to stay out of the radar and kept himself far from any contact with the police, but the police had informants who got paid to give them information on all the big-time drug dealers. Because Trey always stayed on the move, it took them some time to catch up to him. When one of his workers had gotten arrested, he snitched on Trey to get time knocked off his sentence. This helped the police bang the final nail in the coffin.

No one from his crew even came to bail him out. They all took advantage of his stash. They knew that Trey would be going away for a long time, so they began to branch off and do their own thing with his money.

"All rise! All rise!" the bailiff said.

Everyone stood.

"The Honorable Judge Lewis D. Fritz presiding!"

"Please be seated." Judge Fritz banged his gavel.

Everyone sat down and got comfortable. Another door opened, and in walked the jurors, who filed into the two rows and took their seats.

When the room became quiet, Judge Fritz asked, "Has the jury reached a decision?"

The foreman of the jury, an older white male, stated, "Yes, Your Honor."

"Let me see the verdict," Judge Fritz said.

The verdict sheet was passed to the judge. Once he read it, he had the bailiff pass the sheet back to the foreman.

Judge Fritz said, "The jury will now read the verdict on the defendant Dante Reed at this time." He told Dante. "Please stand."

Dante and Kendall both stood to await his fate. Dante was nervous, but he carefully hid his emotions.

Judge Fritz gave the jury foreman a nod, letting him know it was time to read the verdict.

"In the case of *The State versus Dante Reed* on the charge of insurance fraud, we the jury find the defendant guilty."

Dante's shoulders and head dropped in defeat, and he took a deep breath, as he had been holding it in. Kendall patted him on the shoulder for comfort.

"In the case of *The State versus Dante Reed* on the charge of welfare fraud, we the jury find the defendant not guilty."

Dante was relieved, but he knew those weren't the worst of the charges against him.

Diamond sat there smiling up at her son. She knew if they found him not guilty, they would definitely find her not guilty.

The juror continued to read the other charges brought against Dante, who immediately held his head low again, fearing the result.

"Don't worry, kid," Kendall whispered. "Hang in there. Hold your head up, man."

Dante lifted his head to face the other charges brought against him.

Judge Fritz had to bang his gavel because of all the buzzing in the room. "Order!" he yelled. Then he told the foreman, "Go on."

Dante's legs weakened. He didn't know if he would be able to keep standing if he was found guilty of any more charges. Not really knowing the amount of time issued for the guilty charge, he just figured the worst. Calculating the time he would have to serve so far, he figured he was gonna be sentenced to at least twenty years.

Kendall gave Dante a pat on his shoulder again to assure him it wasn't as bad as he was thinking.

Diamond, seeing how nervous Dante was, said to him, "It's gonna be all right, son. I'll make sure to come see you."

Dante glared at his mother. She'd never cared before, so he knew she didn't care now. Preacher was right about her, he realized at that moment. He turned his head when the man began to read the verdict for the murder charge, the one he feared the most.

"In the case of *The State versus Dante Reed* on the charge of first degree murder of Dr. Michael Ricci, we the jurors find the defendant not guilty."

Dante and Kendall yelled out in victory and gave each other a hug. Although he would be sentenced on other charge, Dante was thrilled that he was found not guilty on the murder charge.

Judge Fritz continued to bang his gavel to quiet the now noisy courtroom.

Prosecutor Swartz was partially satisfied with the verdict. She didn't have much to go on, as far as Dante was concerned, but she desperately wanted to put Diamond behind bars for life. She knew that woman was pure evil.

"Order in my courtroom!" Judge Fritz yelled.

Everyone finally began to settle down.

"Your sentencing will take place next month, Mr. Reed," the judge said. "Until then you will remain in custody."

Dante and Kendall shook hands again before they sat down and awaited Diamond's fate.

"Diamond Reed, please stand," Judge Fritz said. Then he told the foreman, "You may read the verdict on Diamond Reed."

"In the case of *The State versus Diamond Reed* on one count of murder in the first degree, we the jury find the defendant not guilty."

"Yes!" Diamond jumped up and down, making sure she poured it on extra thick. She knew she would beat out the Dr. Ricci murder.

Prosecutor Swartz simply rolled her eyes. There was still more to come.

"In the case of *The State versus Diamond Reed* on two counts of fraud, we the jury find the defendant guilty."

"What!" Diamond yelled.

A smirk spread across Prosecutor Swartz's lips.

"Order!" Judge Fritz banged his gavel.

"Diamond, you need to calm your ass down right now!" Kyle whispered. "Let them read the verdict. You have not been sentenced yet. If anything, I can file an appeal, so chill out!"

Diamond breathed heavily, not happy that Kyle was giving her commands.

Judge Fritz watched the defense table to see what was going to happen.

The bailiffs were ready this time for anything Diamond might do, moving closer to the defense table, just in case she decided to leap over it again.

"Go on," Judge Fritz told the foreman after he saw that Diamond was settled.

The jury foreman was hesitant to move forward. He didn't know what Diamond's reaction was going to be to hearing another guilty verdict. The other jurors studied her intently, waiting for her to jump so that they could run. The spectators in the courtroom groaned.

Diamond stood still, fuming with anger.

The foreman continued. "In the case of *The State versus Diamond Reed* on one count of conspiracy, we the jury find the defendant guilty."

Dante looked at his mother and felt sorry for her. He did love her, but he couldn't help her now. She needed to answer for her own wrongdoings.

"In the case of *The State versus Diamond Reed* on one count of extortion, we the jury find the defendant guilty."

Diamond looked over at Prosecutor Swartz, who was already looking at her and smiling. Prosecutor Swartz was satisfied beyond belief. Peter and the other two attorneys at the prosecution table began to shake hands and give each other high-fives in celebration of their victory.

"This is bullshit, Kyle!" Diamond yelled. "All that damn money I paid you, and you ain't do shit! You are fired!" She turned to Kendall, who had stood, not sure what to expect from her. "Kendall, I want to hire you to handle my appeal!"

Judge Fritz banged his gavel. "Order!"

The spectators all stood, hoping to see another show, courtesy of Diamond. The noise in the courtroom intensified. The bailiffs moved closer to the defense table, waiting for Diamond to make a move. More police entered the courtroom, having been on standby because of the last incident.

As the jurors started out of the courtroom, Diamond jumped on top of the table, trying to elude the bailiffs, and the jurors, fearing for their lives, rushed out of the courtroom.

Bang! Bang!

Judge Fritz banged his gavel, but the sound fell on deaf ears. The courtroom erupted with shouts.

Diamond kicked one of the bailiffs in the face, creating an opening for her to jump through. The way she was acting, no one would have known Diamond was in her fifties. The bailiff hit the ground, and Diamond pounced on him and swiped his gun from him.

Everyone in the courtroom hit the deck.

Dante yelled. "Ma! No, Ma!"

Every armed person in the courtroom pointed their gun at Diamond. One of the bailiffs pushed the judge to the floor for his safety.

"Dante, get your mother!" Kendall said. "They will shoot her dead, man!"

Dante walked toward her. "Ma! Please, Ma, put down the gun."

"Hold your fire!" a police officer told everyone as he saw Dante trying to talk his mother down.

"Ma, please."

"Dante, get back! I ain't going to jail! Come on, you can escape with me," she said, panting.

"No, Ma, I ain't gonna go with you."

"What? I'm your mother, boy. You do what I tell you!"

"Not anymore, Ma. I'm a grown man. I gotta think on my own, and I don't want to do this with you anymore."

"Do what? Obey me like you supposed to? I raised you by myself, boy. I gave up my life for you! You will do what I tell you to do, and that's that!"

"Ma, I want to thank you for all that you have done for me when I couldn't do for myself, but at some point in life, you have to allow me to move on so that I can have kids of my own to care for. Ma, if you want me to say it, then I will. I owe you, Ma. I owe you my life, but life is something no human being can pay back. I love you with every ounce of me, but I can no longer be held accountable for you doing what you was supposed to have done as a mother, and that's care for her child." Dante stood there with tears streaming down his face.

Diamond also began to cry because her baby, her son, had told her something she'd never considered. She was selfish and never thought about anybody but herself. She cursed herself for not protecting her mother from her father and for being the cause of running the one person off she knew would have given her love, her mother. She hated her father at that very moment for teaching her to take what she wanted. Dreams that she'd had throughout her life of a normal life came flooding back into her mind as her life flashed before her. But she knew her life was over.

"Come on, Ma, give me the gun," Dante said, moving a little closer to her.

"I never got a chance to do what I wanted to do." She cried. "I didn't get my prince. I was supposed to marry a prince." She continued to talk incoherently. "I never meant to hurt people. My father told me to do it. He is the one that should be going to jail. It is all his fault!" Tears began to fall from her eyes. "I want my mommy! Where is my mother?"

A police officer slowly crept up behind her. Dante saw him and continued to talk to his mother as tears fell from his eyes like a faucet. He felt sorry for his mother because she lived in a fantasy world. She had been chasing a fantasy all her life. He realized his mother never had love and didn't know how to return it. He tried to give her love, but she didn't know how to receive it.

The officer suddenly bolted for Diamond and tackled her to the ground, and the gun flew from her hands, slid across the floor, and stopped at Dante's feet.

"Freeze! Don't move!" the officers yelled, their guns now trained on Dante. They were expecting him to pick up the gun.

Dante looked down at the gun. He held up his hands and slowly backed away from it. He shook his head. *When is a black man ever gonna get a chance?*

Diamond kicked and screamed as four officers worked to restrain her. They took her out of the courtroom and out of her fantasy world forever.

✦∗ ✦∗ **THIRTY-SEVEN** ✦∗ ✦∗

The Sentencing
One Month Later

Dante and Kendall stood as Judge Fritz read Dante's sentence.

"Dante Reed, on the count of insurance fraud, you are sentenced to the maximum of three hundred and sixty-five days. With time served subtracted from your sentence, you have served your time. However, you will remain in custody here in county jail until your next hearing. You will return in one to two months for the hearing on the charges of you eluding the police, aggravated assault on an officer, and unlawful possession of a firearm."

"Thank you, Your Honor," Kendall said.

Judge Fritz then looked at Kyle and began to read Diamond's sentence.

Diamond received twenty years to life for all of her charges. She wasn't in court to hear her sentence because Judge Fritz had ordered her to stay locked up, fearing her reaction. Kyle would be the one to break the news to her.

When Judge Fritz ended the sentencing, Dante leaned toward Kendall and whispered, "Thank you, man."

"It's all good, kid."

"I know they gonna throw the book at me when I come back."

"They might not, now that you have been acquitted of the murder charges and also I got the attempted murder charges knocked down to aggravated assault. Let's just see what happens. But I wouldn't worry about that just yet. I'll do what I can for you."

"A'ight, thanks again, man."

"Look . . . be good in there, and you'll back on the streets before you know it. Call me if you need anything." Kendall shook his hand before the bailiff came to take him away.

"Thanks, man," Dante said over his shoulder, while walking away with the bailiff.

Meanwhile, Diamond, in solitary confinement in a straight jacket, lay on the floor talking to herself. "My prince will come rescue me. Here I am, Prince Charming. Come and get me. I have been waiting for you," she said.

✦✦ ✦✦ **THIRTY-EIGHT** ✦✦ ✦✦

Two Months Later

Dante stood before the same Judge Fritz to be sentenced on the charges of aggravated assault on a police officer, eluding police, and unlawful possession of a firearm. The charge of possession of a firearm was thrown out of court because a weapon was never found.

The courtroom housed only minimal spectators. It wasn't like it had been when Dante and his mother were on trial only months prior. There were no reporters or photographers there. In fact, it was quiet and surreal in the courtroom.

It didn't take the jury long to deliberate at all.

Kyle, there to give his brother support, sat in the first row behind the defense table, and Prosecutor Swartz and her team sat at their table awaiting the sentencing as well.

"On one count of aggravated assault on a police officer, you are sentenced to a minimum for first offense of one hundred and eighty days, not to exceed a maximum of three hundred and sixty-five days.

"On the one count of eluding police you are sentenced to a minimum for first offense of one hundred and eighty days, not to exceed a maximum of three hundred and sixty-five days."

Dante groaned and held his head low. He just knew Kendall was gonna be able to get him off just like he did before, but with the numbers the judge throwing at him, he felt he was gonna die in jail. Dante didn't have any knowledge of jail-time numbers, but it sounded bad to him.

"Each sentence will run concurrently. Your sentence amounts to three hundred and sixty

days, not to exceed seven hundred and thirty," Judge Fritz announced.

Dante thought he was gonna pass out. He couldn't even count up in his head how many years that was. All he knew was, it was a long time. He wanted to cry like a baby, but he didn't. He stood there and waited for Judge Fritz to finish shuffling through pages he was looking at.

Dante leaned over and whispered to Kendall, "Yo, man, how long is five hundred days?"

Kendall laughed after seeing Dante's face turn pale with sickness. "You only gotta do a little under a year if you stay outta trouble in there. The rest you will do on parole when you come out."

"Well, why didn't he just say that? Spitting numbers at me like that sounded like a hell of a lot of time."

"I know, kid."

"With your time already served, you will do the remaining two hundred forty days and then be released. But you will do three hundred and sixty-five days of parole and report to your parole officer faithfully." Judge Fritz looked over the top of his glasses at Dante. "Consider yourself a lucky young man. When you get out, do something positive with your life. You are still a young man and still have a chance to make a change." Judge Fritz banged his gavel.

"Thank you, Your Honor," Kendall said.

"Thank you, Your Honor," Dante said as well.

Before the court officers took Dante back to his cell, he turned to shake Kyle's hand. "Have you heard anything about my mother?"

"Yes." Kyle looked over at Kendall, not sure if he should tell Dante the full story.

Kendall shook his head, letting Kyle know it was OK to tell him.

"Your mother tried to kill a CO and then tried to kill herself."

"What?"

"She shanked a guard in the face and then stabbed herself in the neck with the shank. But they were able to save her. She's in a coma, Dante." Kyle hated to reveal such horrible news to the young man.

Dante stood there looking down at the floor in deep thought when the court officer came over to escort him away. His face was saddened as the officer grabbed his arm gently to take him away.

"Are you gonna be all right, kid?" Kendall asked.

Dante lifted his head and looked back at the two brothers. "I'll never tell," he said, turning and walking away with the officers.

MELODRAMA PUBLISHING ORDER FORM
WWW.MELODRAMAPUBLISHING.COM

Title	ISBN	Qty	Price	Total
Wifey by Kiki Swinson (Pt 1)	0-971702-18-7		$15.00	$
I'm Still Wifey by Kiki Swinson (Pt 2)	0-971702-15-2		$15.00	$
Life After Wifey by Kiki Swinson (Pt 3)	1-934157-04-X		$15.00	$
Still Wifey Material by Kiki Swinson (Pt 4)	1-934157-10-4		$15.00	$
Wifey 4 Life by Kiki Swinson (Pt 5)	1-934157-61-9		$14.99	$
A Sticky Situation by Kiki Swinson	1-934157-09-0		$15.00	$
Tale of a Train Wreck Lifestyle by Crystal Lacey Winslow	1-934157-15-5		$15.00	$
Sex, Sin & Brooklyn by Crystal Lacey Winslow	0-971702-16-0		$15.00	$
Histress by Crystal Lacey Winslow	1-934157-03-1		$15.00	$
Life, Love & Lonliness by Crystal Lacey Winslow	0-971702-10-1		$15.00	$
The Criss Cross by Crystal Lacey Winslow	0-971702-12-8		$15.00	$
In My Hood by Endy	0-971702-19-5		$15.00	$
In My Hood 2 by Endy	1-934157-06-6		$15.00	$
In My Hood 3 by Endy	1-934157-62-7		$14.99	$
A Deal With Death by Endy	1-934157-12-0		$15.00	$
Dirty Little Angel by Erica Hilton	1-934157-19-8		$15.00	$
10 Crack Commandments by Erica Hilton	1-934157-10-X		$15.00	$
The Diamond Syndicate by Erica Hilton	1-934157-60-0		$14.99	$
Den of Sin by Storm	1-934157-08-2		$15.00	$
Eva: First Lady of Sin by Storm	1-934157-01-5		$15.00	$
Shot Glass Diva by Jacki Simmons	1-934157-14-7		$15.00	$
Stripped by Jacki Simmons	1-934157-00-7		$15.00	$
Cartier Cartel by Nisa Santiago	1-934157-18-X		$15.00	$
Jealousy the Complete Saga by Linda Brickhouse	1-934157-13-9		$15.00	$
Menace by Erick S. Gray, Mark Anthony, Crystal Lacey Winslow, Al-Saadiq Banks, JM Benjamin	1-934157-13-9		$15.00	$
Myra by Amaleka McCall	1-934157-20-1		$15.00	$

(GO TO THE NEXT PAGE)

Instructions:

*NY residents please add $1.79 Tax per book.

**Shipping costs: $3.00 first book, any additional books please add $1.00 per book.

Incarcerated readers receive a 25% discount. Please pay $11.25 per book and apply the same shipping terms as stated above.

Mail to:

MELODRAMA PUBLISHING

P.O. BOX 522

BELLPORT, NY 11713

Please provide your shipping address and phone number:

Name:_____

Address: _____

Apt. No: _____ Inmate No: _____

City: _____ State: _____ Zip: _____

Phone: (   ) _____-_____

Allow 2 - 4 weeks for delivery

Now Available

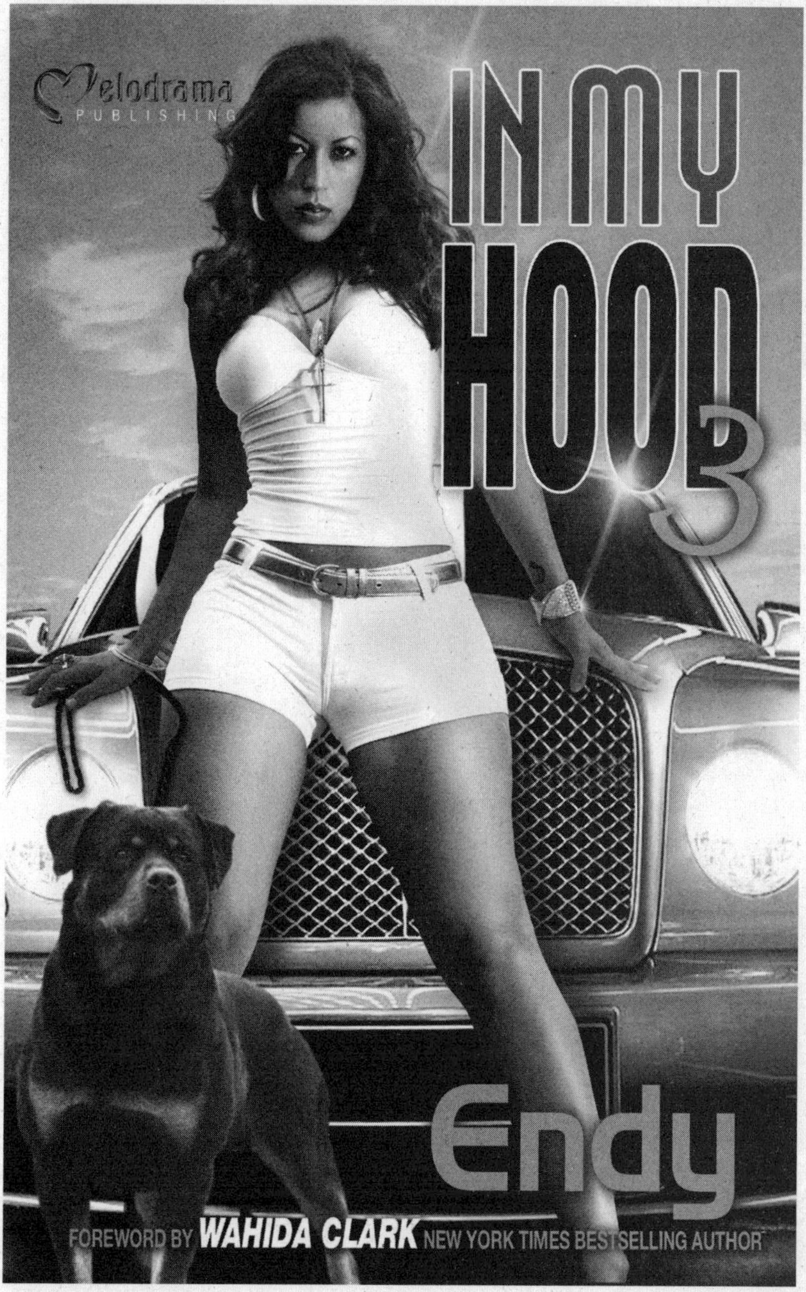